Quickening

Also by Liza Wieland

FICTION
A Watch of Nightingales
Bombshell
You Can Sleep While I Drive
Discovering America
The Names of the Lost

POETRY
Near Alcatraz

stories

LIZA WIELAND

Southern Methodist University Press
Dallas

This collection of stories is a work of fiction. Names, characters, places, and incidents are either the product of the author's imagination or are used fictitiously.

Copyright © 2011 by Liza Wieland
First edition
2011 All rights reserved

Requests for permission to reproduce material from this work should be sent to:
Rights and Permissions
Southern Methodist University Press
PO Box 750415
Dallas, Texas 75275-0415

Grateful acknowledgment is made to the following publications, in which some of these stories previously appeared: *The Virgin of Guadalupe, Amuse Bouche, The Path Not Taken,* and *The River* first appeared in *The Packinghouse Review;* "First, Marriage" first appeared in *Freightstories;* "Some Churches" first appeared in *Connotation Press;* "The Girl With Radium Eyes" first appeared as "Apparition" in *Sou'wester;* "Out of the Garden" first appeared as "1943: A Dream" in *Literal Latte;* "Vision" first appeared in *North Carolina Literary Review;* "Quickening" first appeared in *New South;* "Body and Engine" first appeared in *The Normal School;* and "Slip Out Back Here" first appeared in the *Bridport Prize Anthology 2007.*

Jacket and text design by Kellye Sanford
Cover photo: "These Boots Are Made for Walking" by Jared Revell, Melbourne, Australia (www.jaredrevell.com.au)

        Library of Congress Cataloging-in-Publication Data
Wieland, Liza.
  Quickening : stories / Liza Wieland. — 1st ed.
    p. cm.
  ISBN 978-0-87074-564-5 (alk. paper)
  I. Title.
  PS3573.I344Q53 2010
  813'.54—dc22
                                                2010024681

Printed in the United States of America on acid-free paper
10   9   8   7   6   5   4   3   2   1

for Jane, Kathy, and Connie

"There isn't any good in promising," he said.

In the early morning on the lake sitting
in the stern of the boat with his father rowing,
he felt quite sure that he would never die.

—Ernest Hemingway, *In Our Time*

Contents

The Virgin of Guadalupe	1
First, Marriage	3
Some Churches	27
La Fenêtre	45
Amuse Bouche	73
Pound in Venice	75
At Wanship	89
The Girl with Radium Eyes	105
The Path Not Taken	119
Out of the Garden	121
Vision	141
Quickening	169
The River	191
Resolution Trust	193
Body and Engine	217
Slip, Out, Back, Here	229

Acknowledgments

My first and most profound debt of thanks goes to my extraordinary editor, Kathryn Lang, who has now guided me through four books in the course of nearly twenty years. I am so very grateful for her faith in my work, her vision, her sense of humor, her kindness and generosity. My gratitude extends to her wise and indefatigable colleagues, Keith Gregory and George Ann Ratchford.

The following people have sustained me with their excellent company and good stories: Linnea Alexander, Jeff Aydelette, Tom DeMarchi, John Hales, Cheryl Huff, Alexis Khoury, Phil and Franny Levine, Dan Marcucci, Kat Meads, Flora Moorman, Neil Nevitt, Tanya Nichols, Rob Roscigno, Carol and Marcus Simmons, Carrie Thies, Karen Tolchin, Dympna Ugwu-Oju, Lee and Linnea Wieland, Paul Wieland, and the fabulous Starlight Women.

This book could not have been completed without a generous research grant from the Thomas Harriott College of Arts and Sciences at East Carolina University. I'm also indebted to my many and delightful colleagues (present and former) in the English Departments at ECU and Fresno State.

Thanks, too, to Melanie Carter for permission to quote from her poem "January," which was originally published in the *Gettysburg Review* and reprinted in *Best New Poets 2008: 50 Poems from Emerging Writers*, edited by Mark Strand. Books about translation by George Steiner, Douglas Robinson, Daniel Balderston, and Marcy Schwartz have also been indispensible.

I'm grateful also to Robin Whitaker for her meticulous and insightful copyediting of the manuscript.

For Dan and Georgia, thanks aren't nearly enough. I love you both, beyond words.

The Virgin of Guadalupe

She was pregnant, but she didn't know quite how.
The generator quit, but the snow didn't.
He could fix anything, but not this.
"There's this one detail, though, that really gets to me," she said. He heard a note in her voice and looked up and saw she was crying. "If you enlarge her eyes—I mean, scientists have done this—they magnified her eyes and you can see a reflection of the bishop, his housekeeper, and another priest—all the people who were in the room when Juan Diego opened his serape and the roses fell to the floor and her image was revealed."

"It's part of the miracle," he said. "She already knew who would be in the room when he got there."

"Maybe," she said. "That's what everyone thinks. But I wonder . . . I was wondering, what if it was alive right then, the image. What if the Virgin of Guadalupe was alive on Juan Diego's serape and looking out into the room?"

"Like a hologram," he said.

"No," she said, "like . . . like human. For an instant, she was alive, in the cloth. She was really there."

Like the moment of conception. You're there and I'm there, and in an instant we become alive in some other way.

"I was in church and I was thinking it makes sense that the Feast of the Immaculate Conception is four days earlier."

"Maybe you're spending too much time in church," he said.

She looked at him, then beyond to the wreck of frozen tree limbs and snow drifts that was their front porch. No light or heat for six days, only the battery-operated radio and the fire. She'd heard the power crews could get through to them tomorrow.

First, Marriage

But then, what next? And after that? I ask myself these questions on the occasion of my fiftieth birthday, here in the dark, with one last glass of champagne. So. I am a woman now squarely in middle age, a translator by occupation, and alone. There was, briefly, a husband, in New York City, but I was not truly in love with him. I was in love with loneliness. So simple, I imagined: a perfectly quiet life, which words could come into and go out changed. I have spoken a great deal about my work over the years, but what I never say to anyone is this: I have always felt a desire to have no voice at all, to say nothing, to keep the words to myself. And isn't it true that translation is about privacy and secrecy? And which of these is the origin of the career? Is a young woman secretive by nature, and so she takes up the work of translation, or does the profession dispose a woman to be secretive? I wanted to be everywhere and nowhere, to elude capture. I wanted silence. And order. What the translator has power over is order. Words in the sentence. Events in sequence.

So: in the beginning was Raymond Alexander, his brother, and God.

In 1988, in New York, Raymond Alexander was a painter and also a student in art history. His paintings were representational, out of fashion then, delicate oils, *windowscapes*, he called them, the view from a small room. I met him through a friend who brought me to a tiny gallery on Cornelia Street. When I saw his canvases, I thought, the light is strange, too much of it, coming out of nowhere. You felt as if you would not want to be in such a room, or else you would never want to leave it. We ran into each other a few weeks later, at Columbia, where I worked in Butler Library, deep in the basement, cataloguing foreign holdings. He lived in a studio apartment, almost directly across from Butler, in a building between two fraternities.

"But it's deceptive," Raymond said when he'd let me in. "I have this extra space." He led me through the main room, where there was a fireplace with a narrow mantel, two metal bookshelves—the kind people who live in the suburbs have in their garages for tools and canned goods—a red butterfly chair, and a frameless futon closed up like a couch. The kitchen was big enough for a table and two chairs. A cookbook was open on the table, the *Moosewood Cookbook*, I knew from the small, careful handwriting of the author, which has made it untranslatable. Green peppers, tomatoes, onions, and parsley were piled on a cutting board. "But this is the best part." He stepped into the bathroom and unbolted a door on the other side, then propped it open with a kitchen chair. "Look at my backyard," he said.

Five wooden steps led down into a wide alley stretching a quarter of a block in length, one of those usually empty echoing spaces made by the backs of tall apartment buildings in New York City. But this one had been transformed into a garden, bordered by middle-sized shade trees, a vegetable bed, shrubs, rose bushes, and two circular, groomed grassy lawns. The whole space was wound with paths filled with small luminous stones. On each end, a wooden bench was set against a high trellis. I did not recognize the vines on the trellises, but each one was just coming into leaf, so it would be possible to sit facing east or west and, with a certain sort of strict vision, see nothing but green. Each of the round lawns was about six feet in diameter, the size of a bed. I wanted to lie down on one of them. I wondered if Raymond ever had.

"This is gorgeous," I said. "Did you do it?"

"No, no," Raymond said. "I haven't been here that long. A woman who lives on the ground floor in the next building—she's been there for years. The widow of a professor. She did it. I'm just lucky."

"Does she let you sit out here?"

"She used to let me paint out here. As long as I'm quiet. And I do a little pruning for her. I cut the grass. She has a push mower by the back door. It's a funny thing to see in the city." He pointed to the mower, and it was surreal, but also like the children's game: find what doesn't belong. "Do you want something to drink, Nora? I was just about to start cooking."

We climbed the steps and passed back into the kitchen. Raymond opened two beers and handed me one. He pointed to a small knife and the peppers. The cookbook was open to a recipe called "Scheherezade Casserole." Two medium green peppers, chopped.

"I'm not a vegetarian," Raymond said, "but I play one on TV. I hope this is okay."

"It's great," I said, not quite getting the joke, not then. "Anything is great."

There was a silence in our working together that was a kind of presence, but comfortable. Two people standing next to each other, with jobs to do. At his opening, there had been noise and so much talk. We never had a chance to finish the conversation. Now there seemed to be so much time, hours, even whole days in which to wash the tomatoes and peppers, rinse the bundle of parsley, really look at Raymond as he moved around the kitchen. I thought he resembled certain pictures of Jesus, though Raymond was tall and muscular: the light brown hair that hung to his shoulders, the neat beard, a softness in his eyes. It was a troubling notion, and as if in response, the floor began to tremble, utensils hung on the peg board rattled against each other. In the other room, books fell off a shelf. Water from the parsley flew into Raymond's face, and he laughed. He opened two more beers, patted my back.

"It's all right, Nora. Don't worry."

"What *is* that?"

"It's the subway. I hardly notice it anymore. Except when the books fall down."

"Does it happen every time a train goes by? Goes under, I guess it is."

"Only the express trains. The trains that stop at 110th Street haven't gotten up enough speed yet."

I walked into the other room intending to pick up the books. I could see the bare bones of how he lived. There are only a few years in most people's lives when that's possible, before meaning is obscured, before they move to bigger apartments, then houses, then into marriages, children, back into their old hobbies. But for a little while, it's right there, out in the open, the truth of what somebody is and wants. Raymond's typewriter sat on a black board he'd balanced on top of the radiator. There were several large books piled to one side, and I went to look at them. The one on top was in French, *École de Barbizon*. The cover was Jean François Millet's *L'Angélus*. I picked up the book and took it into the kitchen.

"Are you studying this?"

"Well," he said, "I'm *teaching* it, but also studying, yes, the period really. The place."

We stood for a moment just outside something. "It's pretty. It's so familiar."

"The light," he said. "He got it just right. It's genius."

And it was. But it was almost too much for me, the way the light shone so hard on the frailties of the people, how fallen it made them, and I took the book back to the desk.

We ate at the little table in the kitchen, talking about our work and holding hands awkwardly around the plates and bottles. I felt elated and afraid. A garden in the middle of an alleyway in New York City, the end of my schooling. I'd been very good at learning languages. I told Raymond my family history: my father's early death, my mother's grief, and mine, which had always felt like making a speech into one end of a long tube, but this time seemed less so. I told him I loved the silence of translating poetry. The process is internal, nearly silent, a slow wreckage, dismemberment. I take something apart in order to put it back together, and I find this strangely soothing. Sometimes I imagined joining a convent, that there was some stillness and quiet I needed to find out what to do with my life: I was thirty, and I had no idea. He nodded and ate—what reply was there to such statements? The casserole tasted very good, *substantial* was the word I used—I remember this because Raymond laughed and repeated it as if he wasn't quite sure he was being complimented. But what I meant was, it was the first food I had really tasted in a long time.

We finished the meal, took our beers and sat outside, on the east-facing bench of the garden so we could see the quarter moon. It was wonderfully dark. A long rectangle of light shone out the back door of Raymond's apartment, illuminating what I thought must be a rose bush, maybe a camellia, but a red flower, in bloom and round like an apple. It was like being outside one of his paintings and looking in, and I said so. Beyond us, the sounds of cars, car horns, voices, the trickling of music from open windows, all of this seemed to quiet and then fade. Raymond's arm was around my shoulders, but I couldn't see him. We weren't talking.

"I thought this feeling might go away," he said suddenly. "But it hasn't." I must have stiffened a little because he held me more tightly. "No, no. Not about you. I mean about painting. There's something about what Millet's seeing. What I'm seeing—"

"Your work is so different from his."

"I know. If I could only really see like that. But I think all I can do is copy. I can't do anything useful. I haven't even wanted to paint in months."

"You'll get back to it." I patted his knee, motherly.

"No. I don't feel that way. I feel relieved. It's fine that I'm not going to be another second- or third-rate American painter. I'll finish school in two years. I love the teaching."

"Art in the dark," I said. "That's what they called it when I was in college. We called it that. The students did."

"Here too," Raymond said.

"And it's true, isn't it? I mean that's how it gets made. In the dark."

"You mean as in 'I have no idea what I'm doing'?"

"That's right. At least that's what I think."

"Or maybe it's *why*. Like 'I have no idea why I'm doing this.'"

"I'm just doing it."

"Right."

"Because I have to."

"Right. Let's go inside, Nora," he said.

I didn't want to leave that garden, but we did. We went inside and unrolled the futon and got down to solving other kinds of mysteries. I loved Raymond Alexander then, but I knew already I did not love him enough. We lay in the dark in the middle of the night, with the windows open, listening to the fraternity boys next door, the anguished, endless barking of a dog, and shouting between men and women, all the ways New York City talks in its sleep. Once or twice, I thought there was a rumbling underneath us as the express train ran north or south, and then the echo of it traveled across the room and into the kitchen.

"Do the trains run all night, Raymond?"

For a while he didn't answer. For a long time.

"I don't think you're convent material, Nora," Raymond said much later. His lips moved against my neck as if he were trying to tell me something.

Raymond and I spent the summer this way. And in the fall I took part-time teaching jobs at Fordham and Hunter College and the New School, and my life became a blur of train rides and vocabulary tests, voices calling for my attention, in French, Spanish, and German. Raymond had nearly finished his course work, had begun to think about a dissertation. He never touched his paints.

Most nights that summer we slept out in the garden, in a sleeping bag when the weather turned colder. Raymond explained to the old widow that we were doing this, and she smiled approvingly, he said, and nodded her head, and she told him it was like having an all-night security guard. Sometimes in the morning, we would wake up to find her a few feet away, pruning, fertilizing, gathering blossoms or late tomatoes. It was hard to say, at those moments, who was guarding whom. She seemed to me an angel, a vision, a message I could not quite read, but didn't have to yet. When I opened my eyes, she was looking at me. Not at us. It appeared that she smiled and shook her head, just once. The sun rose behind her, and her smile brightened when she saw I was awake. Then she turned back to her work.

In December, Raymond's brother Nolan was on the plane that blew up over Lockerbie, Scotland. His parents went over to Lockerbie, but Raymond didn't think he could stand it. In New York, we went to church together for days, staying long after Mass had ended. Raymond was trying to understand, to make a thousand deals with God, deals of understanding. He told me in the coffee shops along Broadway those first weeks of January, the litany: If I could be sure he felt no pain, if I could be sure he wasn't scared, if I could be sure he had no knowledge whatsoever. If someone could promise me these things. If I could be sure he died immediately. If I could be sure what we buried was really him and no other, that he's not alive somewhere. If I could be sure he's gone to heaven. If I could be sure there is a heaven.

"What's the then," I said.

"The *then*?"

"If, then. If you could know these things, what would you give? You have to give something back."

"I was thinking, 'then I could be happy.' Why should I have to give anything back?"

We drank another cup of coffee. We tried to talk about our lives at school, the city, books, but his desolation was too great, and it became mine too. We couldn't stop taking it apart again, our idea of those last moments, or reading the newspaper accounts. We held hands constantly. We sat close to each other in the coffee shop booth and held on.

Finally, Raymond came to believe he had to go see the exact place where his brother had fallen from the sky. Many of the families felt this way. Raymond wrote to some of them, talked on the phone. His parents said they were too old to make the trip again, too broken, and so I agreed to go with him. We made plans all summer, and then left in August. We flew to London, then to Edinburgh, rented a car and drove the rest of the way, through beautiful weather, really more like the end of spring that far north. We were in farm country, where the land had unfolded itself, opened fully for a brief time to admit us. Everywhere we were told we couldn't have come at a better moment. It was the season of life, the season, a priest said, when every tear shall be wiped away. The families stared dumbly at this. We were traveling with two others, two sets of parents and a sister. One of the mothers whispered *I can't bear it*, over and over. Her husband shook his head. Sure, tears could be wiped away, he said, but there was no end to them, would never be.

And then we got to the place in the road, behind a man's house, a place where suddenly eight months before there had been chaos, metal raining from the sky, and flesh, and a child's doll, the sleeve of a sweater, sugar packets, miniature bottles of liquor. We lived through it all again, the crater, the woman on the roof, the other still half-buckled into her seat, the flight attendant whose pulse could be detected for ten minutes, the others who lay in fields, on roads, who looked like they were sleeping.

We went to a house to ask about it: a woman who said Raymond's brother had fallen into her kitchen. Smashed through the ceiling. She opened the door after the explosion and the fireball, and there he was, curled into himself as if he'd dropped there for a bit of rest. The police told them not to touch the bodies, not to move them until there could be an investigation. He lay there, the sleeping laddie, she called him, through the night and all the next day. It was bitterly cold. When evening came on, she said she could not stand it, and she covered him with a blanket, even though she knew he felt nothing.

"I talked to him," she said, tears filling her eyes, "I told him he was a good lad, and I knew he was with God, and I promised I would take care of the flesh until—" She stopped.

"His mother came for him," I said.

"Did she?" the woman said. "I didn't know that. We weren't told anything."

But she petted him, she said, and closed his eyes, even though she wasn't supposed to touch. She wanted us to know that, that he wasn't alone.

It was not survivable, they told us again and again, until the word lost its meaning. The sets of parents nodded, their eyes empty. I could see they were thinking something like: and neither is this. We looked up into the open spaces of the church, the meeting hall. There were three separate memorial services while we were there—the drone of a voice trying to explain. I remembered the sound from the weeks after my father's death, the noise your heart would make if it were a machine and not living tissue. God is building a house, one of them said, and he was exactly right. It was the sound of an adze or a saw, a carpenter's tool that has to repeat its sorry work over and over.

There is a famous golf course at Lockerbie, and some of the wreckage fell there. We came to it quite by accident, driving aimlessly, having seen what we thought was the worst. It was closed, but the guard seemed to recognize the seven of us before anyone spoke or explained. There was something about the open space, the groomed quality of it, that made us separate from one another, fan out, the relatives each seeking some quiet place apart. Husband drifted from wife, father from mother. Raymond let go of my hand and wandered down the first fairway. The sister fell to her knees at the edge of a green and then lay down, perhaps the same way as her own sister who had died.

There is the notion, I think, that you can hear God's voice in an open space like that. But what Raymond said was that the silence on the golf course, over all of Lockerbie, was terrible, unbearable, not survivable. There was no comfort, no voice of God to explain, to soothe him.

"The rest of the world is so loud," I said, and just then an airplane roared overhead. We stood perfectly still and did not look up. As the sound grew louder, one of the mothers bent her head, folded her hands, became the woman in Millet's *L'Angélus*.

We were married in a town just outside Edinburgh, on the way home. We didn't plan. We had two days' layover—though that isn't the right way to explain—we came away from Lockerbie two days earlier than planned, gave up the rented car and rode the train, because we couldn't stand the situation. Not the sorrow, not our sorrow, or the local people's and the strangeness of theirs, inside of which was a thin line of accusation, like strata in rock. Not even the ghostly immanence of the place, the sense that all these American students would suddenly reappear, walk out from the meadows and lanes, clouds of them drifting into the pubs and the chemists' shops, fanning out across the golf course, sweet smiles on their faces, the joy of homecoming. No. It was that, in the end, at the end, we didn't know why we'd come. Raymond didn't know. There was no translation. Our being there didn't translate, wouldn't, not ever.

We stepped off the train in Edinburgh station, and there was the famous music festival. We had forgotten about it, not noticed at all maybe. So there were no rooms. We got back on the train and went to the next town out, really a suburb, South Edinburgh. The weather was warm, the sky a brilliant blue. Everywhere we saw posters advertising the International Music Festival, and even here people on the street had the same joyous, drunken look we'd seen in the city proper. It seemed as though many of them were in costume—we told each other this, but now I don't know how that could have been true. I was reminded of Mardi Gras, all that frenzied pleasure before the solemnity and self-denial of Lent. We walked along the road that ran from the train station until we came to a small place, the Glenora Hotel, and went in. An old woman led us upstairs, where we saw the room was spare, but very white and clean. The bed was soft, which ordinarily would have been uncomfortable. But the events of the previous days, all the attention they required, made us both feel that we wanted to fall backward into something deep, bottomless, a pool of feathers.

"A cave made out of bodies," Raymond said as he was falling asleep. I didn't know what he meant.

When we woke up, light was pouring in the window, and music rang in the street, hum and laughter even at this far edge of the festival. We held each other close, for a long time.

"I'm afraid the world might end right now," he said. "But I'm not afraid too. It would be all right." He touched the side of my face. "Nolan missed out on this."

"How do you know?"

"He told me. He wrote it in a letter. He said he'd gone to bed with a woman, for the first time, but they both knew it was nothing, that they didn't want it to happen again. He said he was waiting for somebody he could just hold in his arms."

Raymond had closed his eyes, but now he opened them, looked at my face. "Let's get married, Nora," he said. "Right now. Here. For Nolan."

I didn't know what to say. I gazed at the details of our little room. The roses on the wall paper, the white washbasin and pitcher—I tried to get some meaning from them.

I reminded Raymond that we weren't citizens.

"Are you saying yes or no?"

I thought about that. I wasn't sure I loved this man, but he'd suffered so much. I knew I was right, that back in the United States, the marriage would be—what? The words seemed strange to apply to marriage: null and void. No good. The marriage would be no good.

"Yes. I'm saying yes."

We got out of bed then, dressed—a kind of fury had seized both of us, though not the same kind, different furies, bound by the same knowledge that right then, in or near Edinburgh, there would be someone crazy enough, happy enough, song-filled enough to marry us. We laughed and kissed and brushed our teeth, looked at ourselves in the mirror, mugged it up like a couple in a photo booth. This seemed significant later, this lack of evidence: how we didn't have any pictures of ourselves that day, only the memory of the tiny hotel bathroom, the cloudy mirror over the sink.

Downstairs, a young man stood behind the reception desk, wearing earphones. His eyes were closed. There's music everywhere near Edinburgh, I thought, even places you can't hear it. Somebody is hearing it, though, and that's what's important. This man was so completely still and pale that he looked not alive. The woman who found Raymond's brother in her kitchen had said he was wearing earphones, and I must have recalled her words a millisecond before Raymond did, because he stopped as if I had noted this resemblance out loud. He clutched my hand, then released it, like pulsing. I could almost feel it myself, his taking note, the way his body seemed to move from this world to a kind of shadowy universe that ran beside it, and then back. He sighed a tiny rasp and took hold of my hand again. The man had already heard us or seen us and pulled the soft discs from his ears, one at a time.

"I have a crazy question for you," Raymond began.

"This is just the place," the man said, smiling.

"We want to get married."

"That's nice."

"Where can we find a magistrate?"

"You're Americans, right? I think you need to go to your embassy."

"Do you know of anyone who might just do it anyway, just for the money?"

"I think there's some waiting period before you can get a license."

"Who could we talk to, do you think?"

"Go over to the Catholic church, St. Anne. And ask for Father Percy. He's visiting from America, and my sister says he's quite mad."

We did as we were told, and the woman who answered the door at the rectory said Father Percy would be right with us. He appeared, as if from nowhere, and stood behind her.

"Come in," he said. "It's me you're looking for. What can I do for you?"

We told him, and told him what the young man's sister had said, and he laughed, then invited us to sit down.

"I probably am quite mad. But not mad enough apparently, because I feel compelled to tell you the marriage wouldn't be legal once you got home. Also, I don't know you, to put it bluntly. I would need to ask a few questions."

"All right," Raymond said.

Father Percy turned to me. "You're awfully quiet and solemn, for one thing. For a woman about to be married. Are you here of your own free will?"

I told him I was.

"What are you doing in Edinburgh then?"

"We've just been up to Lockerbie," Raymond said, and from his tone the priest understood at once.

"A family member?" he said.

"My brother," Raymond told him.

"And it's made you want to marry each other?" Father Percy

looked from Raymond to me. His voice was gentle and full of sorrow, but there was another note in it too. Approval, I thought. Understanding, an appreciation of how it could happen that senseless, violent death might cause two people to want to cleave together. That it might be a way to mourn. That the one might translate the other.

"I'll tell you what," he said. "You'll have to do it all again when you go home, because no one will issue you any paper, any license. There's a waiting period here, several months, I think. But I'll say the words. It will be like a rehearsal. I'll say the words and I'll mean them. God will understand." He looked heavenward. "A rehearsal. Let's go into the chapel."

He led us out a side door, through a small courtyard and into the lady chapel, left us alone for a moment, and came back wearing a stole, holding a prayer book.

"Let me read a gospel first," he said. "I like this one for marriages." He grinned at us. "It's short too."

You are the salt of the earth; but if salt has lost its taste, how shall its saltiness be restored? It is no longer good for anything except to be thrown out and trodden underfoot by men. You are the light of the world. A city set on a hill cannot be hid. Nor do men light a lamp and put it under a bushel.

"Salt," he said, "for you right now comes from your tears. But someday, it will come to have once again the old meaning, flavor—all that makes your lives good and interesting. You will be salt for each other in that way. About the rest of it, the light for the world, I don't know. Show each other the way. Don't let each other down. Light is a tricky thing."

And then the familiar part: do you take this woman, do you take this man. We did. We took. We promised. We kissed each other, there in the Scottish Catholic chapel, in front of the American priest. Afterward, we walked back to the rectory and had a glass of whiskey and a piece of apple pie. Father Percy told us he was from California, but he had become tired of the West, it was so corporeal, so unreflective. There was a thing that happened.

"The chapel was on a college campus, across the street from the football stadium. Sometimes games were going on at the same time as Mass on Saturday evenings, and I don't know the electronics of it, but the sound systems would get crossed over, and the game announcer's voice would come booming through the speakers in the church. Or else there would be this terrible feedback. One day, it just wouldn't stop, and I had to end the Mass. I walked across the street to the announcer's booth, and I went nuts. Yelling. Trying to break things, breaking things, too. I don't know exactly what. I was away from myself. Just out of my head. Afterward, I told the bishop I needed to be alone somewhere, and he said I most certainly did."

As we were leaving, Father Percy said, "Remember, this will be something else when you get home. But try not to let it be."

When we came back, Raymond and I were estranged. The whole world seemed pushed to the sides of my vision, and out of focus, *peripheral* is exactly the word, so that the inside of my head seemed a perfect blank, ready to let in some other language. I moved out of Raymond's apartment, took away my few possessions one day while he was working in the library.

There were questions first, in September, asked very seriously across a desk in the graduate studies office at Fordham. These questions had a certain weightlessness about them, an absence of gravity, in both senses. I was reminded of the process for obtaining a permit to carry a concealed weapon, which I had read about in a story. The director of graduate admissions was a priest, and I was alone with him and the crucified Christ, which hung over his head and appeared very attentive. The sounds of the city seemed to come and go, car horns, shouting, the hum that is thousands of people talking, the forward-going of their lives.

"You are older than most of our Ph.D. candidates," the priest said. "You'll automatically become a mother figure, probably a confidante if you have that skill."

"I don't know if I do," I said. He looked at me for a long moment, as if he were wondering whether I knew anything useful.

"Most of our older graduate students don't make it. Life intervenes. Marriage. Children. They need jobs. But there have been exceptions."

"I'd like to be an exception."

"Is that all?" the priest said. His eyes were closed, or maybe he was staring down at his hands. His fingernails were ringed with something black and unwashable, grease or dirt. I thought he must have been working on some kind of machine.

"That's all," I said.

He looked up, at my face, then took off his glasses and rubbed his eyes. The dirt seemed to sting; he blinked hard, pulled his hands away quickly and stared at them.

"There's something—," he began, then sighed heavily. "But what do I know?" He smiled. "Literary translation is powerful—and sad, too. When it's done, no one needs you anymore, and no one cares. But power and sadness can be the same thing sometimes. Think of Christ."

I nodded. Unaccountably, I said, "It's lonely at the top."

He laughed, shook his head. "You might not like it here. But you'll be good for the others." He folded his hands, signaled that I could go.

"Did you fix your car, Father?" I said.

He glanced at his hands. "I'm not a mechanic," he said. "I can't fix anything."

I went to Raymond's apartment. He was drinking tea and studying his art history text. The Greeks. I thought of all the statuary I'd seen, all those broken bodies. He had made cookies. His place smelled like sweet, tentative life. I told him where I'd been.

He didn't respond for a long time. It was all right. I knew he had to take in such information slowly. I looked around the room, which I believed I'd never enter again, saw the monkishness of it, the futon, the hemp rug, the board over the radiator, the red butterfly chair someone had given him, the metal bookshelves he had assembled badly, without tools.

"Do you want some tea, Nora?" he said finally.

I followed him into the kitchen. The blue kettle, the package of tea bags in the cabinet above. The peg board also inexpertly attached to the wall, the shaking utensils, the sound of falling books. I had not thought of it this way: several times an hour, his whole place rattled, threatened to collapse.

"I'm going to move in with another graduate student. Named Wendy. She lives on 112th Street, so I'll actually be closer to you. Nothing will really change."

"Nothing will really change?" He spun away from the stove toward me. "What do you mean nothing will change? You moved out. It's all already changed."

He handed me a mug of tea and arranged some of the cookies on a plate. We sat down on the futon, which he folded every morning into the nearly S-shape of a couch. He was using a fruit crate for a coffee table. Subway cars rocked under us. The art history book, heavy and glossy and awkward, fell off the table and convulsed briefly on the floor.

"The director of graduate studies said I was too old. He thinks I'm probably not going to last."

"But he let you in anyway?"

"It takes a long time. You have plenty of chances to blow it, fall away."

"Why are you telling me this?"

"I think I'm telling myself."

He nodded and we drank our tea. The cookies were still warm, peanut butter with chocolate chips, the ideal marriage of sweet and salt. I thought that at the time, I really did. The ideal marriage.

"My brother—," Raymond stopped, picked a shard of cookie off the floor. "Nolan is everywhere." He turned to face me. "It's that I talk about him too much. Isn't it, Nora? Is that it? That I can't get over it?"

"No, no. That's not it at all. But there's so much to get over. There should be fewer people in the world with something to get over."

"He's everywhere," Raymond said. "But what good does it do? I can't get to him, I can't talk to him, I can't touch him."

"He can't eat these fabulous cookies," I said.

Tears ran down his face. "That's exactly right. That's it. That's right."

"And he's missing them."

"He is. He *is*."

He bent double, weeping, his face pressed into his knees. I patted his back, then lay sideways across the strong table of his spine, the curve of his ribs, feeling the faint good rumble of his heart.

"This is killing me," Raymond said. "This feels like murder."

I moved in with Wendy and two other students, but downtown, near Fordham. They had all been undergraduates together, and were twenty-two years old. What the priest said was true, that I was their mother, their confidante. They were very sweet girls, and they all spoke several languages, six between us. What they wanted most was to do good in the world, it seemed, by teaching strangers how to talk to one another.

I worked on my translations, substitute taught in the public schools, tutored children, taught classes at Fordham. The high school students did not understand much of what they were learning—I can see that now—a cultural moment was overtaking us all. Good children went bad overnight, brought knives to school, smoked marijuana before Spanish class, so that there was something of the beyond, of the divine, of the immortal about them when they came into the room. It gave them a kind of awe, an appreciation for the miraculous. They said "whoa" when we read in Spanish that the stone was rolled away, the burial garments folded neatly, the body disappeared. They meant it. They did not really need a translation.

For a while, I took the subway uptown to teach a French class at Mother Cabrini. I knew when the car I rode in passed under Raymond's apartment, knew how his place fell apart and then becalmed, fell down and then got up. After I moved, we didn't see each other, but I knew that his brother was still everywhere.

And I came to understand the Millet painting, *L'Angélus*, the strange fade of that light, the storm coming in from the right side of the canvas, close to the village in the distance, the way it burned on the arms of the man and the woman standing together in the foreground. It was she who was facing into the light, and the bridge of her nose and her fingertips glowed red, as if she would feel hot to touch, to kiss. And the light turned the field red too, the ground was burning—it would be impossible to walk across. How would they get home, this man and this woman? I had once asked this of Raymond, but he didn't answer. How would they lift their loaded cart and turn and move toward the village without bursting into flame? And what was there waiting for them anyhow? The place they lived was only a dark steeple, almost black, and a low rectangular structure that seemed to admit the light, a corncrib, a broken-down stable. No wonder she stood frozen, burning, her neck bent as if to take a blow. Allow me to translate: The King James version of the Bible for instance: in French, one reads *"Laissez la lumière."* Let there be the light. In English: "Let there be light." Unspecified, casual. Some light, somewhere, wherever, whenever. This is the difference between the painting and our seeing of it.

Many years later, I heard a story about this painting, that the man and the woman had just buried their child, who had died in an accident on the road outside the town. Millet knew them, loved the child also. In English: "The child has been run over." No one's fault. Accidents happen. In German: *"Das Kind ist unter die Rader gedommen."* The child is under the car's wheels. Such drama, and a terrible vision in the mind's eye. In French: *"L'enfant s'est fait écraser."* The child has caused himself to be crushed. This is what Millet would have said when his wife asked him what had happened to the child. This is how I have to make him say the words, this is my violent occupation.

The translator brings her own language into the machinery of another language. She enters into that language and smashes her way to the center, the heart, and she tries to break that heart open, to see what's inside, see how it all works. And in so doing, she becomes invisible. She leaves the scene.

What the translator has power over is order. Words in the sentence. Events in sequence. What the reader knows when. Otherwise, she's nothing.

I'm nobody. Who are you?

Some Churches

I. OUR LADY OF THE GROTTO

I saw the baby's legs, in light green footed pajamas, dangling outside the window on 114th Street. Her mother's voice drifted down to me from the second floor, a whisper with an edge, from cigarettes, bad air, hard living. I heard her, but I couldn't see her. My breath came out in little clouds that rose, opened, and came back to my face as tears.

"Sister Camille, you take her," the mother called to me. "Right now. I can't stand it no more."

"All right, Nancy," I said. "I will. I will. Come down and let me in."

"Take her now. I ain't letting nobody in. Here."

I heard Nancy sigh, and then she let the baby go. I stood below, inside a still moment of falling, the horror of it like an echo, a baby in midair, a terrible, beautiful flight, divine, awful. Then suddenly, she was in my arms, ten pounds of flesh and bone, this child without wings. I was on the sidewalk with her—the force of her fall had driven me to my knees, my long coat open and bunching at my waist, folds of wool pressing on the baby's left side, pressing her to my belly. I held her there and held myself. A child from heaven, a baby born out of a voice. People on the sidewalk stood a little ways off, respectful of what they didn't understand. A black man with snowy white hair broke from the knot of them and asked if he should call somebody. I told him no, that I would take her to a doctor, I would look after her. I felt powerfully that if anyone tried to take this child from me, I would kill him. I would die first. There was a great heat up along my spine and like an arrow to the top of my head. The world swam in my eyes. This man helped me to my feet and went on his way. I carried the baby down 114th Street, past my apartment, around the corner and into Our Lady of the Grotto. The baby was long and light, like a loaf of bread. Like the baby girl I had given up the year before. Named her Sophie and let her go.

Deep inside the church, behind the altar, is a replica of the grotto at Lourdes, the stone cave where the Virgin appeared. Water drips from some hidden vessel into another, and ordinarily, one has an urge to fix the leak, find the tap and close it. I dragged a cushion off the celebrant's chair and wedged it into a far corner of the grotto. Then I sat down and held the baby, who slept now, warm in my arms. I thought I would like the world to end, before someone found us, before the baby woke up. The sound of falling water took on a shape: straight, vertical, true, while outside, the world shook sideways, wobbled on its axis.

II. NOT ABOUT A CHURCH, NOT EXACTLY

But about a leap of faith, as my mother would tell it.
She would say this: *I lived in a dream, Sophie, only four weeks.*

A job in a bank, in Pittsburgh. Extraordinary amounts of cash money, much more than I had ever seen. Small thefts, three in one week. I am good at this, I find, this slyness. Always, my secret life. On a Friday afternoon, I dressed in three changes of clothes and boarded a train eastbound for Philadelphia. From there, I could go to South America, Europe, or anywhere.

I cannot explain what happened next. The sun set. When full dark came, and then supper, I waited until the car I rode in was nearly empty, until the conductor had just passed, announcing the dining car was open. Then I left my seat, moving away from the dining car, and let myself through to the place where the cars joined, one to the next. Coupled. I did not think that word at the time, but what of that? I am thinking it now—I can be there now, because I am so utterly nowhere, because there is no such thing as the past, no such thing as was. So I stood on that coupling, watching the night stream past. I stand on it now. The stillness of it, how quickly all that black stillness moved and still moves. Then I leapt, far out into the night.

It might be into a river, I told myself, and then I will freeze. Or it might be onto a road, down into a forest from high up, and then I will hit hard, or my clothes and skin will be torn off on the long way down. It might be through the roof of someone's unlit house, and then I will be trespassing. What it most surely will be is the end of you. I must say that I was not unhappy about that, the end of you, Sophie, before you had hardly begun.

But the earth below was none of these things, not river, not road, not forest, not house. But grass. Hay. Winter-yellow, if I could have seen it, and covered over with a blanket of new snow, stiff enough to break my fall and roll me over once so that I came to rest on my back, buoyed up, as if in a bed. I lay there still until the train passed out of hearing, and then after. For a while I didn't feel any cold. I tried to think what I should do. Then it seemed enough time had passed, and so I got up and walked away from the tracks, keeping them exactly behind me, the line of them running perpendicular to my spine. It was steep going, uphill, but I stayed warm at least. Then I came to a lake.

I am telling this as if it were a dream. What I remember most vividly is that I was not afraid. For the first time in my life. I was not afraid because in that hour, my life had taken shape. A woman feels fear when she cannot make a shape for herself, when she does not know who she belongs to, cannot understand that she belongs to herself. But finally I had a shape, and so I got up and walked away.

After some time, I came to a rise and when I crested it, saw what I believed was a lake, frozen and glimmering in the winter night, like a vision of an answered prayer. I could see small houses, wood cabins, places people came to escape the summer's heat, but boarded up now. That was the prayer I didn't even know I was praying, I thought, please God, let there be a place. And here it was, this little village sprung up out of nowhere, just for me. The snow was deep, but I made my way through it, from cabin to cabin, pushing on the doors and windows until one of them gave a little. I pushed harder, opened the window and climbed inside.

I moved from room to room with a kind of drunken happiness, the way a new owner moves through her house, assessing, proud. There were two bedrooms, a kitchen, a sitting room and a screened porch. The people who lived there in the summer had left camp blankets and thin tattered bedspreads, and so I gathered all of these onto one of the beds, took off my boots and the two outer layers of clothes, and lay down underneath. I was warm enough. The house was more silent than anyplace I could remember. There *was wind in the trees, an owl, I thought, asking who, who, who had come into its neighborhood. I lay on my back and then I felt you move inside me. So you had survived.*

That was a certain kind of favor, Sophie, my mother would say, a blessing. She thought she would never again feel blessed in any way, not ever. She wondered how she could possibly deserve to be alive and warm and free, and she decided there must be laws for deserving that humans weren't meant to understand. She thought she would have to give me up and give her life to God.

III. ST. SULPICE

If I say I simply found myself there, in Paris, in the 4th arrondisement, would anyone believe me? 17, rue St. Antoine. The Convent of the Visitation Nuns, the order I would soon leave. It was Christmas Day, and I set out to find St. Sulpice, see its famous unmatched towers and Delacroix's *Jacob Wrestling with the Angel*. A friend suggested I should make a tour of the famous churches and take note of the mistakes, the illusions, the laws of physics that didn't apply, or did, but strangely. All is not orderly in the church, Camille, he had said, raising his eyebrows.

I thought when I saw it, Jacob is not fighting the angel. He is trying to kiss her. Kiss *him*, probably, for the angel had a man's arms and legs. The struggle is delicious now. It made me intensely happy. The forest surrounding the two figures seemed so romantic, so cool and soothing. Who would ever want to leave this place? The longer they carry on this argument, this dance, the longer they get to stay.

After a while, I wandered out and east on rue St. Sulpice to rue de Tournon and north as it becomes rue de Seine, through Place de l'Institut. I say all this as if I am one of those small machines, GPSs. So, no one gets lost anymore. This seems like a terrible precedent. Anyway, I crossed the river over the Pont des Arts, skirting the Louvre on its east end, to rue de Rivoli until it becomes rue St. Antoine.

I saw that the convent's front gate was open, and a line of women and children and a few men was being admitted. A sign outside said *Fête de Noel, 25 décembre.* A Christmas party. Some impulse seized me. I had no place to go until later, a dinner where there would be friends of friends, people I hardly knew. I stood at the end of the line, but very soon, it was not the end. A woman with two small boys waited in front of me, all three of them very quiet. The older of the two boys carried a parcel, wrapped in shiny red paper. When the woman turned to look at me, I smiled and then noticed she was looking at my coat. My good American coat. One of the boys began to whimper, and she lifted him in her arms. Almost immediately, he fell asleep, his head lolling over her shoulder. He was a very beautiful child, pale, blond, like an angel. The other child turned to look up at his mother, then raised his arms and whispered *maman, maman.* His mother said something in French, turning slightly to show the sleeping brother. Behind us was the sound of a small fast car moving up the street. I remember how the noise of it was like a crater cut into the day, and how the young boy in front of me turned toward the sound and then began to run into the street.

I didn't think. I ran and reached out my arms. And then I was holding this boy, surrounded by cars. I saw afterward that he would not have been hurt, but I had chased after him anyway, caught him, launching us both into the air and then to the ground. I must have looked like a giddy, doting relative, desperate for an embrace from this child. One of the cars stopped, a little ways beyond us, and the driver was opening his door. The parcel, which had flown out of the boy's hands when I caught him, lay three feet away, crushed under the wheels. The boy was not crying, only staring at me so that I wondered if something had happened to my face. The woman, the mother, was looking down at me, and I said, in French, without thinking, I am American, I am a Visitation nun. I pointed to the open door of the convent, and then a man took my arm and helped me to my feet. There was an acute silence, into which I stood and retrieved the crushed parcel. *Voilà*, I said to the boy, to the driver, *voilà*, as if that was the only word I knew, which, at that moment, it was. The mother still did not speak until I motioned that I would take the sleeping boy. She looked at my coat again, took a breath, and shifted the boy off her shoulder and onto mine. Then she bent to pick up her other child. We stepped up onto the sidewalk and back in line, standing so that our shoulders touched. Thank you, she said, You are very kind, Sister, and then she did not look at me. The boy she held was crying, and she whispered into his ear, words, a low song.

The line moved, not slowly, not quickly. Something that took time was happening inside in the courtyard, where voices echoed. The child breathed into my neck. He was very light. Not much more than two years old, I would guess. His cloth coat smelled like cigarettes. I am called Camille, I said to the woman. She glanced at me, then at her child, puffed out a breath. I wondered for a second if she knew not to believe me. Thank you, she said again, this time in French, and that was all.

"What does he call himself?" I said in French. I knew it was not the right way to ask the child's name, but I thought she would get my meaning.

"Jody," she said, then, "his father is American."

"*Petit Jody,*" I said. The child stirred in my arms.

The woman said *oui, le mignon,* and something like a quick smile flickered over her mouth.

"*Il fait beau,*" I said, realizing too late that this was a phrase about weather.

"This one is called Patrice," she said, indicating the other boy, the one she held.

"Also beautiful."

She laughed then, I think at my poor French as much as anything. *Joyeux Noël,* she said, slowly, as if teaching me the words, and I wished her the same.

By then we were close enough to the front entrance of the convent. Two women stood greeting the children—I heard them asking and repeating names, and I wondered what I should say, what, exactly, was called for. I was surprised by how much I wanted admission into this world. If I started talking, in any language, I would explain too much, which would mean, of course, stumbling upon the truth; *tomber* is the verb the French use, which doesn't really mean "stumble." It means "fall."

And finally, at the door, it did not matter. The woman—only one now, wearing a simple dark blue dress that might have been a habit, but also might not have been—wished us a happy Christmas and asked the names of our children. So I was a mother with a child in the season of mothers and children. Despite my good American coat, I was a woman who wanted to give my son a nice party and perhaps could not afford to.

The front room was high-ceilinged and deep, with a huge fireplace—big enough to walk into upright—at one end. A great screen, like three confessional doors joined together, stood before the burning fire. No child went anywhere near it, not even to see the nativity scene. The furniture in the room—couches, armchairs, tables with lamps—all of it had been pushed back against the walls, and the children sat on a huge Oriental rug, though a few stood pressed to women who appeared to be their mothers, or leaned against them on the sofas. The walls were decorated with greenery and red and white velvet tapestries. A quiet pandemonium was being created by Père Noël in his great green, ermine-trimmed robe, laughing and talking to the children, or conferring with Père Fouettard, who followed behind and reminded him of each child's behavior during the past year. Père Noël seemed to have a kind of shimmering about him, a reckless joy, and I was reminded of the Ghost of Christmas Present, from Dickens. I could understand enough to hear that he often overturned Père Fouettard's verdict, handing out small packages, proclaiming that this child had been very good, this child is an angel.

They were all angels. They were all sick. I understood that finally, seeing the mass of them. A few were in wheelchairs and on crutches, a boy attached to an oxygen machine, some boys and girls bald and silvery from chemotherapy. Many of them, though, had AIDS. I could see it in the lesions and the listlessness. No wonder Jody's mother had been so willing to let me hold him. Probably no one ever wanted to. I wondered if Patrice was sick as well, thought of their American father. Of course I didn't know the story, not any of it. Who did know, really? Who cared? They were children full of wishes, even Jody, who slept on and on.

One of the Sisters made a show, a beautiful pantomime, of tapping Père Noël on the shoulder, and Père Fouettard exclaimed, She has certainly been very good this year! The children laughed and the Sister whispered something to Père Noël. He thanked her and announced that there was a meal for them in the dining room. Then we all waited for a slow procession to move out of the room. The dining room faced south, and so there was a haze of pale sunlight in the doorway between the two rooms, a glowing cloud these children went walking into. It did not seem they would ever come back. It broke my heart. I believed I saw one of the Sisters take note of the same vision—I could tell by the way her arms dropped to her sides as she watched. I caught her eye and smiled. She walked over at once, patted Jody's back. *Ils pratiquent,* I thought she said.

They are practicing.

Then they were upon us, Father Christmas and his curmudgeonly helper, who was so difficult to please. They spoke to Patrice, asked, I suppose, what he wanted for Christmas, if he had been a good boy. Very naughty, said Père Fouettard, but Patrice's mother spoke, laughed, corrected, saying, no, he was a good boy. It was his father who was a bit devilish.

Then she looked at me, at Père Fouettard. "She is American," she told him. "She is a Sister." Then she told him in French about the car, the crushed gift in the street.

"Oh! Oh no! Patrice, you were very lucky!" Père Fouettard said all this, in perfect English, a flat California accent. He held his son hard against his body. "Thank you Sister," he said to me. "Thank you so much."

"He's light as a feather," I said. "He's a good sleeper."

"Like his father," he said. Then he winked at his wife. Their shared relief seemed suddenly to fill the room. Père Noël was moving on to the next mother and child, the next *pieta*. "Merry Christmas, Sister," Patrice's father said again. "Peace be with you." He touched his wife's cheek. "Peace." And in the twinkling of an eye, he was gruff again, consulting his list, wiggling his eyebrows like Groucho Marx, utterly, happily wrong about all the children. But once or twice, he glanced back at us, at Patrice, and his head seemed to tremble, to shake as if he were trying to get an image out of his mind

His wife turned and smiled, shrugged a little. She asked if Jody was too heavy, if I wanted to get something to eat. I said no and yes, and so we walked into the flood of light, carrying the children. Inside, trestle tables were piled with sandwiches, cookies, cakes, chocolates. There were smaller tables at which one might sit and eat. The sisters moved among the tables, pulling wagons full of wrapped gifts, distributing them. They seemed to know what was inside each package and who should receive it.

"You can have whatever you wish," the boys' mother said to me, gesturing toward the food. "There is so much. The children will not want it."

We sat at a small table at the back of the room, ate sandwiches and cake, while Patrice and Jody wandered back and forth between the tables, observing gifts, commenting on their suitability. His mother translated for me: "They say that is a good car, it goes fast. But the doll is silly. They say that one is not a good present for a boy."

In between, she asked me about my visit, how long I would be in Paris, did I know anyone in the city. I wanted to ask her name, but I was afraid of seeming forward. It was ridiculous, of course: I had fallen in the street with one of her children and then carried the other. But there was a way she stared at me as I spoke, a kind of distance and concern. I wondered briefly if I had something on my face, a mark, a wound, and I patted my cheeks every so often, then looked at my hands for traces of dirt or blood.

"Your family, Camille?" she asked, finally, and I realized that was it, what she was worrying about. Where was my family, on Christmas Day? Where was Sophie, the child I had given away?

"They're back home," I said. "In America. In the South."

"They must be missing you today."

It happened so fast. I tried to stop the tears, but I couldn't. They ran down my cheeks and dropped onto the table between my spread fingers.

"That's good," she said. "You cry for this whole room. You take the sorrow and get rid of it, and then it will be all right. That's what Christmas is."

When it was time to go, the woman told me her name, which was Mirette, and that Père Fouettard's real name was Andrew Place. She said it the American way, with the long *a*. She asked if they could call me, take me to dinner in gratitude for helping her. I told her it was such a small thing, but she said *non, non, non*. She wrote her number on a card from the Hotel Georges V, and it took me some time to understand she was part of the concierge staff. I found this intensely comforting. She would know how to get anywhere, find anything or anybody.

I walked back to St. Sulpice and stood again in front of Delacroix's *Jacob*. I saw it clearly then: they are dancing, Jacob and his angel. Their lovely garments thrown down are like the spill of women's coats in a back bedroom. A winter party, and one couple has danced their way into this place to be alone, apart.

IV. LIKE A CHURCH

The weather was portentous, uncertain, and the night very cold, but I knew somewhere in Paris, somewhere near the Eiffel

Tower, on New Year's Eve, I would surely be able to buy brandy if I wanted to. The wind rose and rose during the evening, until it was nearly screaming, and the streets were empty. As I walked from my apartment, I was frightened. Cut trees and their decorations came zooming at me, shreds of tinsel wrapped around my legs. Above me, on a balcony, I heard children's voices, and the pop, pop of firecrackers. The air was hazy from these small explosions, a blanket of smoke and vapor drifting lower. On rue Garibaldi, the Metro comes out of the ground, and I walked in its shadow. Although this was a wider street, it was darker, slightly uphill, the sidewalk more narrow. The few people coming toward me said *pardon*, whispered the word, and passed close, the leather on our jackets swishing companionably. This proximity, I had been told, meant that I was passing for French. Suspected tourists, a friend had said, were given a wide berth. Wear a leather jacket and boots, Camille, she told me before I left America, wear black. She had laughed then. That part you're used to, I guess, she said.

The spans of the elevated Metro made a roof, a transom, like a church. Underneath, small barrel fires and lanterns burned, and I overheard the click and shuffle of voices and bodies—vagrants, homeless—eating, settling in for the night. Someone had a radio, I could hear it, going on low, crackling talk and then music. The lights looked cheerful, decorative almost, like the paper bag lights called luminarias—such a lovely word. I knew I was probably a fool for thinking this, making this scene romantic. A man's voice called out to me, *Bonne année!* then a figure broke from the shadows and began to keep pace with me. He was young, I thought. In his twenties. I did not want to see his face.

"Don't," I said to him. "Please." I tried my French. "*S'il vous plaît.*" Tears were filling my throat. "Please leave me alone."

I started to run, and then stumbled. He caught me by the arm before I could fall to the ground. "Please don't," I said, wailed, really. I did not want to be hurt in a strange city on the last day of the old century, did not want my life to come to this moment of stupidity.

"*Madame,*" he said, and then something I did not understand.

I stopped moving, because I could not see. I thought I would be sick.

"*Je ne parle pas français,*" I told him.

"American," he said. "You are alone?"

"No," I said. I took a five-franc piece out of my pocket and held it out to him.

"*La belle dame, la plus belle dame,*" he said, the coin in his hand. He said something else I could not translate, but there was a note in his voice, a pitch. Not concern, not at all. Proof. Instruction. He was going to make me understand something. He took my left hand in his, and with the other he pulled my body close. I recall the material of my jacket crunched in his embrace—I remember the sound because I thought it was the last I might hear. The man smelled like burning wood and fish, or maybe more like the river the fish came from. Like the Seine, I thought. He said, "You are okay." Not a question. After a moment though, I did not feel afraid. People behind him watched. It was New Year's Eve, and suddenly it seemed no harm could come to me.

We danced then. This is what happened, though I still cannot quite believe it. The others behind him hooted, called out in French. He lifted me high into the air; I saw rue Garibaldi move slowly around us, and I felt amazed. This was the way to see Paris, see it all, to look literally around, dancing in the arms of a stranger who smelled like the Seine.

After two slow circles, he stopped, set me on my feet, let go my hand and my waist, stepped back.

"*Merci, Madame,*" he said, then again, holding up the five-franc piece that had been pressed between our palms. He was a shadow again, in the shadows.

"*De rien,*" I said. It is nothing.

But this is not true.

V. BUT OF COURSE

You could leap from the Pont Neuf, I thought, but almost no one does; no suicides jump from any of the bridges or *quais* in Paris. It wasn't far enough a drop—you'd just get smacked by the water, monumentally wet. Parisians would laugh at the silliness, the impurity of the gesture. Nearly twenty years ago, on my last retreat, one of the priests had said to me, *think why you cannot take the pure leap.* But I couldn't think, couldn't answer him. I could only think of it as falling. I could only think of it in a painting: Bruegel's *The Fall of Icarus.* The water, far down, falling—what did it mean in the world, which took so little notice? The city of Paris has this motto: *It floats but does not sink.*

So we crossed over the river, my almost-grown daughter and I, and then there it was, the place I'd seen all my life, so much larger than one expected, Notre Dame, lit from inside, by light, but also by music, strains of *"Adeste Fidelis."* Here, I thought, gazing at the pure leap of the flying buttress, here if you did not leap, you could enter the house of God.

Outside, tourists with candles waited in line. "Even at this hour," I said, pointing to them.

"Especially at this hour, Mother," Sophie answered.

We drifted into the crowd, and for some minutes we were gone from ourselves. We were part of an idea, part of a house, of the famous birth, longing for peace, celebration. Briefly we were separated, and I knew I could have wandered into the mingling of tourists and faithful, but I stayed where I was. I wanted Sophie to find me again, to have to look, to be afraid for me, to miss me. She was off to college in a few months, and I missed her already. A café on the corner was still open, still filled with revelers. I wanted to go there later, sit down inside, have a drink. Or maybe sit outside under the heat lamps and look up at the gargoyles, and thumb my nose at them, like a child, say you don't scare me anymore.

In a few minutes Sophie was beside me again, laughing.

"There you are," she said. "Thunderstruck."

"I am."

"Mother?" Sophie said. She put her hand near my shoulder but didn't quite touch me, as if she were afraid. "Do you want to go in?"

"No. Not right now. That's all right."

"Yes, you do," she said. "Notre Dame at the end of the century. Even I want to go in."

"The place might fall down around us if I went in."

"Of course it won't," she said.

We joined the end of the line. A young boy selling candles approached us. He said something very quickly, and Sophie laughed. She said okay in English and paid for two candles.

"He says we have to put them out before we go in. But it's pretty for now."

When the line was nearly to the doors of the nave, Sophie pressed forward to listen, then returned to me. "If you can say,

'I've come for the concert,' in French, you can get in," she said.

"You'll have to say it for me, Sophie. I can't say it."

She looked at me for a moment, right into my head, it seemed. "Can you go in, Mother?" Then she asked the question as my mother would have. "Will you allow yourself to go in?"

I nodded, unable to speak. She took my arm in hers, the material of our coats whispering darkly. Then she spoke the magic words to the man at the gate. Inside was a murmurous silence. The pews were filled, and people stood clustered in the side chapels. A boys' choir sang somewhere. I could not see them, but I thought I recognized the song—I had learned it in school—*un flambeau, Jeanette, Isabella, un flambeau, j'arrive au berceau*. That's what French waiters say, *j'arrive*. I'm coming. I'll be right there.

Beside us, pressed close to the wall, a man held a child on his shoulders. Little by little, as the boys' silvery notes rose into the air, I watched this child fall asleep, his head leaning forward over his father's, and then back finally to rest against the stone cloak of—who was it? I could not see the name at the foot of the statue—a female saint. The child's lips moved a little in his sleep, visions of sugarplums, is what I thought, what I hoped. The father seemed aware of his son's shift and stillness. He smiled, touched the woman next to him with his elbow, rolled his eyes upward when she looked at his face. She saw her child sleeping and smiled too. Our eyes met, and she gave a little shrug, closed her eyes, exhaled.

How easy it is, I thought, to get her meaning. I was astounded. For many years, many years ago, I'd lived in a house of women religious, a place where the signs and gestures nearly always eluded me. What did it mean, I was always asking, this sign, that look, this little voice, that hurried promise? And here, now, in a foreign land, the expression on a woman's face, the smallest shift in her body, all of it was so clear. They need to be held aloft, she was telling me, children need to be kept from falling. And they sleep anywhere. Wouldn't you like that? she was asking. Wouldn't we all like it, to be held in the air, to be so at peace? She put her arm around her husband's waist. This will end, I thought; we will go in peace. The people who were standing began to mill about, shift, compose themselves back into the world, make a crowd. I took Sophie's hand and she squeezed mine. I would need to hold on to get out.

La Fenêtre

Madame Rouffanche wrote beautiful, excruciating letters. This was in 1952, eight years after the Germans burned my town, Oradour sur Glane, and murdered nearly everyone in it. She wrote about those who survived, the five men and herself. She recalled her leap from the window of the burning church. She knew the death of my father, that he did not suffer. Robert Hébras had been standing behind him and saw a bullet pierce his chest. *He died quickly,* she wrote, *in Robert's arms, for he fell backward. He said a few words. Then they set the barns on fire. I buried your sister, Josephine, whom we could still identify, and buried your mother, who had been burned almost beyond recognition. There are photographs.* So the trial will be difficult, she explained, because there was so much horrifying evidence. For instance, a box containing the remains of a baby had been discovered in one of the ovens in my father's bakery. And there would be Alsatian defendants, conscripts after the Nazis annexed Alsace. *These were Frenchmen,* she wrote, *who killed their brothers.* She wrote all this without emotion, except for her last question, which rang off the page as if she were screaming, *How did you escape, Mirande, when so many others could not?*

I wrote back—I could not help myself. I told her I was married now and had a son. I told her something of my reasons for not coming to the trial, that I could not bear it, that my life was in Normandy, in the seaside town of Port-en-Bessin. My father's sister, who had taken care of me all these years, needed me in her restaurant. I told Madame Rouffanche I loved the sea, that it was hard on my spirit to be away from water. She replied that she had suspected this—my discontent had always been palpable. Everyone knew I would get away, that Oradour could not hold me. But, if I would not come to her, Madame Rouffanche wrote, she would come to me. She would bring the photographs.

She had asked us to meet her outside the cathedral in Bayeux, which is called Notre Dame, though it bears little resemblance to its sister in Paris. I remember that it seemed strange not to have my son, Bertrand, with me on this excursion, and I found myself turning to look for him, as if he had fallen behind. I did not leave him very often, though of course he was in school. And so it was in the act of turning to look that I saw Madame Rouffanche, eight years and many lifetimes older, but still every bit herself in a black dress and boots and an electrifyingly white lace collar just visible beneath the top of her coat. She gripped a large black bag with red handles, and walked with a slight limp, which may have been caused by the weight of what she was carrying. I mean this literally of course, the bag, but it is also true that she walked in the places of the dead, all who had perished in the church and the barns, and this would have made for a strangeness in her gait.

My aunt Genevieve turned and gasped. We stopped and waited. The sky seemed to darken suddenly. Then Madame Rouffanche recognized me. She put her hand to her mouth, not in horror, but as one would move to hide part of an uncontrollable expression, and stood perfectly still. When I embraced her, I felt her tears on my cheek.

"You are the vision of your mother," she said finally. "And you"—here she turned to Genevieve—"are your brother's image."

We stood in silence for a moment, awkwardly. Madame Rouffanche shifted the bag to her other hand, and then Genevieve took it from her. Madame Rouffanche wiped her eyes. "I have not wept over it in some years. I do not like to. It seems dishonorable."

"It's not," Genevieve said quickly. "This is heavy, Madame. I hope you did not have to carry it far."

"Just from the hotel. But where shall we go?"

"There is a café, La Fermie, in the next street."

"Yes, of course. But about the photographs what will we do? They should not be seen by others. They are—difficult. Maybe . . ." She looked up then, at the cathedral, the high windows. "We are right here. I think at this hour, there will be enough light. Then afterward we can have quiet, or you may do as you like."

So we went into this Notre Dame, down the eight steep steps from the street. We sat down in three chairs in the back row, where daylight filtered in over our shoulders, illuminating our hands. We waited a moment, and then Madame Rouffanche closed her eyes and spoke disconnectedly of what we would see, who had taken the photographs and how she had come to have them. She said she had chosen the role of historian, since she no longer had a husband, children, or grandchildren. There were pictures of my father, she said, and my mother, and Josephine. She reached into her bag then and drew out a large envelope, which she laid on my lap. On the front was written the family name "Duqueroix."

I thought I should hand the envelope to Genevieve, but then I opened it quickly. The photograph of Papa was on top. He was unmistakable, his face singed but not burned. It was plain that he had lain tangled with other bodies, near the bottom of a heap, and the fire in the barn had burned itself out before it reached him. I thought I would be sick, but then all sensation left me. He looked peaceful; I told myself this lie. He looked as if he had gone to sleep with his face half in shadow, in an old shirt with a dark smudge on the front, wine perhaps, or oil from his car. He had been working on his car and had fallen asleep, that was all. I might go to Oradour and wake him, or find him already awake, refreshed, at work in the bakery, his face and body white with flour, pure white, from head to foot.

I did not linger over the other pictures, my sister, Josephine, holding the child, who looked like a dark-furred stuffed toy in her arms, the face seared away except for the round mouth, open in a scream. Mama, whom I could not recognize at all, lying half on top of a child, who was barely burned, though it appeared their bodies had fused together. The altar was beside them, its remains, rather, and a stone crucifix. I felt a terrible thing then: envy. I envied this child my mother's body, that they held each other so closely, that this death had been the perfect reverse of birth. I gave the pictures to Genevieve and she looked too, then put them away and handed the envelope to me.

I heard the rain begin, and then come harder, and I listened to it with every part of my body, with blood, with flesh, with bone, as if the force of this rain were the sum total of my parts. There was a flash across our three pairs of clasped hands, and then a single splintering crack of thunder, but just one, and then the rain, only the rain, a steady gentle pattering, as if it had been going on forever and would never stop. The day darkened further. We did not move.

Behind us, the vestibule of the cathedral filled with murmuring voices, the surprised citizens of Bayeux, or visitors, as we three were. We heard the soft shufflings and muted rattle of coats removed and shaken and put back on. There was, in all these sounds, the particular consternation that sudden weather brings as it makes adults children and makes children more so. To be in a church because one cannot go out. I turned and saw that the people behind us faced away from the altar, looking out of the cathedral and up at the sky. Where has this come from? they seemed to be asking. Why here? Why now, when we are so unprepared?

Madame Rouffanche took my right hand in both of hers. "It seems we must stay a little longer," she whispered and glanced up toward the windows. They were quite high, and all were closed.

Genevieve turned and looked past me. "I am very glad to have seen these," she said. She paused while Madame Rouffanche nodded slowly. "For some years, I have thought that my brother might not be dead. I thought perhaps he might have lost his mind or his memory."

I recalled what Madame Rouffanche had written, that someone had seen my father shot, but I did not say anything.

"But this," she continued, patting the envelope, "this has shown me. This has ended it." She began to cry, but spoke through her tears. "I am really quite relieved," she said. "I am at peace."

In the café we spoke quietly. All this time, Madame Rouffanche's gaze drifted over the other people there, as if she were looking for someone. The wine she drank seemed to make her sleepy, and her eyes had a stealth to them, as if they were trying to be quiet. Then suddenly they opened very wide.

"How did you do it, Mirande?" she asked me. "Josephine saw you that morning at home. How did you get away?"

"I pretended to be dead."

"But where?"

"In Limoges."

"So you weren't in Oradour? But how did you get to Limoges by that time? And why should you have to be dead? There was no attack in Limoges."

"They knew where I lived."

"Who?"

"The Germans I worked for."

"I don't understand," Madame Rouffanche said. She exchanged a glance with Genevieve. Their faces were full of wonder and sympathy.

"I don't either," I said.

"I had not heard this part," Genevieve said.

"Perhaps you were hurt. Perhaps you don't remember."

"There was a deep gash on her forehead," Genevieve said, "when she came to us."

"But how did you do it? All on your own. With the Germans marching in the same direction. How did you manage it?"

"I don't know. We traveled those roads every summer. I just kept going."

Again, Madame Rouffanche and Genevieve looked at each other. I thought they must suspect the truth, that the Germans had saved me.

LA FENÊTRE

~

Madame Rouffanche stayed in Bayeux for a few days. I did not invite her to Port-en-Bessin, and it seemed she did not want especially to go there. I was relieved. I felt oddly enough as if she were unlucky, a talisman of ill fortune. This is absurd, of course, because she had the good luck to find the open window in the church and climb through it, survive the fall to the ground and hide from the Germans and live to testify against them at the trial. But I did not want her inside my house.

I went to Bayeux for one last time to see her, and even then I was not sure I would go to Bordeaux for the trial. She had not mentioned my going, not once; the trial, yes, she had spoken of often. She knew who the judge would most likely be; she knew the hotel the journalists would stay in; she knew even that the courthouse was small, and outside Bordeaux, in case there was a disturbance. That afternoon we wandered in the shops admiring lace, and she bought a few pieces to take home. She did not say to whom she would give them, only the phrase, *she would like these.* She spoke these words as if dreaming, as if she were thinking of her daughter, Marie-Louise. We were very nearly the same age. And it came to me then that I had been thinking of Madame Rouffanche as my mother, not the woman who behaved so badly and broke my father's heart, but the mother who seemed in her last years to recognize something of herself in me, who strove to treat this resemblance very carefully, with great attention.

Just before we parted, Madame Rouffanche took my hand, opened it, and dropped a small parcel into the palm. "I saw this," she said, "from where I was lying with my face in the tomatoes. I saw the German, Diekmann, come out of your house. His hands were full of banknotes and bottles of wine, other things. He could not carry it all, and so he dropped this, without knowing. It rolled to the side of the road, and I kept my eye fixed on it. Fixed. For an hour, for five hours until the sun set. This shiny little thing. I believe it kept me from losing my mind. So I have not wanted to part with it. But it is yours really. You should have it."

I opened the cloth and there was my mother's wedding ring. I knew it instantly from the date inside, *12 juillet 1922*, and my father's name. My vision blurred. I knew there was only one occasion for which my mother took off her wedding ring, and this was when she went to help my father at the bakery. This she did very rarely, but it meant that relations between them were peaceful. I remembered she had gone more often that spring—Josephine and I had remarked upon this to each other. It seemed her infidelities might finally be put behind them. I placed the ring on my own left index finger, where it fit.

"I have heard," Madame Rouffanche said, "there is a vein in that finger which runs straight to the heart. And there is a saying that one ties a string around this finger in order to be reminded to do something."

"What should I be reminded to do?"

She did not say anything for a moment. "You should come to the trial. At the very least you might identify some of the Germans. Perhaps they passed by you at work."

"I don't know."

"It is my last wish, Mirande. There is something you know that you haven't told. I am afraid if you don't go voluntarily, you will be summoned and you will be treated like a fugitive."

A German had come into our house and taken our things. This had happened all over France. I kissed my mother's wedding ring. I had missed her for eight years, but I had not really felt her loss until now.

"I'll go," I said. "Someone from the family should be there. Genevieve would like to, but she cannot leave the restaurant. I will go."

It happened, strangely, that I still had the Oradour photographs when I arrived at home. I had meant to return them to Madame Rouffanche. I thought in fact I had given them to her, but there was the envelope stuffed into my bag. I could not think what to do with them, and impulsively I ran out the door and down to the harbor, intending to weight the envelope with rocks and cast it into the sea.

On the *quai,* though, another desire took hold of me, and I turned back to the house, where I went into our water closet and locked the door. A small shelf and drawer on the wall held toiletries, grooming items, combs. I found a pair of fingernail scissors and set to work on the top two photographs, cutting carefully around the faces of my father and then my sister, liberating them from their deaths. These I hid in the back of my dresser drawer. The rest I threw into the incinerator. Thus my family was twice consumed by fire, this last time to ashes, as I looked on.

Before the trial began, I found I could not stop thinking of a certain detail I had heard about the judge, repeated over and over in the news so that its repetition came to be more meaningful than the information itself. This was not even about the judge himself, actually, but about his uncle, the composer Camille Saint-Saëns, who was an eccentric genius and heard music more accurately than what the world could accommodate. For his

"Organ Symphony," it was written in *Le Figaro*, 33-rpm vinyl records had to be specially cut, because the bass notes have such fullness, and the needle could not track them otherwise. There was, I thought, the suggestion that the nephew might have a similar talent, though manifested judicially, that he would hear in the testimonies at Bordeaux what no one else could. There was the sense of bass notes as comparable to truth, or maybe evil. This last was the comparison I fixed upon, I should admit.

I arrived at Bordeaux a few days before the Germans were scheduled to appear, because I wanted to see them right away, make sure I knew none of them. I felt certain Fleigel would not be there. But if he were, I knew I would have to behave differently, though I did not know how. I tried to think of it, this alternate course of action, but nothing came into my head. I wondered if I would be able to go home afterward, home to Port-en-Bessin. Madame Rouffanche had booked a room for me in the hotel where she was staying, a very comfortable place, where the French and European press were also lodged. I thought I might stay there and not ever leave, that Fleigel would find me, now or in ten, twenty, thirty years, and we would have a final scene, and he would explain why he had not sent me home to die with the others.

In the early morning of January 12, 1953, I was awakened by many shouting voices. At first, this did not surprise me, for the hotel was filled with a contentious group of Alsatians, Limousins, and others from all over France who argued loudly in the hallways. But as I came into full consciousness, what I heard sounded quite different from the usual disagreements. There was a great clomping of hurried footsteps and slamming of doors, and finally the muted shout, from outside the hotel, *They have arrived!*

I dressed and went out with the journalists, the partisans, failing to understand for a time that these were the Alsatian prisoners on the train and not the Germans. But I had not experienced such a fury in the night since the war. It was very cold, but still many men wore only shirtsleeves or thin sweaters, and no one seemed to feel the chill. The shouting grew to a roar as the train pulled into the station, and then approached the apocalyptic as eleven men stepped out of the second car and onto the platform. They blinked in the bright lights and huddled together, saying nothing at first. Then one made an inquiry, and the press shouted at him to speak up. I could hear that he was asking for his legal representative, and then some of the others took up the cry. "Monsieur Boerner!" first a call, then a question, and it seemed the whole crowd in the station held its one breath to listen. No one answered or came forward, and the shouting began again.

I began to be afraid for these eleven. The members of the press had kept their distance at first, but now there was a surge forward and the explosion of cameras flashing. The Alsatians began to inch their way along the platform. One of them seemed ready to collapse and had to be half-carried by the others. Two members of the Alsatian press broke away and went looking for taxis, while the eleven moved slowly out of the station and into the street. There were lampposts, and I thought I saw the journalists from Limoges look up at them and whisper to one another. I was seized by a terrible dread that had at its core a fine prickling of guilt. I thought if I didn't say what I knew, these men would be hanged in street.

Police appeared, but stood away from the crowd, waiting to see what would happen. We all stood in the high, false light from the street lamps and from the battery-powered torches that some men waved over the faces and bodies of the accused. The garble of accents calling out questions, the mist of our exhaled breath in the cold, the intermittent silence and the crablike scuttling of the Alsatians. It was a vision of hell, anyone would have said this, but I thought it was worse. At least in hell one knows who will suffer and why.

At last, as if it were what we had been waiting for, there was a gunshot, the crowd dispersed, and in the same instant, the taxis, three of them arrived. The Alsatians climbed in and sped away to the hotel where their lawyers had slept through the *zinzin*, journalist's argot, which sounds to me like the whiz of a bullet against one's head. After this came silence and extraordinary darkness, an illusion created by the held breath of dawn, the moment when everyone in the world, in every language, wonders if the sun will come up again. The journalists seemed to have turned inside out, gone to shadow, shivering, mute.

In the morning, just as the German defendants arrived, I received a telegram from Madame Rouffanche, explaining that she was too ill to attend at present, but hoped to join me in ten days. At first, I felt lost, but then a kind of visceral relief took over, and I wondered if I might sit in the courtroom without being recognized. I had the documents required to gain admittance, and a bailiff let me in to the courtroom at three o'clock in the afternoon. There was no place to sit, so I wedged myself into a corner of the back wall, trying not to look anyone in the eye. The judge, Saint-Saëns, was speaking, his voice even and pitched low, though not quite so low, I imagined, as his uncle's musical compositions. From that distance, it was difficult to see much of him, but my overwhelming impression was of calm. I stared at the judge a long time, gathering the courage to look elsewhere.

And then I did, as Saint-Saëns read out the names of the defendants, eleven Alsatians and seven Germans. My vision darkened at the edges, and I leaned heavily on the arm of the man next to me, which caused him to peer into my face. I turned my cheek, as if from a strong wind.

"My God!" he said, then cleared his throat. "You are Mirande Duqueroix." Then he lowered his voice. "I am Marcel Belliers, Mirande. Do you remember me?"

I did. Madame Rouffanche had told me Marcel escaped by hiding in a cow stall. He was younger than I, the age of Josephine. I wondered why he was back here, instead of at the front of the courtroom with the witnesses, the other families.

"Diekmann," Marcel said, as if in answer to my question. "Just there, left of Weber. He is the one who led my mother away."

"Are you sure?"

"Yes. That face. Did you see it when he turned? Like a pig's. He doesn't look like any of the others. Anyway, how could I ever forget it." This was not a question.

"No," I said. "One cannot forget the faces. But why are you here, so far back?"

"I am afraid to be so close."

"Afraid?"

"Afraid of them and afraid of myself."

"I see."

"But it is a miracle that you escaped," Marcel said. "How did you do it? And you have never come back," Marcel said. "After all these years. So why have you come now?"

"Madame Rouffanche—"

"She is very ill. We are worried that she won't be able to testify."

"I think she'll manage," I said. "I saw her in Bayeux a month ago. This trial is the meaning of her life."

Marcel looked at me oddly and repeated his question, "How did you get away?"

"I'm not sure. I don't remember."

"Perhaps something happened." He stopped speaking and put a finger to his temple, the gesture for madness.

"Perhaps," I said.

The Germans testified for two weeks. They were brutal in their speech, in their arrogant defenses. They looked to be jaundiced, some of them, or anemic. I thought perhaps they had suffered. But there were occasional moments of tenderness: when he finished speaking, Weber touched his daughter's cheek. Boos wept and bent toward his wife, and she kissed him, gently, on his balding head. Most days I went to the courtroom, but when I felt tired or unsettled by the testimony or by Marcel's endless inquiries, I stayed at the hotel. One afternoon, I traveled to Bordeaux, which I found to be a pleasant enough city, perhaps a little dull. Without my family around me, I missed the sea, and so I went to the port, but the vista of the Atlantic Ocean was too vast. This is nonsense of course, all in my head. Still, I felt there was something manageable about looking out across the English Channel. There was an end to it, another side, a few hours away. This was how the trial cast its long shadow: *another side, an end to it.* These were the things I wished for.

At the beginning of the third week, much of the testimony was given by Jean Canon, a Maquisard. He said he believed the

Germans had made a mistake, that the town they meant to destroy was Oradour-sur-Vayres, twenty kilometers away. This other Oradour, he said, was a known center for the Resistance. Where Diekmann was captured by the Maquis, he saw a sign for Oradour, and he reported this after his escape, but incompletely. After he spoke, there was silence. What did it mean, except that the Germans were careless? Did we not already know this about them?

Beside me, Marcel was trembling, and then he began to shout, "That is the man who killed my mother!" His voice became an unworldly shriek. He said the words again and again, as if he'd gone mad, and no one made a move to stop him. The silence continued otherwise, as if it had been merely translated, as if this were silence turned inside out. Marcel left his place beside me and moved down the center aisle of the courtroom.

"For God's sake, *who?*" Saint-Saëns called. He did not tell Marcel to stop or go back. Marcel came to the row of defendants and pointed at Diekmann, who stood and turned toward Marcel and then the rest of the courtroom. His face was stark white.

"I was never in Oradour!" he shouted. "I was a sentry outside."

One of the conscripts, Boos, rose then, shaking with anger, and raised his fist. "No!" he said. "All the Alsatians were in the town."

"It's not true," Weber said. "I was not there."

"Don't be a liar," Boos called to him. "Don't add that to your sins."

Saint-Saëns demanded order and asked Marcel to approach. When he did, I could see that Marcel looked terribly, mortally ill. He was younger than I by a few years, as I have said, and had always been a fine athlete, a football player. Now he appeared as helpless as a child, the child he was then, as if he would see his mother led away all the rest of his life. Saint-Saëns asked if he was sure, suggesting memories could fade with time.

"No," Marcel said and touched his heart. "I remember here. Forget? It's not possible." He pointed once again at Diekmann.

The next day it was announced that the deposition of Madame Rouffanche would have to be read, as she was too ill to attend. Then Saint-Saëns did a very strange thing, though to know his family would have been to expect this. He began to speak about sound. Did we know what sound was? he asked. Of course we did: waves, particles, reverberation, echo, pitch, volume, all working together to produce that which we understand through our ears. Did we know, he wondered, that the sense of sound, hearing, was the one of the five senses least likely to give a false impression? The eye might cloud, the palate dull and take the nose along with it, the touch go numb. But sound—if one is not deaf—is a kind of truth, a center of gravity.

"I could read Madame Rouffanche's deposition, or have it read by M. Brouillard, the lawyer for the prosecution, but I do not think this would be right," he said. "This testimony, by the only woman who survived the fire in the church, where all the other women died, ought not to be read by a man. I have conferred with Madame Rouffanche on this point and she agreed."

I felt a pain under my ribs, a burning there as I began to understand his intention.

"Madame Rouffanche suggested her deposition be read by Mirande Duqueroix Bruhot. If Madame would be so kind as to approach."

I stood up immediately, perhaps before Saint-Saëns had finished speaking, so great was my distress. I believed he had only made a request, and I would tell him I could not do it. I moved into the aisle and forward, past the gendarmes, past the legal representatives, the Germans and Alsatians. I wanted, strangely, to reach out and touch the coats of Dagenhardt and Daab on my right, Prestel and Ochs on my left. Graff looked up at me, and I saw the patch over his left eye was dark green, not black as I had thought. I stepped before Saint-Saëns and whispered, no, please. I can't.

"I am not asking you," he said. "I am telling you."

"I'm sorry, but my sister . . ." Surely he had read the deposition, and would know what had happened to Josephine.

"*S'il vous plaît, Madame.*" I think now he was not imploring me, not really.

Saint-Saëns handed me the printed deposition, and I turned to face the courtroom. A very particular sensation came over me, a kind of tingling and the sort of separation from my body I feel if I have gone a long time without food. I saw before me not the courtroom but the face of Madame Rouffanche, and then a misty darkness, so that I had to glance down at the paper to steady myself.

"About two o'clock in the afternoon," I began, "on the 10th of June 1944, German soldiers burst into my house and told me to go to the fairground, together with my husband, my son, two daughters, and my grandson. A number from the village were already assembled, and men and women were flocking in from all directions. They were followed by the schoolchildren, who arrived separately. The Germans divided us into two groups, women and children on one side, men on the other. The first group, of which I was one, was taken under armed escort to the church. This was all the women of the town, especially mothers, who arrived at the house of God with their babies in their arms or pushing them in their prams. All the schoolchildren were there as well. We must have numbered several hundred. Crammed inside the church, we waited in growing anxiety to see what would happen next. Around 4 p.m., a few soldiers, about twenty years of age, brought into the nave, close to the choir, a large kind of box, from which hung strings, which trailed on the ground."

Here, I paused and looked up from the page. The courtroom was perfectly still. A stranger, even a visitor from some other world, would have immediately understood who was guilty and who was not. The Germans in front of me, and the Alsatians, every one of them had bowed his head. Even when I stopped speaking they did not look up. The rest of the throng, the French especially, stared at me, their faces raised, their mouths forming the round O's of terror, as if I were one of the women in the church, who would have been, at this moment, just beginning to understand her fate.

"When the trailing strings were lit, the device suddenly exploded with a loud bang and gave off a thick, black suffocating smoke. Women and children, half-choking and screaming in terror, rushed to those parts of the church where the air was still breathable."

Something happened to my voice here; I could not help it. I felt the smoke in my own lungs. I tried not to cough and then glanced up at Saint-Saëns, whose eyes had gone wide with horror. I wondered what sort of transformation was taking place, if my hair and skin and clothes had turned black with soot.

"It was then that the door to the sacristy was broken down, under the irresistible pressure of a terrified crowd. I followed them and sat down on a step. My daughter joined me. The Germans saw that people had escaped into the room and cold-bloodedly shot everyone who was hiding there. My daughter was killed where she was, by a shot from outside. I owe my life to my closing my eyes and feigning death. A volley was fired in the church; then straw, firewood, and chairs were thrown in a heap over the flagstones. I had escaped the slaughter unwounded and took advantage of a cloud of smoke to hide behind the main altar. In that part of the church, there were three windows. I went to the middle one, the biggest, and with the aid of the stool used for lighting the candles, tried to climb up. I don't know how I managed it, but terror gave me strength. I heaved myself up as best I could and fell about ten feet through the broken glass. Looking back up, I saw I had been followed in my climb by Josephine Duqueroix."

I had been waiting for this part, her name, my sister and the story of her last minutes alive, but I had forgotten too. I felt a great pain in my chest, a log rammed against my breastbone. I believed I could not go on. Saint-Saëns leaned his forehead on his hand. I walked to the bench.

"This is my sister," I whispered to him. "I cannot read any further."

"Yes, you can," he said, his voice also lowered. "This is how you will revenge her death. This is how you will make it worth something."

"I can't."

"You can. Turn around."

"No."

"*Madame.*" The judge did not raise his voice, but somehow it grew louder in my head. "Remember how to know the truth. Remember what sense does not lie. Now turn around."

I turned. I found Marcel in the crowd, who appeared to me

again, as a child in want of its mother. "Josephine Duqueroix," I repeated, "who from the height of the window was holding out a child, my grandson, who had been badly burned. She, they, fell next to me. Alerted by the child's crying, the Germans fired at us. Josephine and the baby were killed instantly."

I read these words, but I was not there, present in the courtroom. I was myself, eight and a half years before, escaping out the window of an office in Limoges, traveling on a train from there to Paris, Paris to Caen, along the road to Bayeux, to Arromanches, to Porte-en-Bessin, a great gash on my forehead where my German lover had put his boot.

"I was myself wounded, as I crawled away to a nearby garden," I read on, but I was in Limoges, standing below the window while this German held traveling papers aloft. Then he sent them into the air, one page at a time. As if they were ashes, the wind took them a little ways, and I had to run after them. When I turned back to the window, he was still there, leaning on the sill, holding my shoes, which he then dropped, straight down. *You will need these*, he called in German, then *run* and *don't ever come back*.

I read the rest of the deposition: "I hid among rows of peas and tomatoes, and I waited in terror for help to arrive. I was not rescued until the following day, in the early evening."

There was no more writing on the paper. I seemed to be falling into that white margin at the bottom of the page, then I reached behind and placed it on the judge's desk. He thanked me and I returned to my seat. He spoke, but I did not hear the words. I was not in that place. Perhaps he was wrong about sound. What if there is no one present to hear a sound? What then? It seemed to me then the only way to keep myself in one piece was to keep Madame Rouffanche's page from turning white, keep the words coming onto it, marching across it in their neat rows, though the words would now have to be mine. My lover had said it, every day that I worked for him, over and over, *Write this down. I promise I will keep you safe. Write this down. Your writing is very beautiful. I will keep you safe. You are a fine writer. I will keep you.*

When Madame Rouffanche came the next day, I wondered at her good health. She had entered the courtroom through a side door before anyone else, and occupied a large armchair in front of the Germans. The chair was so much bigger than she that from behind, it appeared as if no one sat there. She had thought of it herself, I felt sure, that a ghost would seem to be speaking against the defendants, a person who was missing, a true representative of Oradour. When the court convened, Saint-Saëns asked if she had anything to add to her written statement.

"I have nothing more to say," her voice intoned from the empty chair.

Jean Brouillard, the lawyer for the plaintiffs, began to question Robert Hébras, one of the five men who had survived, asking him to describe what had happened in Laudy's barn. This was, I knew, where my father had died.

"It was stifling hot," Robert began. "We were herded together while the Germans set up a pair of machine guns."

"How long did this take?" Brouillard asked.

"Some minutes. Maybe twenty."

"And then?"

"We waited."

"At what time did the Germans begin firing the machine guns?"

There was some discussion here, the lawyers for the defense

arguing that Robert had not actually said the Germans fired.

M. Brouillard restated the question. "Then what happened, M. Hébras?"

At four o'clock we heard an explosion, which sounded like a grenade. Then the men behind the machine guns settled into position and fired. The guns were aimed low, so most men were hit in the legs."

"Most men?"

"M. Duqueroix, who stood just in front of me, had been so startled by the explosion that he fell to his knees. He was shot in the chest."

"Go on."

"The guns stopped, but all around me, there were shattered bodies. Men wailed and groaned."

"What did the Germans do then?"

"They covered us with hay and wood and set the barn on fire."

"With living, wounded men inside?"

"Yes."

"Did you know any of the living beside yourself?"

"M. Duqueroix was still alive."

"How do you know this?"

"Because we spoke. As the fire was being lit."

"What did you speak of?"

Robert did not answer for what seemed like a long time. He looked up at the ceiling of the courtroom, and then his face contorted with rage and sickness and deep despair.

"We spoke of music."

"Music?" said Brouillard, and Saint-Saëns echoed him, his

voice full of anger and confusion, as if he believed Robert mocked him.

"Yes," Robert said quietly. "I still hear it sometimes in my dreams. The Germans played music while they executed us. M. Duqueroix and I tried to think where it was coming from. We wondered what it was. We wanted to remember if Laudy had a phonograph. He had a radio; we knew that much. The music was . . . *bullying,* M. Duqueroix said. Then he was quiet."

"He died?"

"No. Yes. He said his wife's name and he took my hand in his, and then he didn't speak anymore after that. I felt his hand grow cold."

"Bullying," Saint-Saëns repeated. "I would like to know what music that was." He looked out at the Germans and the Alsatians. "Does any one of you know?"

Robert went on to tell the rest of his story: how he made his way from under the burning hay and discovered himself to be one of the five survivors, how one of them, the stonemason Matthieu Borie, took a wall apart, stone by stone, to make a gap through which all five escaped. How they hid in the hayloft of another barn, which was then set on fire, and then escaped to the rabbit hutches behind it, moving from the first to the second to the third as each one in turn caught fire. How they ran for their lives and hid near the river all that night and into the next morning, when they returned to silence and smoke.

At 2 a.m. on Friday, February 13, I was awakened by the *boom, boom, boom* of the Great Bell of Bordeaux, and so I knew there was a verdict. I dressed as fast as I could and went to stand in the square outside the court building. The bell rang and rang for long minutes, and then the sentences were read. The wailing from the French began immediately, countered by silence from the Alsatian press, who did not, it seemed, know whether to rejoice or despair. There were two death sentences, for Lenz and Boos, and the rest received hard labor, twelve years for the Germans, eight for the Alsatians.

The crowd exploded in a frenzy of shouting. Someone fired a pistol near my head. It was easy, advisable even, to leave the square, leave the district. I hurried back into the hotel and packed my bag, and ran along a backstreet until I found a taxi—I did not have to go very far. The drivers were arranged off the square, eager to carry the news themselves. I asked the driver to take me to Le Remeyeaux, to the train station. I told him I would pay extra for speed, and he nodded and turned toward the wheel in a manner that suggested he believed the verdicts had driven me mad. He himself was very angry and spoke of the crime and the trial. He was from Tulle, and he remembered the Maquisards' bodies hanging from the lampposts there. He said his mother told him not to look and kept him away from that part of town, but at night, he went to look and saw the families sobbing beneath their dead. He said this had done something grave to him. He said he used to be an auto mechanic, but he could no longer remember how the parts of an engine were supposed to work. He drove me to the train station, and I bought a one-way ticket home.

Madame Rouffanche was there also, waiting for her train. She took my hands in hers and looked down at them, not at my face, turned them over, seemed to examine the palms. "You took dictation for them," she said. "You did their writing. And more." She held my hands to her face. "You always were a beautiful writer. And now you have seen this through to the end." She let go of my hands and put her own palm to my cheek, a slap without force. "You are forgiven."

I felt as if I had fallen through a fissure in the universe. I had entered the past and might be caught there forever if I did not see my son and husband, my aunt. At the station in Caen, I could not stop kissing them, nor weeping. When we came to our house, my husband put me to bed with a glass of brandy and forbade me to get up. When she saw me that evening, Genevieve declared that I looked half dead, and I told her I felt exactly that. I slept and woke and always my son, Bertrand, was there, holding my hand, or placing his hand on my forehead, offering the same cup or glass or bowl. I began to wonder if years had not passed and the son had grown into the father, into his image. In the middle of the night, when no one was there, it might be that years had passed, and I was old, infirm, alone as I deserved to be.

On Wednesday, when I got out of bed, everyone seemed to be behaving even more oddly. Philippe did not speak. Genevieve turned off the radio as soon as I entered the restaurant. I shrugged and went back out into the street, wandered toward Bertrand's school, opened the front door and went inside. The hall was dry and warm, with boys' breath, I thought. There was the inviting smell of lunch cooking. I sat down on a bench below the round rose window and listened to voices in the classrooms, asking questions, droning their lessons. I thought I could distinguish Bertrand's voice reading a poem, a Lafontaine fable, the fox and the grapes. I thought of Robert Hébras's sister, who kissed him good-bye after their lunch and then went off to be murdered by the Germans, the Alsatians, both of them. I thought of Josephine, climbing ten feet with a crying baby in her arms, and my father, whose last words were about music.

My head dropped into my hand, and then there was an insistent finger tapping on my shoulder, on the back of my neck. "Mama," Bernard was saying. "Wake up! Why are you sleeping here?"

"Oh my darling boy!" I said. "I was so tired. But I wanted to see you." I brushed his dark hair out of his eyes.

"Have you come for me, Mama? I have already heard the news."

Suddenly I was quite awake. "What news?" I pulled Bernard roughly onto the bench. "What do you mean? Tell me!"

"The National Assembly has passed an act of amnesty. All the conscripts are pardoned. Your mayor—"

"Who?"

"The mayor of Oradour has returned the Legion of Honor medals. He says France has made a mockery of the victims, and his city will no longer be a part of France."

My body went cold. "Can you take me home?"

Bernard nodded, but we did not move.

"Mama," he whispered, "they say your father is dishonored."

"No," I said. "Not in himself. Not that way, not because of something he *did*." Bertrand stared at me, not comprehending.

"Then what?"

"No one is being punished for a large crime. No one has learned a lesson."

Bertrand sat beside me and I held him for a long time. I stroked my son's hair and kissed the top of his head. No one disturbed us. The school seemed to have emptied out, through the back door. No more lessons to be learned today.

"Maman?" Bertrand said. "Did your papa and mama do that when you sat together?"

"Do what?"

"What you're doing now. Touching my hair. Kissing my head."

"Yes, my darling boy. Yes, they did."

"Then I have an idea. Close your eyes, and let me do it, and you can pretend it's them."

As we sat there, I did as he suggested. I did pretend. Bertrand asked me to tell him a story about my father, my mother, my sister. "Pretend they are still alive." I did that too.

In my recent letters to Madame Rouffanche, I mention that I have begun writing stories for children, that she might like to read them, these stories about girls and boys who were in Occupied France and had acted heroically during the war. Small acts of heroism, I explained, such as taking food to the elderly, rarely anything to do with combat, but set in the atmosphere of vague dread that we lived through. Most of the stories concerned a family like mine, two parents, two sisters. Sometimes the father was away, fighting in Germany or Belgium or Poland. There is always a window, in each of these tales, a window high up, which someone must open. Sometimes this is an important part of the heroism, and sometimes it is not. But the window is always there, always mentioned. I try to write a story without a window in it, I told her in one letter, but then I feel as if I am suffocating, as if the story will be meaningless, a failure. When I put the window in, even at the very end, even a window that a young girl glances out of into the sky, I am relieved, and I know the story is finished.

Amuse Bouche

"I've been having these dreams about intimacy," she said.

"I've been having these dreams about flying," he said.

Both thought this, but neither one said it: *That's the same dream.*

"What happens in your dreams?" he asked.

"A man puts his arm around me. His arm is very long. Don't laugh. This arm is almost inhuman. We're very warm and comfortable. I'm happy."

They were making sushi, which they would feed to each other, later. The sticky rice, the dark ribbon of seaweed, the shining, nearly fluorescent disks of tuna and avocado.

"In mine," he said, then stopped and spread his arms wide and closed his eyes. He smiled.

They heard a sound then, like a step on the front porch, like music, someone singing. They stopped to listen, their hands still, palms up, open. Nothing. The wind.

Later, he read her a poem called "January." She loved the sounds of the words in his mouth, the way his voice gave them dimension, *viscera, color. She thought she would like to put her mouth very close to his as he spoke, especially when he said the words, "These songs unfastened" and "I had not thought possible this plenty."*

Pound in Venice

This is the end of the story.

It began beside the Canale della Guidecca, when I was sixteen, an American exchange student, a lost girl. I passed a man and a woman. He was quite old, his skin pale as candle wax, and as opaque. She was younger, smaller, his guardian, it seemed, though what gave me that impression, I'm not sure. They were Americans, and this I could tell by their clothes and their accents as they spoke to each other. "Did it go all the way down?" he asked her, and she replied, "I believe it sank to the very bottom." They glanced at one another and then back into the dark canal. "Look where the light comes," he said, and she nodded. "Now we are looking at ourselves," she said, but he was silent. And they stayed that way, bent over the water, for some minutes. Once she stabbed her finger at the water to show him, but that was all. When they straightened up to walk away, the woman saw me. "It's nothing," she called to me. "Come have a look," and so I did. I crossed the bridge—I had been stopped midway—and came to where this couple stood. "It's nothing," the woman said again, and I bent my head as they had theirs and stared. "This water is an unforgiving ooze," the old man said. "Would you like to have a drink? I'll tell you what we were doing." The woman gasped and tightened her grip on the man's arm, but he did not seem to notice.

I had nowhere, or maybe everywhere, to go. This was early April, still quite cold. I was traveling with other American students, and after nine days, I'd grown bone tired of them, their manic wit, their lack of interest in anything except drinking in the cafés and smoking European cigarettes. That afternoon, I'd left them, slipped out of a shop unnoticed, turned two or three corners, as one can do in Venice to be completely, definitively lost. Now I had an hour before the bus would leave to take us back to the campground just outside the city. I had not made up my mind that I would get on that bus. I dreaded the dirty barracks, the stacked bunks, the latrine with its endless fluorescence. I'd been sick the night before under those humming lights.

The couple led me to a restaurant where, they said, they took most of their meals. The maitre d' smiled warmly and gave us a table by the window. No one came to ask what we wanted, but a carafe of wine was brought, and water, and three glasses.

"So," the woman said. "My name is Olga." She did not introduce the old man. Her speech was unaccented, but oddly so, as if some former music in her voice had been excised, and what was left ran sleek and smooth, like scar tissue. Not mechanical, though. Clean, was the word I thought of. "You're young to be on your own."

"I'm sixteen," I said. "That's not so young. I'm on school holiday."

The old man laughed and said, "A spotted lamb." He poured some wine into a glass and pushed it toward me. The wine was the color of wheat, of hay, if that color could be seen through. I drank and felt the little bubbles in my mouth. "They'll come looking for you," he said, "your makers, your creditors, but we won't let them take you."

The woman petted his hand, the rough knuckles. "Why have you come to Venice?" she asked me.

"To see it," I said. "The buses brought us. The company chose the itinerary. But I'm glad." We all drank. "Are you Americans?"

"Yes," Olga said. "But we've escaped ours too."

"Yours?" I said.

"Dinner is on the table," the old man said. "Ham and chickens?"

Outside, the light had turned violet and glittering. I've seen eyes like that. There was half a loaf of bread on the table. I felt that I was here with this couple, but also in another room, another city. If I missed the bus, anything could happen, and would. This couple might take me home with them. This evening was years ago, I should say, and I have seen it reflected since in many lights, a thousand mirrors. The woman cut a large slice of bread and fed it to the man, bit by bit. The end of the loaf she offered to me, and I took it.

"Usurpations, jealousies, taxes," the old man said.

"What were you looking at back there in the canal?" I asked.

"Well," Olga began and folded her hands on the table. "The water itself, of course, the reflection of it." She giggled a little then, girlish. "It's good to check every so often, make sure it's still you you're carrying around."

"Tell her," the old man said. "Tell her I was right about some of it."

"Some papers," Olga continued as if she had not heard him. "It's a good way to get rid of them. They lie along the bottom. They spread out like handkerchiefs. Then they dissolve."

"What kind of papers?" I said.

The door to the restaurant flew open. "There you are!" a voice boomed behind me. "You need to be on the bus. We're ready to go back."

Go back.

That was the driver of the bus, whose name was James. He was English, from the East End of London he'd told us, proudly. I'd discovered a certain thing about him and his partner, Robbie, the other driver. I'd fallen asleep one night in Istanbul, and when the others went to find a bar, they let me stay in my seat. I woke up on a dark road where James and Robbie were accepting a stack of drachmas in exchange for radios, cameras, cassette players, goods I realized then had traveled on top of the buses, under the black tarp with our duffel bags and backpacks.

So James was keeping me close. There in the restaurant his hand went under my hair and his index finger traced a line from the bottom of my skull down the back of my neck, proprietary, warning. The old man saw this and frowned. Olga looked away.

"She's here," the old man said. "She's all right with us. She's got vino to drink."

"And I've a bloody bus to drive," James said. As I rose from the chair, James's hand slid down my spine. He leaned over my shoulder and whispered to Olga and the old man, "Their parents get ticked off if we lose them." I said good-bye and thank you. I wondered if the police would question them after my body was discovered in the lagoon where James must surely be planning to dump it.

That's not what happened, though. James seemed, in fact, to be near tears. "Don't do that again," he said when we were outside the restaurant. "I thought I'd never find you." He put his arms around me and kissed the top of my right ear. He didn't let go.

I could see past his shoulder the old man, leaning across Olga, watching us. I asked James how he found me.

"Some people saw you by the bridge," he said. "Do you know who that man is?"

"No. Her name is Olga."

"He's a writer. Called Pound. He's loony. Off his nut. Everybody seems to know him."

James took my hand and led me back to the meeting place, a car park behind the Doge's Palace. The others were waiting, hungry, not curious, already a little drunk.

The next day, above the Palazzo san Marco, on the cathedral parapet, he found me. I was sitting with another American student, named Margaret, who was writing a letter to her brother. I noticed she'd adopted the slightly boxy, canted, perfectly decipherable handwriting of all English schoolgirls. When James sat down, she said something about finding the *poste restante* and left us.

After a moment, he said, "I've probably done this trip twenty times. The kids always like Venice best, but not me. You know what city I like?"

"Istanbul?"

His eyes flashed violently into mine. "I like Sofia. Bulgaria. It's another world. This!" Here he threw his hands into the air, as if releasing birds, waving away all of San Marco, all of Venice. "This is just London over again. But Sofia is *strange*."

"I noticed," I said, "that we didn't exchange any currency at the border. So we were illegal the whole time."

"You don't miss anything, do you?"

"I try not to."

James stood up. "Let's walk. There's places I always go here." I followed him down the dark stone steps, through the cathedral, and out into the sunlight. "Why is it that Americans in Europe are always looking for fucking ice cream?"

There is a Rodin museum in Venice. At least that's what I remember. In the middle of the largest room is *The Kiss,* or maybe a copy—I'm not sure. I thought all the famous Rodins were in Paris or New York. I could find out, but I'd rather remember it wrong. Couples were supposed to kiss in front of *The Kiss,* that's what James said, but I refused. What I remember, too, is the city like a roller coaster or a serpent—we were forever walking across small, arched bridges made of stone, making for a kind of constant undulation below us. The sky, though, as it appeared above roofs and around the corners of buildings, was all geometry, all angles and planes. And blue. No clouds. Glassmakers worked every corner, preying on tourists, like the carpet sellers in Istanbul. My carpets fly, they had called to us, for you, special student rate. The *fabbri di verieri* made a more astonishing claim: I have caught the light of Venice, they whispered, so you will have it always.

After a while we didn't speak much, except to say "Look" or "I like that one," which James mostly said about a bridge, a building, a woman. Later, one or the other of us would just point at the admired person or object. I marveled that we never met any of the other students or Robbie, but when I asked about him, James said Robbie had a woman in every port. I kept watch for Olga and the old man, the loony writer, and I tried to lead James to the Guidecca Canal, but he seemed determined to walk in the other direction, north toward the Cannaregio, the Jewish ghetto.

"All these narrow streets," he said. "Makes you feel safe." We stopped in front of a pastry shop, admiring the golden, glazed *dolci ebaichi.* "I like that star," he said, "the two perfect triangles. It always reminds me of Christmas."

I laughed then, but the sound of it was wrong, cruel.

James turned toward me, made himself larger. "You're so smart. You think you know what Robbie and I do on the side, don't you?"

I said I had an idea, but he told me I was wrong, whatever it was. The cameras and radios and other goods weren't new, he said; they were *antiquities*. I thought of statues with the noses broken off, gleaming eyeless women with one bared breast, shards of pottery, an onyx cat. "They fetch a nice sum," he said. "From collectors. Sometimes the governments are interested. A bunch of junk," he marveled.

"Where do you get these *antiquities*?"

"That's for me to know," he said. Then his voice softened and he took my hand. "You'd be amazed what people don't keep watch over."

So they were thieves. Who would fall for a man like that? I understand now it wasn't the man I fell for. It was the bus, by which I mean synecdoche, metonymy, words from *antiquity*. I mean the conveyance, the conveying. It was camping in Salzburg and waking up in snow, and eating breakfast right there, standing up beside our tents—good bread and marmalade from an industrial-sized can, and instant coffee. "Saves money," Robbie said. "Don't tell your parents." Stopping in northern Greece, pitch dark, and waking up in an olive grove. No hotels, not one. Saves money. Don't tell. Sleeping on a beach outside Athens, near a town where the men welcomed James and Robbie like prodigal sons. The cathedral in Cologne, jeweled and spiky as a rich matron. Not eating cheese in Limburger. The Black Forest, alive with enchantments. Don't tell. Spending a night at the foot of Mt. Olympus, and the promise of Zeus casting himself into my tent, not as a swan or a bull, but as a bus driver. That dark road near Istanbul, the shiver of fear inside the borders of Bulgaria, none of their money in our wallets. Easter Sunday at a Turkish army base, soldiers and their families generous with boiled eggs and bread, oranges and chocolate. Too much beer and Greek retsina, sleeping off the hangover on the island of Thassos. All of it. The ferry back to Dover, the locked lavatory, the fumbling press inside. The kiss. The train home, my wallet, watch, and passport gone.

Years later, I went back, to the Guidecca Canal, the Doge's Palace, and to Calle Querini, where I knew Olga still lived. I had written to her, and she expected me. "I have been saving something for you," she said as we stood in the doorway. She was very small, white-haired now, with fine, chiseled features, as if she were halfway turned to stone. I thought of Lot's wife, though of course that's the wrong transformation, but it was true of Olga's life, looking back at a tower of babble.

At the end, she said, he just ran out of language. He could sit for hours, days at a time without speaking, clawing at his knuckles. Visitors came, biographers, other writers, and he'd refuse to speak. He'd fix them with his stare, eyes blue as sapphires. I took him to New York, she told me, to the public library. Valerie Eliot showed him her husband's poem, with his notes scrawled all over. He said, *I don't remember a word,* but then he wept onto the pages.

"Wet pages," she said, and reached for a large envelope. We were in a bright yellow room, with columns, like a Greek temple. She asked if I would take it. "It's a novel. Long parts are untranslatable," she said. "I have saved it because all those years ago he was going to tell you what it was."

"But he threw it into the canal."

"I fished it out. The next morning, while he was still asleep."

He hated novels, she said. The structure, the first, the then, the next. He came at ideas from the side or from the bottom. He wrote five chapters of a novel in 1909, and then burned them. But here it is. I drew the pages from the envelope. He had written on the first one, *a novel*.

How had I come to be in possession of this antiquity? Coincidence. My old impulse toward solitude.

My husband was in Venice on a teaching exchange. He was an economist. We joked that I was too—a home economist. All day, I cooked, took classes in Italian cuisine, Italian language, and art. I started painting, still lifes mostly, orderly arrangements of fruits and cloudy wine glasses. I could not get the necks of bottles right. Sometimes I painted Venetian scenes. My husband said my gondolas looked like blackened bananas. I had never myself set foot in a gondola—maybe if I had, I could have painted them more accurately. I preferred subjects that didn't move quickly, or at all.

Olga and I took the ferry to San Michele, to the cemetery. It's in a lagoon, she told me, the very essence of funereal. The dank was everywhere, real, lapping at our ankles. I wondered if the dead lay still underground, if they hadn't all floated away, out to sea. At his grave, Olga bowed her head and spoke to the stone. "I gave it to her," she said. I half expected the earth to split open, but all was silence except for the little waves against the shore.

Then Olga looked up. "Do you have children?"

"No."

"Why not?"

"We didn't want them," I said, though this was, of course, a lie.

"I have one daughter. She believes I'm selfish."

"Are you?"

"I don't know," she said. "I think I don't quite understand what selfish is in the modern world. I think in antiquity it probably meant self-preservation. Selfish came with time." She pointed at the stone, the old man's name. "My daughter loved him. She didn't think he was selfish."

"How do I know he wrote this?" I asked.

"Because I'm giving it to you."

"Have you read it?"

"As much as I could, but as I told you, some of it is in need of translation—and some is beyond translation."

"What is it about?"

"The hospital in Washington. Howard Hall and Chestnut Ward, then back to Venice. At least as far as I can tell."

A young man had got off the next ferry and was walking toward us. He stopped and gazed down at the stone, shaking his head in wonder, I think. He stood still, and I sensed he hoped we would leave so he could be alone at the grave. I said Olga's name and drew her a ways off. At the sound of my voice the young man looked up sharply, then concentrated his gaze on Olga. He seemed to be coming to some conclusion, then walked to where we stood. "Excuse me," he said quietly. "Do you speak English? I couldn't help overhearing." He turned to Olga. "Are you"—here he jerked his thumb over his shoulder to indicate the grave—"*his* Olga?"

I wondered what she would say, what truth she would tell. "Yes," she said finally.

"Really?" he exhaled. "What was he like?"

"Like?" Olga smiled. "Read the poems, read the prose, read the letters, read all the studies."

"Read the novel," I said. The young man looked at me as if I were insane.

"All right," he said carefully, and moved away from us to stand again in front of the stone.

"I've got to get back," Olga said. "I'm very tired now."

"I'll see you home," I said.

"No. I'll be all right. You stay." I walked her to the landing and waited with her until the ferry came. At the top of the gangplank, she turned and said quietly, "It isn't that you don't want children. Well," she nodded her head toward the envelope I still carried. "Now you have one. You'll find it quite unforgiving." Then the boat churned away from the dock. I would not see her again.

When I turned back, I saw the young man had crouched beside the stone. He held something in his hand, and after a moment's hesitation, he placed this object on the grave. He rose quickly then and thrust his hands into his pants pockets, but did not leave. I made my way back to him, and so I saw the offering was an ordinary ink pen, with a blue barrel. He looked at me and smiled. "I just do this," he said. "At certain graves. Writers. Emily Dickinson. Faulkner. I left about six at Père-Lachaise." I wasn't sure I wanted to know why, but he told me. They might need them, he said. Maybe paradise was ill-equipped. Or wherever they were. "I go back," he said, "and the pens are gone. The other things are there, pennies, flowers, postcards, candles. But the pens are always missing."

I handed him the envelope. "This is his novel," I said, pointing at the grave. The young man shook his head, no, no way. "It is. She gave it to me, just today. He tossed it into the canal, but she rescued it, and—you take it. Quick. Before I change my mind." He took the envelope, stammering, stuttering, trying to ask me, I think, who I was, did I want to talk to him about it, shouldn't I think about what I was doing. "No," I said, then, "Wait. I want to see how it ends." I reached in and took the last page of the manuscript. No, no no. It doesn't cohere; it's an error and a wreck. It's vanity. "Take it and go."

And he did. He sprinted to the landing, and because there was no ferry, he practically leapt into a water taxi, which I'm sure he could not afford. I felt a cold breath on my neck. I bent to pick up the pen and slipped it into my pocket.

What did we do in Venice? the end began. *We drank and ate. We walked over a stubbled bridge on San Michele to find the lot where she and I would be buried. I asked her to leave a flower, and she said, soon enough, mi caro. At least a seed? Soon enough. At a distance, a farmer bent over his field, as if he were pleading. We should tell him, she said, we should tell him his harvest lies too near the graves, this tangle of old limbs, she added, glancing at the earth and then at me. This was in April, a month about which quite enough has been said, when the old delirium returns and winks its one good eye in my direction. Once, on Murano, the glassmakers were gods. They carried swords, they paid no taxes. But here's the rub: they couldn't leave. Their prison was sand and flux. Bah! It's as if a girl wrote all this. She was sixteen. Her life was just beginning. She could not say whether she moved forward or backward, nowhere or everywhere. Same as at the end, I'd tell her now.*

Lira buy nothing in this glass city. Think of the rightness. We've come here for the little light beyond the glass. The water carries sounds and they have nothing to do with us. Now old women and their musty lace back in upon my tomb. A ferry howls us back. I see the line of your cheek, even in the dark, and that is some comfort, that I can still see you, even in the dark. Come back when there is a little light. Look for splendor.

At Wanship

She was sleeping in my bed, and I was lying on the floor beside her, wrapped in my heavy coat. At daybreak, I got up without disturbing her, walked through the old snow into town for coffee and a roll, then back to school to teach my class in Western civilization. The lesson was Browning, but I couldn't resist a lecture on Ezra Pound, *Personnae* and the Pisan Cantos, for a half hour anyway, until the frowning students in the front row set me straight.

I walked back to the boardinghouse slowly, thinking all the while about my own poems, and the ring of mountains around Salt Lake City, and how these mountains drive one's gaze heavenward. I was thinking, too, that this job gave me abundant free time, but even so, how much I resented the few hours of classroom vaudeville, the students who seemed to think of me as their servant—no, their entertainment, but only as long as I kept to the script. I wasn't, quite honestly, thinking at all of the woman asleep in my bed, an actress of sorts I had discovered the night before, lying in the snow, half frozen and starving. She'd lost her room in another house for nonpayment of rent—at one time I had lived in that house, and she across the hall, and we'd had some illuminating conversation about drama. She loved the plays of G. B. Shaw. I'd often fed her toast and coffee when she was out of work.

I should say here that my name is Stearns, and I had gone to that (though the citizenry still doesn't know it yet) god-forsaken place for work. I seemed an odd duck there in the American West, though Utah was, and perhaps still is, its own region, its own direction, not one of the four we commonly invoke—North, South, East, etc. All those mountains: let's call it *up*. I was raised in the downward-tending East, in the Middle Atlantic States, but the job was there. In teaching, a man follows the job. And it was all right, really. It wasn't forever. I didn't drink, so no one was upset. I did smoke, did entertain the hidden sylph of filmy veils, as Pound puts it, gliding where the breath hath glided, veils of shade our dream dividing, even in the classroom, though I had been asked not to. I was unmarried, which prompted a certain, different suspicion.

At the boardinghouse, they were waiting for me in the parlor, five of them, the landlord and men from his ward. I did not like the look of it. They asked me to sit facing them, so that the sun, reflected through the glass door of the entryway, zoomed into my face. I couldn't see them, not at all. The voices seemed to come out of a tunnel of light, as it's described by people who start to die and then don't finish the job. "This is a religious house," the landlord said. And I thought (but did not say) oh, religion, ah, another failure from an attempt to popularize art. "This morning," he continued, "when my wife went to clean your room, she found you had—a visitor."

"Alice Hamilton," I told him.

"Maybe," he said. "In any case, it's not proper. It's in the lease you signed. Imagine my wife's shock. And there are children in this house."

"Yes," I said, "but she was out in the snow. Freezing and starving both. I don't know which would have killed her first." I explained who had slept where, that I had left early for my class.

They were unmoved. "We'll have to ask you to go. The college will want this too."

"I probably saved her life," I said. "Wouldn't you have done the same?"

"Not quite this way," they said.

"Well, how then?"

We went on like this for hours, it seemed. They would not let me go. The college had been summoned, and so I had to wait. We sat. The sun was moving, and one by one the faces came into view, all of them soft, peach-colored, clean-shaven, blue-eyed. I wondered if these men were related, maybe shared a wife or two. I was on the verge of asking, but thought I should pose the question in French or Italian. I would say I was quoting from their good Book, in Latin, in Hebrew; then I remembered they had a different good book. They stared at me, and I stared back. Then one by one, they dropped their eyes and began to talk among themselves—a meeting, an election, a business proposition. The landlord's wife brought in a tray, water with no ice, some oddly shaped pale cookies. She waited a moment, I thought maybe to see if her husband or one of the others would thank her, but no one said a word. So I spoke up, but she did not turn toward me or otherwise acknowledge my presence.

How could she not know she was a fixture, her printed dress twin to the chintz on the sofa? I thought when I was dismissed, as

I was surely going to be, I ought to ask if she'd like to come along. She would say no, of course, but the notion passing through her brain might rattle something else around.

Two deans arrived, Tweedledum and Tweedledean, I might have called them, for they were dressed identically in blue suits and red striped ties. They asked for a full explanation, and I told my same story. They talked to the other five, and some, it seemed, were for dismissing me then and there. Tweedledean, who wore the duller tie, actually said the words, "You are dismissed."

But they had given me too much time to think. "Can you prove anything?" I asked. "Can you show any immorality?"

"The appearance is enough," they said.

"But proof!" I said. "It's what we teach. Innocent until proven."

They admitted finally they could not prove. By five o'clock, I'd been reinstated; by six, I'd thought of another way. By seven, I was packing my bags, with a whole year's salary in my pocket, for severance.

I should say something here about Alice Hamilton. She was an English girl, about twenty, with an indecipherable accent. Her face was long, equine, her arms and legs sinewy, like those of a manual laborer. She was an actress of a sort, her routine being the impersonation of an upper-class Englishman. I don't believe anyone in the entire state of Utah understood a word she said. I took the money from the college, and I took Alice, and we took the train east out of Salt Lake City. At Wanship, Utah, I saw the mountains for the last time. No—I should say I felt them, the long, jagged shadows falling over our shoulders and into our hands. I thought Alice looked lovely in this light. After that, I think we must have slept almost the whole way across to Philadelphia, though I do recall the sight of Lake Michigan and the dawning idea that I must never again let myself live so far away from water. Alice disputed this memory in Pittsburgh, telling me that all we saw of Illinois were cornfields and stockyards and the sooty, shining train station in Chicago.

"Shining?" I asked her.

"Because it was raining," I think she said. "But afterward, the light made the sheep look like fluffy angels, and the sun was a big gold eye."

We hurtled toward Philadelphia. I had the sense we might have to leap off before the train rushed over the Walt Whitman Bridge and thence out to sea. Or we might decide to transfer underground to the airport and keep going, to London, to Paris.

"Tell me what it's like," Alice said. "Your City of Brotherly Love. Tell me what I should expect to find."

"All right," I said. "First you'll meet my parents. They're kind, clever, and well-read. Then you'll meet the woman I'm engaged to marry." Her face fell a little, I thought, but she smiled through it. "Then," I said, "you'll meet the other one."

"The other one what?"

"The other woman I'm engaged to marry."

"*Two*? Why didn't you stay in Utah then?"

"Well," I stammered, "why didn't *you*?"

She hurried out of the train and disappeared into the morning crowd at 30th Street Station. I would not see her again.

I lied about my parents, of course, and perhaps Alice could tell. My father was dead, and my mother was not kind. She was, however, well-read in popular novels and current events publications, so I suppose she possessed a sort of cleverness. She had a monstrous and eccentric vocabulary, though that's really not the right word (she would know the right word, and she would waste no time telling you what it was). I loved her and feared her, and I had not the faintest idea how she would view my dismissal-reinstatement-resignation.

From City Center, the trolley carried me back out to Lansdowne, where I'd grown up. It was a steep walk from the trolley stop to our house, but luckily a neighbor stepped off the car when I did, and he offered to help with my trunk and bags. "Does your mother know you're coming?" he asked slowly. I could tell he was trying to keep his voice as even, as toneless as possible.

"No," I told him and asked the most innocuous question I could think of: "Is she away?" If there was strange news, I didn't want to hear it from this neighbor, whose daughter I'd once been in love with (she had made a better match and lived in one of those grand houses on the banks of the Schuylkill).

"I'm not sure," he said, his eyes on the ground. We were standing in front of my house, and I could tell that my mother was most emphatically in residence. The windows were flung open—in December!—and we could hear the frenetic crashing of piano keys. We hauled my baggage onto the porch, and I thanked him for his kindness. He lingered a moment, hoping, I suspect, to be asked inside, but I thought this might not be the good moment.

The front door, as I pushed it open, did not creak or stick or release a waft of foul air, as I'd expected. On the contrary, the entrance hall gleamed back at me. The wood floor was polished, the table and small chairs had been dusted, and the prisms on the lamp twinkled, casting spectra of light in patches on the walls. The piano continued in the next room—I was sure my mother had not heard me. I thought the music was Beethoven, dark but manic, played a little too fast. The entryway mirror hung so that it gave back not only the person standing before it, about to go out, but also most of the music room and those who stayed in. And so I could watch my mother for a moment. She wore black trousers and a white sweater I knew, a knit so soft it made you want to close your eyes, even from across the room. I saw her head in profile, her graying hair caught up off her neck in a haphazard twist, as she'd worn it on school mornings, when she made our breakfast, mine and my father's. Her skin was still a color I'd once called "milk with crumbs," meaning pale but freckled. It appeared she wore color on her eyelids and mascara on her lashes, neither of which I'd ever known her to do. She played on, furiously, oblivious. When she put out her foot to press the pedal, I saw she wasn't wearing shoes or stockings.

"Mother," I called then, and entered the room, but as I did so, I heard a faint cough and a sighing of the cushions on the sofa behind me. Even before I turned, I guessed who this would be: Emily, the girl I was to marry. The first one. And so it was.

"David!" she said, yelped really, an undignified canine sound. "What are you doing home?" Emily stood up as if she'd been ejected from the sofa. She was wearing a dress I'd always liked, red and green plaid, flannel like a man's shirt. This dress reminded me that Christmas was a few days away. Still, there was something disconcerting about Emily in that dress. I tried to think what it was, but my brain was fogged from the long train ride.

My mother said my name then, not a yelp, but low and oddly soothing. When I turned, she was directly in front of me, and she took me in her arms. My mother is quite small, really about half my size, and very thin. In an embrace, though, she seems to have suddenly put on flesh and stature. She smelled of lemons and vanilla, as always. She held me at arm's length then, and her expression darkened. It's too early," she said. "You couldn't come until January. What's happened?"

"I wanted to surprise you," I said. I turned to Emily. "And you too."

That dress.

"You haven't been fired, have you, David?" my mother said. Emily coughed again. I supposed she must have a cold. I thought I should be careful not to kiss her.

"No." I tried to laugh, succeeded. "It's an interesting story, though. I've been paid to leave."

My mother shot a look at Emily, and then sat down heavily on the piano bench, her back to the keys. Emily began to move sideways, like a crab, but slowly. "I should go," she said.

"No." I went to her, took her hand. "It's all right. It's not really too bad. A misunderstanding." Emily stood frozen, not looking at me.

"But how did you get here?" my mother said suddenly.

"On the train."

"All the way across? But you must be starved. Do you want something? How long a trip?"

"Three days. It sailed by," I said. "Actually, I'm unbelievably thirsty. I've been in Utah for five months. I need a drink."

"I'll get it," Emily said, in motion again, this time toward the kitchen.

"We have wine," my mother said. I followed Emily. "We have gin, vodka, port. Oh!" I heard her say, and it sounded as if she were stifling a sob. "We have champagne."

"I want it all," I called back to her, wondering at the same time what it was I really wanted.

The kitchen, too, was awash with light, as if fires blazed in the windows. Emily bent into the refrigerator and drew out a bottle of champagne. She set it on the counter and reached up into the cabinet for glasses. As her arm stretched over her head, I realized what was odd about the dress she wore, and familiar: that dress belonged to my mother.

And so we passed two somewhat strained days until Christmas Eve. I slept a great deal. I told the story of my semester at the college and its Alice Hamilton finale, but I felt neither my mother nor Emily believed me, or rather they believed I was leaving something out. And I was, I suppose, though this omission was not part of the narrative. I said nothing about feeling adrift, lost. I gazed out at the world, at Emily, and my mother, but I did not know them. I did not recognize rooms in the house, or the facades of other houses on our street. It came to this: in college and in graduate school, I had studied or taught myself seven languages, but that Christmas season, I felt I could not understand a word in any one of them.

On Christmas morning, I walked into town to see the other girl, named Katherine, who did receive me, but less than happily, even though I had brought a gift. "Your reputation precedes you," she said as she let me in. "My parents are in church," she added, "but I said I had a headache." Then she led me through the kitchen to the maid's small bedroom.

"Well," she said afterward, as we dressed, "you don't seem confused." I thought I should let her talk. "The story is, you were—" she pointed to the unmade bed, "with a woman who was really a man."

I smiled and shook my head. "You won't believe me either, but I'll tell you." She listened carefully. As I spoke, I thought, this is the one I ought to marry. She pays attention. I have a clear sense of her, like looking through a window.

"Well," Katherine said when I'd come to the end of the story, "that may be. But I've spoken to Emily and to your mother, and I think you and I are—" Here she drew her index finger slowly across her throat. "But thank you for all the poems. I'll keep them in case you're ever famous." I think she might have said *now run along*, but I was stuck on the idea of Katherine's reconnaissance with my mother and Emily, the vision of it, the three of them together. Whose parlor? What café or sidewalk or park bench? I should say here that the thought of it struck me much more vividly as a poem than as actual fact or event. And so I put on my coat and *ran along*. But not home, not to my mother's house, where she would be cooking the Christmas dinner, the English version she preferred: roast beef, Yorkshire pudding, and a trifle. No. I wanted to get at this picture: the three fates together spinning and measuring the skein of me. Or some other dark triad: the trinity, the parts of the eye, the three crosses on Golgatha. Means *Skull Hill*, I thought, makes a sound like *Schuylkill*. I imagined the three of them somewhere distant, ancient, a rocky plain, a windswept hilltop, a frozen river.

I knew how to walk out Katherine's road to the park that runs beside the Schuylkill. At the far south end of the park were old loading docks, about all Philadelphia had to offer in the way of abandoned and ancient. I thought this place would be deserted on Christmas Day, though I knew at night it was not. The walk was exhilarating, rather exotic. Along this part of the river, the boathouses were decorated for the holiday, with lights and wreaths and jolly, bobbing Santas, reindeer, an electric crèche or two. Electric crèche, I said quietly, enjoying the sounds of the words in my mouth. These were all still lit and, in some cases, moving, since no one had come Christmas morning to turn them off. I was reminded of Las Vegas, how haggard that place seemed in daylight, how exposed. I had only been there once and had not enjoyed myself, night or day. Now, as I passed each boathouse, I saw the single and double sculls, the crew boats stacked neatly as long coffins. I imagined some kind of Viking burial, the body shrouded, draped with evergreen boughs, the small ship pushed out into open water, knocking its way through the ice floes. The twinkling lights made a mockery of my vision.

After a mile, though, I was past the boathouses and into the abandoned commercial district. The docks had been left to rot for the most part—storms and high water had done their work as well. I was mindful of this but not afraid. I felt some need to be on the water, out as far as possible, so I made my way to the farthest pier. I had not been here for two or three years, and I was surprised at the ruin, the smashed windows of the old ferry terminal and customs house, the garbage blown up against the walls and doors. I heard footsteps then and saw a couple move out of an embrace and disappear behind one of the old storehouses. They looked like children. I hoped they would not come too close to the water and perhaps fall in, and drown.

This pier shook as I stepped on, but it held, for a few feet.

I noticed the missing crosspieces. Slowly, one at a time, like the lines of a poem.

I heard a long creak, a snap. Echoed on the water, a rhyme.

The boards below me gave way.

They tipped into the water, and so did I.

For a long moment, I had the sense that this little spit of wood might hold me up.

Venus in her half shell.

But no. The water was sickeningly, deathly cold.

I felt as if I'd turned into a block of ice. I kicked my legs once and came nearer to the splintered end of the pier, reached for it and missed. My heavy coat weighed me down, and I tried to shrug it off, but these movements only caused me to sink. I flung my arm up again toward the pier and managed to grab hold and pull my body closer, but I did not see how I could possibly heave myself up and out of the water. Hand over hand, I moved along the length of the pier toward the bulkhead. This was exhausting. I began to close my eyes, drift into sleep, then cried out loudly to wake myself. I hoped the children were close enough to hear, and then to my great relief, I saw them running toward me.

They were not children, but women. I noticed first this detail, that they both wore bright wool hats, with ear flaps, and the price tags were still attached. Christmas presents. They wore heavy parkas, trousers, and boots, but no gloves. They looked—I hardly know how to say this, even now, years later—they looked like waxwork angels. I knew they would save me and that I would live. I thought at first I only imagined them to be my mother and Emily, because I was delirious with cold. But as they called my name, David, and put their ungloved hands on my shoulders, under my arms, I saw the truth of who they were and what they were to each other. Their cheeks bloomed crimson in the cold, but not with shame. They were indeed children, girls again, with secrets and knowledge and power. And I was already an ignorant old man.

Four decades later, I traveled to London for an event honoring the publication of my selected poems and plays. I was two years divorced from Katherine, who had, I discovered, lived a whole life apart from ours, complete with lover and his children. When I asked her how this could have happened, how I could have been so deceived, she said, "You were writing your poems. You didn't want to be disturbed." I am disturbed, I howled at her, banging my fists on the dining room table, my whole universe is disturbed. She had delivered this news over Christmas dinner. I told her I had never been so disturbed in all my life.

"I bet that's not true," she said calmly. "Before we were married. Your mother and Emily. Their . . . relations. Pretty disturbing, I'll wager."

So I was growing used to Katherine's absence from events like this one, in London at Foyle's bookshop. Usually, she was a point of focus, the one face in a crowd I could see clearly, cling to. Often at these large readings, I'd feel as if I were drowning. The words of my poems would float up out of my mouth like the air bubbles in cartoons, and letting go of the lines was a literal asphyxiation. Katherine's face was my raft, a promise of safe landing. That night in Foyle's, the crowd seemed like floodwaters, moving in relentlessly to fill up every open space, the stairways, the narrow alcoves between shelves, the new café, the aisles of trinkets—why did bookstores sell coffee mugs?—even the restrooms, I imagined. My British editor seemed to know every man there and have a sly, sidelong relationship with every woman. I could not keep up with the introductions, publication histories, and gossip. "Oh, Ian! So good of you to come." "Anne, darling, do say hello to Ian." Anne would not say hello. "Poets only have little tiffs," I said, "because their books are thinner." This remark was greeted with silence, and so I excused myself to find the men's room.

As I stood washing my hands, I looked in the mirror and

thought how oddly unchanged my face appeared. My hair was gray and sparse and my skin lined, but the flesh had not fallen much. I felt calmer, smiled ruefully. If only I could look at this face as I read, I wouldn't need the raft of Katherine. The man washing up next to me glanced over as I smiled and then took a longer look. He opened his mouth to speak then changed his mind. I thought he must have recognized me from one of the advertisements in Foyle's window, and I turned toward him, ready to make a joke, though I really didn't know what about, reminding myself it was sometimes dangerous to joke in a public restroom. There was something familiar about this man; he was a former student, perhaps, another poet, but I couldn't dredge it up, the exact memory, the name. We turned, each to a towel dispenser, and he preceded me out into the store.

A few minutes later, the pretty professor of rhetoric gave her gushing introduction. I had enjoyed her attention at dinner but now felt somewhat embarrassed. There was applause, a kiss at the lectern, and then I began, with an old poem, but perhaps my best known, "Vision at Wanship." When I let out the last line and glanced up, I saw again the man who had seemed so familiar. I had the not wholly unwelcome sensation of years and landscape rushing past me. My eyes wanted to close. Keeping them open took all my attention. Look down, I told myself, find the next poem. I had got into the habit these past two years of following "Vision" with the less well known "Golgotha," because I liked it, because I could often, as I read, picture myself in the act of writing it, early morning in northern France, a few weeks after Katherine and I were married.

As I read the poem this time, my eyes fell on a phrase a few lines ahead. The words, I realized suddenly, were completely wrong, flat, false. The right lines sprang fully formed into my head, and so I said them. I looked up at the man I thought I knew and saw him blink, and startle, and put his head to the side as if he had misunderstood. I thought then he must surely be a former student, someone who had learned my poems out of hope or gratitude. I read more poems, then answered questions. A woman asked if this were my last book, and I surprised even myself by telling her that every book was the poet's last.

I was then led to a small table where my books were stacked in rows, twenty volumes high. When I sat down to sign them, I felt I was in grade school, and a great wall had been erected to prevent me from copying my neighbor's work. I signed and smiled for hours, it seemed. Then, at the end of the line was the man I thought I knew. "Who shall I sign this to?" I said, and he answered, "Alan Hamilton."

"After I left you in the train station," he began, "I went to New York." We were seated in the bar at my hotel. "But the high-class gent impersonation was becoming less and less an act. Alice went to Stockholm for a few years and came back Alan. I teach theater. I've followed your career, particularly the plays, of course. They're all dramatic monologues, really. Even the poems. Don't you think so?"

I nodded. I couldn't stop looking, staring, trying to find Alice, and wondering, too, how to describe this change: an echo? a shadow? a whisper? We had whispered in the dark, that night in my room in Salt Lake City. We had wondered about greatness, I recall, what greatness was, how we would get it, or would it have to find us. I remember we had used the word *ambition*. We had used the word *misunderstood*.

"There is so much drowning in your plays," Alan said. "And in your poems there is so much left out."

I felt such ease in the presence of Alan Hamilton. I felt I should like to sit there all night talking about a past we did not share. Every so often I slipped and said "Alice," but Alan didn't seem to mind. In fact, he smiled, and it was there, that same sweet, desperate, half-frozen flash of white teeth. "In your poems," Alan said, "there are always goddesses. But they change into something lesser. They disappear."

"Yes," I said. "They do."

"And there are never any children."

"No," I said. "Never."

"Why is that?" Alan asked.

"They aren't interesting. They grow up. They can be disturbed."

But I feel this answer is insufficient. I'll have to think further about it. There is so much unsaid. I have all morning. Alan is coming to lunch at noon.

The Girl with Radium Eyes

At his trial in Washington, DC, Ezra Pound studied the jury intently, fearlessly, as a child would. He was dressed neatly, in a black suit, a blazing white shirt, a tie so dark and thin it appeared from a distance to be a snake making its way slowly, imperceptibly toward the old man's mouth.

I use too many adverbs; it has always been the case, my mentors and critics have said so. I think my love of this part of speech stems from my childhood, the daughter of inventors and scientists, Pierre and Marie Curie, a man and a woman always in the act of taking the world apart to see how it worked—or didn't. I inherited a bit of this impulse from them, a desire to know precisely *how* a thing *moves,* and so the adverb is my favorite tool, my ally. But I will try to improve here, now, as I tell this story.

I had been sent to cover this trial for my paper in Paris. Actually, I sent myself, since I was editor. My mother knew Mr. Pound in the 1920s. He wrote about my father in his twenty-third Canto, my father testing radium, my father who would very soon be crushed under the wheels of a carriage—*se fait écraser; he made himself to be crushed.* And so I was delighted to be there, to see him, to see what the Americans would make of him, which was, so far, a kind of demon.

These proceedings were difficult to watch, and some moments I had to grip the arms of my chair in order to keep quiet. When they were being gentle—his advocates, even—they said he was eccentric, but sometimes they called him neurotic, paranoid, delusional, terms that are, at their core, quite empty, for they name spiritual emptiness. Others called him grandiose, vituperative, a "confabulist." I saw him smile at that one, and I reached forward to touch his shoulder. I am sorry to say he did not like that very much; he twitched violently and slapped at the place where my hand had been. His solicitor leaned in and whispered a few words, and then the two of them shifted in their seats to look at me. "Eve Curie," Pound said, his voice like an old stone breaking open, and then he grinned. "Got yer apple, Eve? Waal, I ain't bitin'." The smile drifted out of his eyes, off his face. *"Merci,"* he said. "Thanks for coming. Appearing. *Grazie* for the apparition."

For the lunch recess, I had to walk a ways from the court. I was nervous and distracted, for I was to meet—I hardly know what to call him now—Dr. Langevin, whom I had not seen for twelve years. I wasn't sure how I would know him, how I would recognize his face, his neck, and chest above a white cloth and silver and glassware in the restaurant where he had reserved a table. I had always known him by smell: tobacco, brandy, the tang of the laboratory. He had come to my mother's funeral in 1934, but I understood I was not supposed to greet him with anything more than a handshake.

He stood as I entered, so I had not the burden of recognition. We embraced, and I imagined—so much, too much, the scent of my mother, the particular odors she carried in her hair and on her clothes.

"How is the trial?" he said, and I told him. Very unscientific. The defense opens a variety of yawning caverns for dispute, but the prosecution ignores them. No one seems really to want to try him for treason. "Then he'll rot in that institution," Dr. Langevin continued. "If he recovers enough to be released, he'll have to stand trial, so he must never recover."

"He knew me," I said. "In two languages. Three, if you count English."

Langevin smiled. We ordered our meal. He reached across the table and patted my hand, fatherly, as always. "You left me out of her biography. Which is quite beautiful—the book, I mean. You render her so . . . It's perfect. She would be delighted."

"Thank you," I said. I tore open a round bit of bread, contemplated its soft interior.

"Why did you?"

I knew he was gazing at me with a sort of adoration, and I did not look up. "Why did I what?"

"Leave me out of it?" His voice broke on the final hard "t."

"For my father. For his honor."

Langevin laughed, a little, and his face worked strangely, as if all his physical senses must, one by one, take in this information. "I thought," he began, "I thought otherwise."

"You should go on thinking it, then. If doing so makes you happy."

"I won't last the year," he said.

"You have had a very great life."

"Yes," he said. "Because of your parents. But no one will remember my name. They will use my work—"

"It is used now. Sonar helped to win the war."

"But no one will remember my name."

"And now it is not even in any book," I said, chiding him, making a bit of a pout.

"Oh some books, yes, but not yours." He sighed. "So. What will they do with this Pound?"

"I suppose they will judge him insane."

"He is a Fascist dog. Why are you interested in him?"

"I think he is a man of strong opinions. I think there are too few names for ideologies, and they are all inadequate. A molecular system in the real world is unlikely to be present in a vacuum."

"I wrote that."

"I know. I take it to mean also that the world is beyond our complete understanding."

Langevin did not say anything, not wanting, I suppose, to illuminate my ignorance of quantum mechanics.

So I would illuminate it myself. "I'm only a musician," I said. "I expect to be the only member of my family not to win the Nobel."

Langevin asked then about my sister. Direct, as always, I told him, brilliant. Likely to die before she reaches old age. "The radium, you know. It killed my mother and father. There's already a kind of hesitation in her walk." I poured more wine into my glass. "She has beautiful children. They are so full of life."

"And you?" he asked. "No husband? No children?"

When I shook my head, he said, "You have music," and I thought I would like to slap his face, slap the pity out of his voice.

"Yes," I said. "And tomorrow, I play for President Truman and his family."

"Very good. What will you give them?"

"The president has asked for something French, but I think he would rather hear Irving Berlin."

We had come to the end of the meal. I realized I had put food in my mouth, but I did not taste any of it. The court proceedings would resume soon, and I wanted to be there for Pound's entrance.

"If you could hear Pound's voice," I said to Langevin, "I think you would revise your opinion of him."

"Perhaps," he said. "But would I even be allowed into the courtroom?"

"Ah," I said as gently as I could manage, "I might introduce you as my husband. I don't think anyone present would get the joke."

Langevin smiled, though his face looked as if he would weep. "I would very much like to hear a woman called Curie introduce me as her husband. But look at us—our ages—no one will believe you."

The prevailing winds had changed during the lunch recess; this was clear as we entered the courtroom. There was a frenzied whispering, particularly among the first rows of spectators. The legal advocates and physicians, however, sat perfectly still, as if they had been cast in stone. Only Pound moved, restlessly, his bony white hands going over each other, the parody of washing. He leaned forward and then back. The effect was odd—I want to use the word *apocalyptic*—I remember it to this day. One might have seen his restlessness as a symbol: American law and medicine gone dead, and Pound trying to extricate himself from under the pile of corpses.

Langevin listened to the journalists seated nearby. His hearing was still very good—not surprising given his studies—and he seemed to pick up all the currents of conversation and weave them together. He understood the Americans' politics better than I. After a few minutes, he turned to me. "I think I know what it is," he said. "The Department of Justice has altered its view. They want him declared insane. They believe it will be difficult to prove his Rome broadcasts were treasonous. That man says"—here he pointed across the aisle to Albert Deutsch, a writer for one of the New York papers—"there must be two witnesses produced for each count of treason. Who will find them?"

"That might be difficult," I said.

"Yes," Langevin replied, "and expensive. And think if he were tried and acquitted? The Americans would howl. Truman would be shamed."

We listened to the parade of doctors. I began to understand that Pound was not insane at all. He was simply acting as any persecuted person would. I thought that Americans who had not been in Europe during the war should not be conducting this trial. Any man who did not have to flee his home, any man or woman who had never lain in hiding, or been in prison or in an open cage for three weeks or a camp for six months, such people should not be judging this man. He had some detestable opinions, yes. Well, didn't we all?

"Why doesn't either side call him as a witness?" Langevin asked a man sitting beside him. "They might just ask outright if he was a Fascist." His voice rose—I do not know that he intended this—on that last word, *Fascist,* all its *esses* hissing boldly into a silence between the cross-examination questions.

Pound stood. *Shot up* is the truth of how he moved. He did not look at Langevin, but he cried out, "I never did believe in fascism,

God damn it. I am opposed to fascism." He sat down abruptly and leaned back in his chair. He glared at the judge, who did not reply or even acknowledge the outburst.

The jury took three minutes to return a verdict. The foreman said only two words: *unsound mind*. Pound's protest had provided enough evidence.

I walked Langevin back to his hotel. "He once put my father in a poem," I said. "The lines are in French. My father is saying, 'I have obtained a burn which has cost me six months of recovery.'"

"It is difficult to believe they did that," Langevin began. "No. I should say it is difficult to imagine that they did that, your mother and father, that they applied radium to their skin."

"Sometimes I remember pieces of it, though I couldn't really," I said. To think of this always causes me to look at my hands, my fingers, which are thick and strong.

"No, you couldn't," he said. "You weren't born."

"The way they described the burn, though, the destruction of the flesh. It must have been my mother, though. I don't remember my father's voice at all."

"I do," Langevin said. "He was a wonderful teacher. Very generous."

"So it must be you. It must be your voice I remember. You and Maman talking about—" Here I stopped, for it suddenly occurred to me that their conversation had been in code, that the peeling away of flesh was how they described their other relations. I felt something very peculiar then, a certain commingling of all my senses, the sweetish odor of burning flesh, the sound of my mother's voice, the shadowy outlines of two people in a dark hallway, the prickle and perfume of brandy in my mouth and nose, the taste of the chocolate Langevin always brought for my sister and me. And the pressure of a hand on my back, slight but still insistent. Langevin's hand, now, in the lobby of his hotel.

"Come upstairs," he said, in a voice so low I wasn't certain at first that he had spoken. "We are two people alone in the world. Come with me. I would like to hold you in my arms. Only that."

When I woke, Langevin's left arm lay stretched across my chest and shoulder, angled upward, his hand resting gently over my ear, as if there was something he did not want me to hear. We were fully clothed. After one or two rather chaste kisses, we had fallen asleep, into our separate dreams. In my dream, Pound stood up slowly, his curled hands pressed so hard against the table they turned white and then flew off the ends of his arms as doves, gathered, then nested in the judge's hair. Pound began to speak in French, the lines about my father. Then he spoke English, "Tropisms!" he shouted. "We believe the attraction is chemical." He lowered himself into the defendant's chair.

As I woke out of this deep sleep, I began to understand it was Langevin who was speaking, and that his right hand covered my other ear, so he was holding my head between his hands. His voice went on, quite low, but I found if I held my breath, I could just make out the words.

". . . around her whole body," he was saying, "a glow, from the radium, particularly at the tips of her fingers and at her temples where she would use her hands to push her hair out of her eyes. Sometimes the whites of her eyes, in the darkest rooms, became two oddly shaped triangles at the top of her face, pointing away. I could not look, and then I had to look. She was luminous. She said, 'Use a mosaic of quartz crystals for the sonar. Glue them between two steel plates,' and so sound gave birth to sight, an apparition. She wore her discoveries like jewelry. But only for Pierre and for me, only in the dark."

I lay very still. After a little while, Langevin's breathing turned hoarse and even, and so I knew he slept. I lifted the left arm gently and rolled out of his embrace. His breathing changed, and I thought perhaps he was awake, but he did not speak. I gathered my coat and boots, lifted the safety latch as quietly as I could. I stepped into the corridor. As I closed the door, I thought I heard him whisper my mother's name.

I saw the photographs in the Washington paper the next morning. There was a picture of Pound with Langevin sitting behind him. Langevin is looking at me, but I am not in the frame. Pound is looking at nothing. Their profiles make a curious replication. I find I am deeply drawn to both of them in a way I may never be able to explain. They are part of my history, and all history is visceral. It is clear to me now, what Pound wrote in Canto XXIII; energy and matter cannot really be lost because the attraction is chemical.

President Truman was himself a fine pianist, and his daughter, Margaret, possessed a charming alto, though I forget now what she sang. I do recall he said he favored the works of Mozart, because they were really very simple: one could see exactly how the music works. "I think that is why Mozart is so popular," the president said, "because there's kind of a transparent way about it." I played Chopin preludes, then we had a lovely supper. There was more music after. The president and I played a duet. We spoke about the trial, and the president assured me they would make Pound very comfortable at St. Elizabeth's. He asked what my interest was, and I replied that my mother had known Pound in Paris, in the twenties, and I had met him too, when I was ten. Margaret Truman, who would herself become a writer, did not say anything. She opened her mouth only to sing, which caused me to feel as if we were all in an opera or a melodrama, players on a stage. I thought how odd it must be to impersonate someone famous. I thought of myself and Langevin. While we played, the White House photographer took a picture, and when I received a copy, some months later, I noticed our hands were not visible.

"When you leave office," I said, "whenever that is, you should pardon him if he is still—not free." The president said he would remember this conversation, but I knew he would not. The war was behind us, and we believed nothing like it would come again. It was as if the molecular composition of the universe had changed, particles spun in the opposite direction, or more slowly, or faster. Piano keys felt different when I touched them, softer, as if I might push through the ivory into another dimension. The notes rose out of Margaret Truman's throat and shattered their way into the new air. My father and mother and Langevin, my mother's lover, had made this world. One might say they had discovered it, but I think this about other endeavors, too. Poetry, for example. Does the writer discover a poem? The words are most assuredly already there, waiting. I wanted to ask Mr. Pound about this. I would ask, too, about his Canto, the lines about my father and radium, the line in which the discovery is made: *j'ai obtenu une brulure*. That verb, *obtenir*, to obtain, why? Why, I would ask, and not *souffrir*, to suffer? For that is usual, that one suffers a burn, feels the pain of it.

And so I went, myself, the next day to St. Elizabeth's, and

asked for an audience. I explained who I was, all the whos that I am. But Pound would not grant such an audience. And so I went home, to Paris, and filed my story on the trial, and tried not to think of Pound and Langevin, though both troubled me greatly. When Langevin died in December, I remembered he said he would not live out the year. I attended his funeral and interment at the Pantheon. Before the ceremony, I stood in the rain and thought how much better for a coffin to be lowered into wet, black earth than into the cellar of a stone building. The day grew cold and still, the sky like a sheet of metal, so that sounds fell against it and were magnified as they shattered into a million fragments. I felt this inside my body, a curious splintering, as if my mother were being reft from me, again and finally. How would she get out? I wondered. How would she work that particular miracle? Would she rise out through my flesh, appearing first as a red circle, a burn spreading out from the region of my heart? As the ropes around the coffin squealed, and the men holding them grunted softly, one of Langevin's daughters stepped back and took my hand. In that gesture, I felt that I understood something else about discovery, but I wanted to be sure, so I went back and waited until Pound would see me. I did not expect that he would speak, but I hoped he would listen.

I understand it now, I told Pound as he stared and then blinked his great blue eyes. I understand the verb, *obtenir*. It's about possession, about force, active rather than passive. I understood finally, holding the hand of a woman who might have been my sister, but wasn't. *Obtain* is to take hold of. I said this first in French and then in English. *Suffer* is to bear, to be at the mercy of. He took hold of the radium burn, he and my mother. The burns did not happen to them, like accidents or mistakes. They did not *bear*, as one would a misunderstanding, an insult, a degradation, as you, Mr. Pound, are doing now.

"So," I continued, "I have another, more difficult question. Do you think they began it all?"

"It?" he whispered.

"Hiroshima, Nagasaki. The peeling away of flesh."

"They?"

"My mother and father? My sister?"

"I do not know what you are talking about," Pound said. It was cold in the visiting room, and he shivered. Without thinking, I went to stand behind him and draped my arms over his shoulders, around his neck.

"You were a child," he said slowly. "Do you remember what they called you when you came to America in 1921? They called you 'the girl with radium eyes.'"

~

"How does it work?" I asked my husband in Oslo, in 1965, just before he accepted the Peace Prize for UNICEF. "What will the king of Norway say to you, and in what language will you hear it?"

"It won't be the king," he said. "It will be a woman from the Parliament." We had crowded together into the tiny hotel bathroom. We were brushing our teeth. "The flash of cameras may be unnerving. You may not want to look directly at them to save your eyes. There will be speeches; she will talk, and then I will."

"It will be rather like a courtroom, then?" I asked, and he looked puzzled momentarily.

"I have heard," he continued gently, searching my face in the mirror, "that one feels the presence of all the previous laureates."

When my mother won the second time, she said she felt my father's hand on her arm, even though he was six years dead. And when my sister won, she said she felt both of them beside her, my father's hand on her right shoulder, my mother's on her left. She said when she looked at the photographs later, there was a kind of glow emanating from her body. That was the radium of course, though no one wanted to say so.

"I want you to accept the prize with me," my husband said. "You have worked just as hard. You have given up just as much. You have had a lot to bear."

"Given up?" I said. "As much as whom?"

"I want you to be next to me. You can receive the medal, take hold of it for me. I will have the diploma. Or the other way around, if you like. I cannot carry both of them."

"Yes, you can," I said. "They'll put the medal around your neck."

How could I explain it to him—that the glowing, radium-filled ghosts of my parents and my sister already stood behind him, skin peeled away, expressions of horror. You've been left out of the picture, Eve, they seemed to say out of their gaping mouths. That's why you're alive. Langevin, too. All the dead. And Pound, who lived still, in Venice.

"No, darling," I said. "You must take hold of them yourself."

The Path Not Taken

 While they were in Paris that spring, the leaves on the plane trees opened. She was six months' pregnant. They had a bed that was like sleeping in a cloud. They went to the cemetery at Montmartre one afternoon after lunch, wandering between the graves of Nijinski and Berlioz and Degas. The entire cemetery was empty, but for the two of them and the dead. They came to a tunnel, and she knew they must not go through. She felt this as strongly as she felt the baby inside her. The sky was the same blue the baby's eyes would be. "We can't go in there," she said. Her husband laughed at this pronouncement, then he looked on their map and found another way out.

 Earlier that morning, she'd had a small seizure but came out of it all right. Her husband was frightened. Afterward they joked that he would not know how to call 911 in French. They thought they should visit Montmartre Cemetery that day to set things straight, though she can't see the logic of that now. She read to him from the guidebook: they were standing inside an old quarry, and she felt it, a subterranean calm, a long exhalation.

 She didn't know what it was about the tunnel, only that she was right, that some violence waited for them inside.

Out of the Garden

I was told only this by my contact in Algiers: I would find a woman living in Barbizon, the old artists' colony outside Paris, who had information. Her name was Louise Valmet. She was a charming, quiet person who spoke perfect English. Her farmhouse was at the edge of the forest of Fontainebleau, perhaps a mile and a half outside of the town. It was a pleasant walk at first, and then increasingly ominous as the woods appeared to come in closer to the road. One repeats to oneself the words in French—*forêt, marcher, chemin*—as a kind of prayer against the sinister aspect of the landscape. But I did not feel comforted. I felt acutely what I was, an intermediary, an instrument. A sexless thing, a woman without husband or children. As perhaps I deserved.

The house itself was squat and tidy, made of gray stone, but with a surprising pale lavender door. Mlle Valmet had planted a low ground cover that bloomed with tiny blue flowers in summer, perhaps violets, which seemed to launch one's eye toward the door like an invitation. Before the war, she had rented rooms, but it was difficult to imagine now. The place seemed so still, quiet, frozen, almost, as if caught in a painting. In America, the house would be full of lodgers coming and going, the place a hive of gossip and cutlery on plates, chairs being pushed across the floor, heels on the stairway.

The person who answered my knock was someone I felt I had seen before but only vaguely taken note of: a woman, about sixty, round soft arms, pink skin flushed over her chest and neck and up into her face. Which was lovely, I saw, but also somewhat secretive, a jewel-like face, with round cheeks, and almond-shaped eyes so dark they seemed to have come out of the forest. Her nose was long and straight, her lips full. The sum of her expression was a profound but decades-old fright, as if she had been taken captive as a girl, and raised gently enough, but by strangers. She was wearing a kind of light shift. I noticed she was panting slightly. She has been in the sun, I thought, working in her garden.

"Je vous en prie," I began. *"Mademoiselle Valmet?"*

"Oui," the woman said, and then she laughed like scales on a flute. "But you are an American, and I speak English."

"Thank you," I said. Then the code: "I was told you have rooms to rent."

"I know who you are," Louise Valmet said. "I have heard"—she paused slightly—"that you are now alone. Please. Come in."

Louise Valmet opened the door and stepped back, and I walked into a room that seemed mysteriously filled with light. From the outside the house had appeared to be deeply shadowed, but tall windows on the south side brought in the noon sun. It was quite warm. I understood why Louise Valmet wore a sleeveless shift.

Just inside the lavender door stood a polished wooden chest of drawers. Brass candlesticks had been set on top, and a brass-framed mirror hung over them, at a height that would reflect the little flames. Just beyond, a staircase ran straight up to a small landing. A hallway led out of sight, and I decided the house must be deeper than I had thought at first. To my right was a kind of drawing room filled, crowded with chairs, two side chairs with red leather seats, upholstered white armchairs, a larger, deeper armchair, and a sofa, covered in dark chintz. Every inch of wall was hung with paintings, watercolor landscapes mostly, a few oils, human figures I recognized slowly as American Indians.

"My friend," Louise Valmet said. "A Swiss painter, called Karl Bodmer. He did these. In America. In your country. He was only twenty-five."

"They're very nice," I said, though I felt a deep twinge of fear. I had not expected to see so much America inside a farmhouse in France.

Mlle Valmet led me down another short hallway and into the kitchen, which was cooler. A stone fireplace opened at one end, and two long oak tables stretched the length of the room. I prepared myself to decline tea or coffee or whatever Mlle Valmet would offer.

"This would be your kitchen too," she said. "Just as you like."

"The room?" I asked this, but my eyes were drawn out the large window to the garden, a tangle of greenery, shot here and there with red and violet and yellow.

"Upstairs. You will see. You can work in the garden to pay for it. Cook some of the meals perhaps. I'll send for your things from town."

"It's just two small bags."

"Very good, then." Mlle Valmet put out her right hand. I took her hand and held it, felt that the fingers and her palm were quite warm. I thought of my children and my husband, how their hands had always been icy cold, the pressure of a block of ice on my body, at night, during the day, night after night, day after day. And now this.

I had been living with Mlle Valmet for two days. Both mornings, we woke early, before dawn, drank a cup of strong coffee and went out to work—I to learn—the garden, weeding, harvesting the vegetables and herbs to be sold at market. Mlle Valmet went out by herself in the afternoon. She didn't tell me where she was going or invite me along. In the evening, we rested indoors and went to bed early. The Germans in Paris, the war itself seemed very far away. We had been quiet together, aside from instructions, names for plants, names for animals, exchanged in French and English.

This evening I had got up from my place on the sofa to look at Karl Bodmer's paintings and sketches.

"Karl went to America in 1832." Louise Valmet appeared to be mending a dress or a shawl and did not look up. "He was a traveling artist in the company of an adventurous German prince. It sounds as though I am making up a story, yes?"

The question was surprising. "Are you?" I asked.

"You will see." Mlle Valmet flashed a secret smile down at the garment in her lap. "Their boat was called the *Janus,* the god with two faces. He was always under the spell of that boat. Their passage was more than forty days, and he was terribly sick. They came into Boston Harbor on your Independence Day, and there was cholera everywhere, and his baggage was delayed. Then they left him behind in Pennsylvania, where there were many dead."

I returned to my seat. "He must have felt . . . ," I began.

"He looked at some of the corpses for anatomical drawings.

The ghosts never left him. He detested the settlements also. It was abhorrent to him how the beginning of a settlement is always the destruction of everything."

"But these paintings are so lovely." I drank my tea, though it had gone quite cold.

"Something burst inside him. It is all like a dream in some of them. Hallucination."

It was true, I thought, as though the pencil and brush could not keep up with the force of what he had seen. One watercolor in particular fascinated me—*Citadel Rock,* it was called—a dismal but exotic towering stone structure that looked like a huge, headless reptilian creature. I felt as though I could stand in front of it for hours. Or that I *should.* There was something in the picture to be seen, to be found. It was a rendering of my heart.

Mlle Valmet went on with her mending. I envied her this activity and thought I might help her. I leaned forward to ask.

"He once preserved a rattlesnake in a brandy keg," she said, quite suddenly, roughly, "and sent it back to Europe."

I sat back, chastened. "When did you become his friend?" I was careful to use the word Mlle Valmet had used herself.

"At first, in Paris. He was a very old man. Then I moved to Barbizon, and soon after, he came to my house, lost. He said, 'Where are the Assiniboin? Where is Mahchsi-Karehde?' He called me by a name I didn't understand but now know to be the name of the chief's wife, Itsichaika. He had a terrible fever, and he stayed here, and when the fever broke, he did not return to the house of his wife."

Later, Louise Valmet began again. She said:

"When I started my shockingly brief career as a painter, I met Karl Bodmer, and he said this to me: the rocks break open with light. I never forgot his words, because I could never make it happen like that on the canvas. As a consequence, I was a minor painter, then none. Now, I am as you see, an old woman, thought to be of no use. So I am quite valuable to the Resistance. The rocks break open with light. I am haunted. Bodmer was haunted too when I met him, an old man, a local colorist, haunted. When I first spoke to him, which was in Paris, I saw him thus, and I know now he was showing me what I would become.

"Years before, he had traveled to America. But that part of the story could wait, Bodmer told me. Instead, he said, *Je dois vous raconter quelquechose d'autre. La lumière.* I should tell you about something else. The light. How it killed us, how it made us see we were already killed. The light in America.

"I myself have been to America only once, to Boston, briefly, to take painting lessons. That too is another story, a story of intrigue and the favors that come from loving certain men without asking them for too much. Without their knowing how much is being asked. Perhaps it is a story about how soulless I am. Another story. But I remembered what Bodmer had said when I stepped off the boat, no, before, when the light suddenly changed, two days off the coast of New England. I thought how wrong he must be. This light seemed the light of simpletons, of children. Morning light. I knew I could never paint in light like this. How odd that Bodmer had been frightened by it. The Swiss, I thought. What are their great achievements, anyway? Neutrality, you will say, or cheese. I thought my year in Boston would go badly, which it did.

"But of course this was not the light Karl Bodmer meant. Nor the people on whom it fell when he saw it.

"I was nineteen when I met Bodmer. My father was a shopkeeper in Paris. *Poisonnier.* It has a second meaning, a rude meaning, about the profession of the fishmonger's daughter. Nevertheless, the house I grew up in stank of fish. I met Bodmer and Rousseau at a salon in Paris. Women were there, though not as artists. I knew how to get in. That is another story also, dull, usual. I could not talk to Rousseau, though I wanted to, but not even men of my age and training could talk to him. But Bodmer, yes, Bodmer the clown, the cartoonist, the man who believed the squirrels in America were so wise. He was seated in another room, away from Rousseau, who, it was said, loved Bodmer like his own father, a grandfather, but often forgot him in the presence of money. Karl was wearing a thick brown coat, very old, and a strange kind of headdress, a tall black hat with an odd sign, a deer's head, painted on the front. It was favored, he told me, by the Hidatsa chief Addih-Hiddisch, which means Maker of Roads. It was a hat like nothing in this world. Bodmer held an empty glass and waited. That was how it seemed to me. Not that he was thinking of anything, but rather waiting for something to end.

"'Sir,' I said. 'I have seen your paintings and admire them very much.' He turned his eyes toward me without moving his head. 'I am thinking,' I went on, 'of moving to Barbizon. How do you find it there?'

"'Very nice,' he said. 'It is good to be with one's own kind.'

"'Yes,' I said.

"Suddenly his whole head swiveled toward me, and his eyes opened wide. 'Mademoiselle,' he said, 'what are you doing here?' And before I could answer, he continued, 'Will you take me away? Will you take me downstairs to get a brandy?' He waved his hands in irritation, as if the room were too warm, the company excruciating. 'Please. I cannot go alone.'

"So we went down a curved stairway from the second floor, and out into the street. The year was 1892. In nine months, Bodmer would be dead. We were in rue des Beaux Arts. He showed me where Corot lived.

"'He was not famous until the age of fifty,' Bodmer said.

"'That distresses me,' I said.

"'As it should.'

"As we walked slowly toward the café he had in mind, I noticed that Bodmer held his face still—his head moved, taking in the sounds around him, but his face was motionless and blank, like a blind man's. 'Everything here is so beautiful,' he said, 'but it is beauty that is easy to look at. Think if beauty were a horrifying spectacle.' I thought I knew what he was talking about. 'Is that how it is in America?' I said.

"'Parts. Yes.' He looked at me a long time then, as long a time as is possible while walking. 'I had not expected it. I had expected something else. Insipid.' He said the word in English. 'I did not know myself.'

"'I don't understand,' I said.

"'No, of course not.' He seemed to shake something off then, a blanket, a fog. 'You're very young. You're a very young woman. There is not much chance for your work. But I would like to see it. Though I cannot, of course, see it very well. But you can tell me what I should see.' I said I would like that. He told me then there was something in my voice that he recognized, and after that, he did not say anything more until we were seated and he had his brandy.

"'You must be self-taught,' he said.

"'Girls are given painting lessons. I have always had a gift. I have always seen things in a certain way.'

"'Describe it to me.'

"'I don't know if I can. I see things as if they are composed, already painted. My hand knows what to make of what my eyes see. I am inspired to make scenes.'

"'Everything is a painting?'

"'Yes.'

"'That's very good. And whom do you admire?'

"'Corot of course.'

"'Of course.'

"'Dupré, Michel, Millet.'

"'Why? Why these three?'

"'I don't know. Though I do know. They haunt me in some way. I see something terrifying in the landscapes. Simple scenes, but the colors frighten me, the darkness.'

"'The land is not open and sunlit, as the English painters show it.'

"'Yes. It's not insipid.'

"'Ah. Very wise.'

"I grew confident under this praise. Bodmer had another brandy. I began to forget the time, the rest of the world. I was in the presence of a painter I admired and a man about whom there was talk, a kind of legend, the hint of a terrible secret. After some time, we were the only ones left in the café, and then all I could think of was the burden of my question. Which at last I asked.

"'I have heard—' I began steadily. 'It is said—'

"Bodmer smiled dreamily, nodded his head. His body, his corporeal presence, seemed suddenly to be gone, to be thousands of miles away. I have seen a man's attention drift off, but this was very different. Bodmer was almost entirely gone. If I'd reached over then, I might have passed my hand through his body.

"'Why do you not paint American scenes?'

"'Surely you know the answer to that question. I am not there. I live here.'

"'But I have heard you refuse to speak about America. So I am quite surprised now—'

"He held up his hand.

"'I will not tell everyone,' he said with a smile. 'But I will tell you.'

"There in the café, Bodmer swore me to secrecy, though as he did so, he laughed and said there was no one left to tell. Perhaps when I was an old woman, I would recall his story, see fit to tell it to someone. But, he said, I should change some parts, make it less strange. Or more strange. He told me to consider my listener and act accordingly. So that is what I will do."

"One day," Mlle Valmet said to me later, "you will tell me such things about your life."

Mlle Valmet had written down almost everything Bodmer told her, and she read it to me. He said that in the spring of his second year in America, he witnessed the ceremony called *oq-uipa*, where a young brave puts hooks into his back, into the flesh and hangs himself from a tree, for hours. Sometimes for days. Not until death, though. For purification, for vision.

But not unto death. There was some evidence, some scarification, Louise Valmet said, to indicate that Bodmer underwent the same ritual himself. He had long, deep scars on his back. Where the wings would be, *où les ailes seront*. Sometimes he ranted and cried out in his sleep. Sometimes he said, "The forest is burning." He thought something horrible would happen to the Assiniboin, the Blackfeet, all of America, really. Something about language. No one would be able to be understood by anyone else.

"I know what you mean, Mlle Valmet," I said. *"Je comprends tout que vous avez me dire."* Mlle Valmet smiled, her eyes still on her needlework. But I did not really know if the story was true.

"Madame," she said to me, "you speak your little bit of French with great happiness. Your pronunciation is very good." I loved the way the last word eased itself out of her mouth, to rhyme with *food*.

"I'm happy to talk to you. It is hard to be alone," I said.

"Yes, this is true. But I am not away from home, as you are."

"Yes," I said. I had been watching Mlle Valmet sew, and now I turned back to Bodmer's painting, *Citadel Rock,* and suddenly saw my family there, in that desolate place.

"I do not know how it has been with you, or how you have come to this work." She said *with* like *wiss,* like air out of a balloon, a sigh out of a body.

"Perdue," I said, *"tombée."* The word for lost, the word for fallen.

"No, no. You say this, *perdue, tombé,* for a necklace or a coin perhaps. She pushed her sewing onto the floor at her feet. "Come now. We must go to work."

Mlle Valmet's garden ran right up to the forest, into it really, and as she weeded, transplanted, harvested over the next five weeks, I came to understand how the garden kept the forest at bay, kept its darkness away from us. At the easternmost edge of the property, she grew willow trees, white willow, she told me, *Salix alba*. The chemist in Barbizon taught her how to extract the active constituent and mix it with honey to use as an analgesic. "These are Karl's trees," she said. The extract soothed his headaches, his rheumatism and neuralgia. He would sometimes drink an infusion of *le saule* after meals. It was good for digestion.

She grew a long hedge of sage. The row of soft sea green and purple plants seemed to have sprung from the weeping of the willows, growing as they did from the foot of these trees. Louise told me how a tea of sage and rosemary had cured Bodmer's fever and helped lift clouds of forgetfulness and confusion. She had hoped it would make him live longer, and perhaps it did. An infusion of lavender helped him sleep, and the scent of it drifted over us all day, released whenever our skirts brushed one of the plants. I supposed there must have been fifty, maybe more. I kept its scent at night, in the fabric of my sleep, like the sheets on the bed in Louise Valmet's guest room.

There was also yarrow, its tiny cream-colored flowers, a row of it for bleeding and toothache, and lady's mantle for female complaints. The leaves, Louise said, looked like *la matrice*, the opening of the womb, and so she explained to me Paracelsus's Doctrine of Signatures, slowly and patiently, half in English and half in French, the belief that the outward appearance of a plant gives an indication of what ailments it will cure. Hollyhock flowers for the throat. Angelica root for the joints, and to make Benedictine. Burdock leaves for indigestion and inflammation of the skin. Often I took burdock upstairs without meaning to; the hooked burrs hid at the hem of my dress and on my elbows.

As we worked, she told me more: in the beginning, Bodmer had answered an advertisement put out by a certain Prince Maximilian of Wied. Maximilian was an interesting man. In another place, he might have been a great philosopher, a political figure, but his great wealth made him into something of a dilettante. He did not have to earn a living, and so he was drawn to wander down many paths. The Mandan called him that,

Wanders Down Many Paths. He was obsessed with the human skull. His teacher at Göttingen, Johann Blumenbach, had the finest collection of skulls in all of Europe, eighty-two of them in all. Maximilian learned from Blumenbach and his skulls that there were five races of the single human species: Mongolian, American, Caucasian, Malay, and Ethiopian. He would often stare at Bodmer's skull, at the skulls of strangers, as if to divine their origins. He talked to the bones of Bodmer's forehead, rather than to his eyes, as most people do. He told Bodmer he had spent hours alone with Blumenbach's skulls, and that perhaps it had made him a little mad. But this honesty was what one loved and admired in Maximilian. He said it was impossible not to handle the skulls a great deal, turning them this way and that way under the light. And then one began to feel fond of them individually. Instead of lifting a skull up for a closer look, and then placing it back in the case, one began to pet the bony heads, and give them names and histories, families, good or bad fortune, easeful or violent deaths.

One evening, Maximilian began to talk about slaves. He said he had purchased two in Brazil, in order to study them. He considered he was setting them free, and they became his friends.

"So the scientist cannot remain impartial," Bodmer said.

"It is a fine theory, Bodmer," the prince said. "You will see."

And so it seemed to Bodmer that he could not paint these Indians, these savages, and remain aloof from them. He believed he would have to become something of a savage in order to get it right. And he hardly knew the meaning of the word, *savage,* his youth had been so tame, so quiet, for the most part.

They landed, Mlle Valmet said, in Boston Harbor on July 4th, 1832. The docks were filled with drunken sailors, and Bodmer and the others had a difficult time moving among them at first. In his feathered cap, Maximilian was at first a figure of fun, but Bodmer watched as the sailors became another kind of indigenous people for him to study. Maximilian looked at each of them, the ones who crossed his path, or at first refused to move out of his way, he looked them in the eye. He touched one or two on the shoulder, and a kind of softening come into their bodies. They stepped back.

They had no guide, so they went to an inn and ordered brandy. Other sailors asked why they had come to America, and when Maximilian told them, they said the West was savage, quite frightening. Others listening shook their heads in agreement, then ran their hands over their hair, meaning scalps, counting coup. There had been stories of apparently friendly Indians suddenly turning hostile. They had customs the white man could never understand.

They have beliefs about the body, a ship's captain said to Bodmer. He would find this when he drew them. When Bodmer asked what beliefs, the man told him, scarring and mortification of the flesh. He said it was all very foreign to them. But Maximilian would have said, they are very like us. And when the captain said, somewhat angrily, they are nothing like us, Bodmer said that it was true. He said they were more beautiful.

Maximilian smiled. He knew Bodmer had never seen Indians. But the captain continued, saying the Indians were a race of slaves. It was Independence Day, he said, when Americans celebrate being free. The Indians, he added, had no sense of this, like the Negro, the African.

Outside Roman candles shrieked, and the crowds cheered

them on their way. Bodmer tried to think what the two things, the coincidence, could possibly mean: American independence, and his arrival in America on that very day. He drank the brandy too quickly; a glass of ale appeared before him, and he drank that too. He began to feel adrift, more than he had at sea. He and Maximilian and the others from the *Janus* went out of the saloon to look for something to eat and a place to stay, as their guide had not arrived. They left their names behind them, everywhere they went, and it seemed to Bodmer that was the truth about American independence: a man was free to leave his name, his name was proof that he existed. Not so for slaves, whose work was this proof. For the Indians, he would discover, proof of existence was something else; it was literal, carved into the flesh.

They lay in their bunks that night, these bunks that did not sway with the sea, the rooming house dark and quiet. The world was elsewhere. They still heard shouts and cheers and small explosions, but only as one would hear them in a dream, the edges frayed and shimmery, a kind of auditory vision. Onboard the *Janus*, Maximilian would speak to Bodmer in the dark; he had grown as used to it as to the sound of the waves. His speaking was a kind of understanding, a pact between them. He knew Bodmer needed it in order to fall asleep.

But on the Fourth of July in 1832, in Boston, Maximilian was silent. Bodmer waited and listened. His friend did not seem to be asleep. Bodmer asked if something was wrong, troubling. For a moment, there was no answer.

From Louise Valmet, I learned to make absinthe from wormwood. She showed me how to put the aerial parts of the plant into a large jar and cover them with water and clear alcohol. I used Russian vodka, which Louise had a store of. The jar would be sealed and stored for a few days, then passed through a small wine press into a jug, then into clean dark glass bottles. Louise called this *teinture*. When we sipped it quietly in the long-shadowed late afternoon, Karl Bodmer's pictures seemed like windows through which the vague shapes of America became alarming to me. The land looked gigantic, the people and animals horribly small and vulnerable. I felt a strange lightness, an astonishment, as if I might float from the earth.

One evening we lingered with our absinthe glasses until the darkness in the house was a sticky pitch. From across the room, I heard Louise sigh.

"How have you come to this work?" she asked.

I thought of my children, and my heart broke again. I was adrift, like Karl Bodmer.

"There is a young man," Louise said, "an American, a pilot, in hiding. He has heard of us. He has information."

From the darkness, Louise's breath seemed to take on color and substance. A breeze rose in a hiss out of the forest, and a ghost of lavender and mint; the lemony tang of sorrel followed it into my brain, as if through a hole in the back of my head. I imagined the shape my husband's body made in the dark, remembered really, for that was how I had known him best, as part of the shadows in the room we slept in together all those years. Here though, inside Louise's garden, I felt calmer than I had ever in my life despite the war, the Germans in Paris, the deprivation. The perfume of the garden would keep it all at bay—there would be a change in the air, almost visible, if anyone came near.

"How many children were there?"

"There were two."

I heard Louise put down her glass. The chink of it against the flagstone was coarse, grating to my ears, as if the glass had broken.

"Do you love your husband?" she asked.

"I promised to love him. But there was a betrayal. And then he took my children away. He was very angry. He left them alone, and they were killed in a fire. I feel sometimes I would like to kill him."

"Ah. That is how it begins. A friend of Bodmer's father's had heard of Maximilian's voyage, and told Bodmer, and there was a story there too. Bodmer had not long before seen this friend in the company of his mother. The circumstances were compromising, and Bodmer knew he had been seen, the seer was seen, a kind of mirror. So his going to America began with a deception, a sort of malice, desperation, secrecy. He said to Bodmer, this friend said, 'Karl, I know you want to travel, and you want to paint, and here is your chance.' Bodmer thought sometimes this man had paid Maximilian to hire him. 'I want you to have this opportunity,' the man said. 'I don't want you to languish at home.' He did not smile as he said this. Bodmer had wanted to kill them, his mother and her lover, come upon them together and flay their bodies alive. Tear their flesh, then show the corpses to his father, crying, see how you are betrayed? Sometimes at night, half asleep, he thought that he really might do it, had already done it. But in the morning, his mother would be sitting prettily by a sunlit window, or readying herself to go out—Bodmer knew where—and he would feel both relief and anguish.

"Karl Bodmer's wife would have killed me," she said, "if she had known how to do it. She could have, really. Quite easily. But she was not that kind of woman. And now I have outlived her. So what does it mean? What is betrayal?"

"I should not have told you anything," I said. "Please forget it all." I put down my glass and let my head fall into my hands. I heard Louise rise and come to stand in front of me, then bend down and pull my right hand to her face.

"*Viens*. Come. I want to show you something." She led me to the middle of the garden, and then the two of us lay down between the rows of thyme and rosemary. "Look up there," she said, and I turned my head past the open mouths of foxglove to stare up at the moon, the thinnest scimitar of light, an eyelash. "Karl Bodmer would say sometimes a very strange thing to me. He would say, '*Tiens*, Louise, there are the stars, there are your children.' I did not understand right away. It seemed cruel to me, because he knew I had no children. And he would not give me any. He was old then. But many of his notions had come from the Assiniboin, very mysterious people, or his ideas had come from the eccentric German prince, Maximilian. Most Germans now are only interested in polite, philosophical questions. The beginning of the world, life after death, such as that. They are little gods. They prefer to judge. Some of it is correct. But not now. Not these Germans. We must get rid of them."

I felt Louise Valmet's garden spin slowly around me, the hedge of creamy moonflowers and an enormous red bloom called mallow, opening like a wound. The sage leaves turned to silver and the green hedge to black. I was at the bottom of the universe looking up, and the undulation of the world was bringing me closer to something, a disorder in my mind bringing itself to clarity. Louise was still speaking, and some of what she said was in French, words like caresses, like little spells. Above us was a configuration of stars I had come to know as the Great Bear, below it the Little Bear and the Pole Star. I remembered finding them on the ship crossing the Atlantic Ocean, a man pointing them out, the two of us looking up from the swaying deck, how I thought the stars in the Bear's tail resembled a gallows. How that man had asked to come to my cabin, how I almost said yes. In the garden, I saw the heavens move, a slow halting turn around the Pole Star, like the tiny hand on a clock that marks the smallest bit of time. *There is something she wants me to do,* I thought. I heard Louise whisper, *digitale, la digitale,* and imagined an absurd cartoon, a bear creeping on all fours with caps of pink foxglove over its sharp toes. "Perhaps, then," Louise said, "he will not make a noise." Then, *"Il va mourir au lit."*

I did not know what Louise said to the young American pilot. "It is arranged," was all that was said to me. A day later, I answered a knock at the door, and a German officer stood there, and I imagined him my husband, gleaming against the darkness, a silvery blade. I said hello and glanced over my shoulder at Louise who had followed us into the room. Her expression seemed innocent and sinister too. Her head seemed to undulate on her neck, like a serpent. I thought suddenly of the first French I had ever learned, *la tête est sur le cou,* the head is on the neck, a phrase full of warning and relief, as if the speaker had just discovered he was still alive.

Between us, Louise Valmet and I poisoned six German officers. We entertained them, gave them an herbal tea, and they died in their beds.

Vision

~1~

My mother stood gazing up the Vanceboro road as if she had known all along, the day and the hour: December 1983, four in the afternoon. She must have seemed smaller than my father remembered her, emptied out, her hands open and empty too. The sun was in her face, but she did not squint against it or hold up her hand for shade. I watched her wait there, in a blue dress, an apron on her hips, the blue a strange, false color, not the sky, not any flower I had ever seen. There was another man walking along the road, a neighbor, named Sampson Lee, who was sixty years old, but seemed ancient to me then. He said good morning and ambled on. I remember thinking there was nothing in his voice, no surprise or happiness that my father had come home, as if he too knew everything already. My father closed the car door and looked again to his wife, my mother, and beyond her to the wet shell of our house. He had flown across half the world, from Beirut to eastern North Carolina, but for now he had stopped moving. In a moment she would see him and understand who he was. I knew what he was waiting for. I knew she would have to tell him how he was supposed to greet her, how to act—she would have to do this with her arms or body. They were strangers to each other. It was like this whenever he came home from a tour of duty. This time, he'd been gone a year.

She stared, her small face wide at the top and pointed at the bottom, like an owl's. She appeared not to move, though when he got close enough, my father could see her eyes were opening and closing rapidly. A slight convulsive shiver ran over her upper body when she let her eyes drop from his face to his clothes. She moved toward him then, but did not open her arms, stopping when six inches of space separated their bodies.

"I knew it would be any time now," she said. "Where did you get this car?"

"Yep," he said. "A friend."

"I wanted to come down to the base, but I couldn't leave Mother." She looked into his face, her eyes going back and forth between his.

She began to cry then, leaning forward to rest her cheek against his chest. "Awful," she said, choking on the word, on the evidence that lay everywhere around her. "It's awful here." My father could not bring himself to hold her—he looked past the clean part in her hair, her bent head, to the yard of what would from then on be his house. It was nothing like the ruin he'd seen in Beirut—at least here was a house, houses all along this road, though he'd prepared himself for weeds growing in through broken windows, a fallen-in chimney, his family taken up residence in a metal storage shed or a tent. But the house did not look abandoned, though it looked ill-used, most of the shutters off in front, the porch rail gone in places, the yard a sea of mud at the height of hurricane season. My father must have prepared himself for that, how we might have let the place go, or sold off parcels of land. He'd heard it from other men whose wives lived away from the base and had written these solemn inventories. He thought of his friend Ronnie Cuthbert, the blown away, sightless face, the twist of his limbs when they brought his body out of the barracks. The aspect of his house reminded him, the sad papered-up windows, with nothing, nothing in this world, to look forward to. He turned and saw me then. I was holding his dog, Birdy.

"You must be tired," my mother said. "And hungry. Are you hungry?" Her face angled up at him was broad and pale, uncomprehending, like his dog, waiting to be led or whipped. Her hairline had receded, exposing fully the barren plain of her forehead. Below it, the thin arched, eyebrows and the brown eyes he knew, a dark, velvety color that caused the whites of her eyes to appear almost blue. He realized it was not precisely age or fear he saw in her face, but thinness. She had caved in.

"Mother has been waiting for you too." She took my father's arm and led him across the wet yard and up the porch steps, which shifted beneath his weight.

"Loose," he said.

"All of it is. Everything."

"The whole damn world."

She stopped then and gripped his hand but did not look at him.

Inside, the front hall appeared shadowy, the beginning of a descent into the nether regions of the house. My father saw that someone had covered the windows with newspaper, and he stopped to look at it for a long time. He had not noticed this before and wondered out loud if there were still glass panes beneath the old news. He said he was afraid to find out. The house smelled heavy, like a damp animal, as if someone else had died in one of the rooms, more recently than his father-in-law, my grandfather, and he thought again of Cuthbert, dead in the marine barracks two months before, blown apart in his sleep.

"It's cold in here," my mother said. "We're using the space heaters."

A voice called out from the front room, my mother's mother, Mary Amos. "Michael?"

"Yes," he said, and went in to her. My grandmother sat as she had for weeks, in a hard chair, midway between the front window and the doorway in which he stood. She turned her whole head toward him, the gesture of it slow and strange, the head tilted slightly backward, as if she were looking at him with her ear. My father realized almost at once that she was blind, and he understood from the sudden pressure of my mother's hand on his arm that her blindness had been sudden and grotesque.

"Mother Amos," he began, and dropped down on one knee beside her. Her hand opened and shut in the empty air.

"It's over, then? If you're home, it must be all over, just like they tell us."

"It's not over," my father said.

"Well," Mother Amos replied, "is there anything to be glad about?"

"I walked." He told her this half-lie, as if it were the answer to her question. "I walked all the way from Jacksonville."

"And what did you see on the way?"

"Nothing," my father said. "I came at night, mostly. It was dark."

"Good," Mother Amos told him. "Then we're going to understand each other."

No one, my mother told my father, was sure what she had done, how she had been blinded. She had stayed at my grandfather Amos's bedside throughout his illness, trying to convince him he would get better. Then one day, she had said, "It's all right. You can go if you need to, if it's your time." Then she had left the room, and, it seems, the house. Nobody saw her go, and she was missing for two whole days and nights; then the neighbor Sampson Lee had discovered her in a field, a mile from the house, lying face down. He thought she was dead, but when he reached to turn her over, Mother Amos said, "Don't," and tried to move out of his grasp. Later they had found her underclothes torn and bloodstained. My mother blushed as she said this, and faced away from him.

"And her eyes were just gone," my mother continued. "Clawed out of her skull. When we asked what happened, she said she had done that herself."

"To herself?" my father asked.

"And then she wouldn't talk. She won't come into the light either. She sits in the front room all day. I bring her supper in there."

My father could see what must have been a faint bruising all the way around both eye sockets, and the way the lids lay concave. She looked like many of the dead he had seen, men who had been buried under the collapsed buildings for days, so that the work of gravity was done upon them, and everything they were or possessed, their hearts, their eyes, their souls, had begun to fall toward the center of the earth.

"If it's not over," Mother Amos said, "who's winning?" She waited patiently for an answer.

"They are," my father said, and left the room.

~2~

I was the child of his youth and his favorite. When I was born, in 1963, my father, Michael Devallee Williams, was seventeen. Then he was gone to boot camp, then he joined the 1st Battalion, 8th Marines, and shipped out to Lebanon from Camp Lejeune, North Carolina. Nineteen years later, he was dead. So I imagined I was the vessel for his old age, all the years he did not get to have, that I was living my own life, but my father's as well. I've kept a picture of him since his death, carried it with me, even to school, and so I remember more of it than I do of my father himself. The picture mouthed words I'd heard from him when I was a child, the picture kissed my mother good-bye when he went overseas, and on the day he was killed, the picture was the man buried in his coffin in the cemetery near Vanceboro. For as long as I can remember, everyone who knew him had told me I was the very image of Michael Devallee Williams, the soul and the voice and the character of him lingering on in this world. But it was no pretty thing to say. My father had been mean, bad to drink, bad to cuss, bad to everybody, my mother used to tell me, and I should know, she would claim, I lived with him longest. But I think that's not true. I see him in my dreams. I live with him today.

But I thought he had the face of a man with good sense, a man who had seen the world for all it was worth and had found it lacking. *This isn't enough,* his countenance seemed to say; *I can't see why anybody would think it was.* His expression was of sorrow and disbelief, and some horror that was just about to bring him to speech. In the photograph, he wore a high white collar and a dull colored jacket that looked like it must have had silver buttons from the way they gleamed. Underneath, though, was an embroidered vest—I remember it from life—dark green with a border on the lapels and down the front beside the buttons, flowers, five petals cross-stitched in white thread. It made the photograph into a puzzle—the serious, nearly aghast expression above such jaunty clothing. The mountains in Germany, Mother said, *Tyrolean,* using a word I did not believe she knew the meaning of. And she said what explained my father was that he had been stationed at the Marine Headquarters at Beirut International Airport on October 23, 1983, when a man drove a car filled with explosives through the front gate. Two hundred forty-one soldiers died, but my father had been at the far end of a landing strip, walking patrol, out of harm's way. Not long after, he found himself standing next to the commandant, watching the dead dug out of the ruined buildings. And when the commandant said, "I am responsible. These were my people," my mother thought Michael DeVallee Williams must have whispered back, *Maybe so, but I'm not your people. I'm not anybody's.*

There were other stories, too, chief among them that he walked almost all the way home to Reelsboro from Camp Lejeune, then rode the last miles with a man from New York, and just south of Oriental, North Carolina, my father killed this man, a retired army officer, took his car and drove the rest of the way in. The car itself disappeared the day after he came home. All I ever saw of it was the license tag, the bottom edge, under a pile of shirts in a drawer: *The Empire State.* But I always defended him: Why shouldn't he hate that officer when it was men like that who ruined the whole world, tore it apart beam by beam? Why should that man have a car, and not Daddy? He'd walked a long way, seen men die, and worse. Why not have a car? Was he a deserter? "You don't understand any of it, what goes on over there," my sister Mattie said years later. "Well, what do you know about it?" I said, "What in the world have you ever had to suffer?" and Mattie replied quietly, "I ought to slap your face, but as it is, you'll come to your own bad end."

And so after my father died, I carried his memory in my side like a stone or an extra rib, heavy and burdensome but impossible to break off or cast out. I watched my own countenance take shape as his—almost daily, I compared the one photograph of him to my own face. I have his eyes, I told myself, his nose, his mouth that was always about to speak to me from the grave, tell me everything I needed to know about the rest of my life. I dreamed often of our old walks in the cotton and soybean fields behind the house, during which this vision of my father said to me, *You should have everything you want,* as we moved through the rows, the bolls glowing around us like little moons, lights with no light of their own. Why should I? I asked, and my father's image kept silent. The little orbs of no-light trembled. My father's image turned its face to me, and I saw it was gray and withered. The old skin hung off the bones in folds, the eye sockets glowed and convulsed as if each held a cotton boll crawling with weevils. *Because you are good,* my father's image seemed to say, though the slack flesh could not make those words or any words.

I imagined this death's head of my father saying what he told me when he was alive.

"We're done in, Nina," he said. "Look around, and remember what you see, because it's going to be lost. It already is lost to you, this property. The family can't work it or pay to have it worked. You don't remember what these fields looked like before, when they could be planted and picked, all of them."

He looked down to the house.

"And I'm locked in with my bad luck, my own fool self. Four

children and not a one to help me. Charlie and Frank useless, doting on their mother."

He pulled me close, held me to his chest. I could feel his heart going like a train when you're standing still beside it, passing out of sight, clackety, clackety, clackety.

"I can hear your heart, Daddy," I said.

"Well you're the only one," he said. "You're mine, Miss Nina. You're just like me, even if you are a girl."

Someone called him from the house, Mother or Mattie. Sometimes it was hard to tell their voices apart.

"Where can I go? In Raleigh, a man can go to work for himself, get lost in that size city. Or north. Canada. I could go out to sea. I'm a goddamn marine."

The field we walked was set somewhat higher than the rest, on the only rise in Pamlico County, so that my father could survey almost all of his property. When he was home, he liked to walk there, above the house, looking down at it, the drive in from the road. He planted a garden on this rise, and when he did work that little bit of soil, he'd straighten up every so often, and glance around wildly like somebody just awakened out of a deep sleep.

I knew why. Even as a young girl, in the years before my father's death, I'd heard it spoken of. When my father barked at my mother to lock the door, she would sometimes turn on him, a vicious smile playing at the corners of her mouth.

"Lock the door, lock the door," she mocked. "Lock it yourself, Michael. And what are you so afraid of, I wonder? Ghosts? The ghost of that man with the car? I'll tell you, Michael, a ghost can get in any way it wants. Locks can't keep out the ghost of a man beat to death for his cheap car."

"Shut your mouth, Laura," my father said.

"Or is it his kin? Real live kin from New York come to find you? He had sons and daughters. He told you so, didn't he? Well, these won't be kept out either."

"Enough!"

"I'll open the door for them, throw it wide. Come and get him, all of you. Here he is, the wreck of him. He's no good to me. He's no good to his own children. Doesn't even speak to them, but the big girl. Turning her strange. Doesn't like to work. Just watching all day. For you all. Waiting for you to come from New York after him."

Sometimes her voice would drop here, while my father grew utterly still.

"You never should have done it, Michael. Never should have killed him. What'd you need that car for? He was going to bring you on home. Jesus, Michael."

And then she'd leave him alone in the room, not rushing, but slow so he could see it, feel it, the full weight of her scorn. Only once did she say the words that went with the act of walking away, only once that I ever heard: *I never loved you, Michael.* But she was afraid of him, and that fear kept her quiet and still, at least for a time.

He didn't go to church with her and the little ones, and kept me out with him. The first times, there was trouble about it, and once they grabbed hold of me—he held one of my arms and she the other, and they pulled until my blouse ripped, until Mattie said, "Momma, he would kill her over this," and Mother said, "I believe he would," and that was the end.

While the others were away on Sunday mornings, my father and I sat at the table in the kitchen. He put a bottle between us, and I watched while he drank. Sometimes there would be a Bible on the table too, and he opened it at random. *I am hemmed in by darkness,* he read, *and thick darkness covers my face.*

Before everybody came home, he would put the bottle away, take my hand or touch my shoulder if I'd fallen asleep, and we would walk outside to the top of the rise behind the house.

"Let's watch them come in, Nina. Let's see their holiness carry them up the road without making a cloud of dust to soil their shoes. Let's us watch."

And in high cotton season, we stood, shielding our eyes from the sun. In winter, we could sit. I sometimes fell back to sleep, but my father never did.

Vigilance. From my father, I learned how to wait.

~3~

And so the story, finally, of Mary Amos's trouble, of her blindness. After we heard about the bombing in Beirut, that day, when all of Jacksonville and northwards was hearing the story, and wives and mothers were running out of their houses into the street, Grandmother Amos was coming home late, at supper time. She said she had felt dogged by something all day, a ghostly trouble, she called it to herself, inescapable, whatever it was. Grandmother Amos was not a tall woman, never had been, but she was still strong, and not afraid of anybody, so she did not move with uncertainty or fear in her bones. She cut across the fields between town and her husband's house. She says she was not despairing exactly, but perhaps a little unconscious. She knew then that something would happen to my father. *In the war of aggression,* she said, for the rest of her life.

She knew there would never be any peace. It seemed at that moment as devastating as the gathering death of her husband.

For death gathers—she said this later, from out of her blindness—death gathers like storm clouds or blackbirds on a fence, even if nobody sees it. And she thought she felt another gathering—the probable death of her son-in-law, Michael Williams, who was keeping the peace in Lebanon, whose headquarters at the Beirut airport had been blown to pieces that morning. Grandmother Amos and her daughter would be widows in the same year, the same week, she predicted, though they had not yet had any news about Michael. She may have said it out loud, walking across that field. She looked toward her house, still two hundred yards away, and saw no light in the bedroom window. A kind of knowledge came to her without words, she said later, and then she felt arms hard about her waist, and heard low voices and a laugh and found herself on her back in the middle of the cotton crop. October, and this field still snowy with bolls. A man tore at her clothes, and another called to him to hurry. She knew who they were by their speech and what she could see of their clothes. The first one smelled bad, and the second one worse. She did not know there was a third until he was on her, but by that time, she felt no more pain. Later, she wondered if there might have been a fourth and a fifth, or more. When it all seemed to have ended, the men stood over her, whispering, and then one knelt down and held her still by placing his palms on either side of her forehead. For a wild moment she thought he would kiss her. Then another knelt down and with the point of a knife made one quick stab, like a puncturing, into each of her eyes. She felt it anciently, pain come into her head as if from years before, dull, long-forgotten until something jars it loose.

The men stood quiet for a moment, and Grandmother Amos wondered if it would start all over again. She made her body hold very still. Then one of them spat, but not on her, and all three or four or seventeen ran off. Grandmother Amos said she heard their voices for a long time, and their footfalls across the field. She thought they might consider and come back and kill her all the way, and so she tried to move but could not. She felt her eyes, and her fingers touched wetness. She did not understand why she could not will herself to open her eyes, get up and go home.

Her daughter, my mother, missed her and set out to search, but before she even left the front porch, Sampson Lee, her father's boyhood friend, came downstairs to say her father, my grandfather, was much worse, and so through half the night, Grandmother Amos went unlooked-for in a cotton field a mile beyond the house.

"His spirit passed over me on the way," she said later, "and told me I would live and all manner of wisdom that I spent the rest of my life trying to make sense of." So she knew when Sampson Lee found her the next morning that Amos was dead. "It's a blessing," she said. "He would not have wanted me, defiled and blind. He will want me in the next world, but he would not have wanted me in this life."

After that, Grandmother Amos lived in the downstairs front room, in the dark, with her head full of visions. One day she said to my father, "I know all about the invisible empire state, Michael. I know all about the unseen world. Ghosts will come for you," she said, "with firearms, riding at night. You'll think it's your kin, your brothers."

He knew what had happened to Grandmother Amos, and like men of his breed, he could not help blaming her for it. He believed she had brought it on herself, wandering alone in the evening, without a coat, coming across that cotton field, where she had no business. Like that breed of men, his vision was divided. He thought somewhere off to the side of reason that she must have looked beautiful picking her way through the stumps of cotton growth—she must have appeared like a goddess or an angel risen out of fire and destruction. Like a pure force that could save them from all the meanness and horror they had seen and made and become. They wanted to be inside all that goodness and beauty. He understood it, Michael Williams did, and he wondered she did not know it herself. And so after October 23, 1983, Grandmother Amos never again saw the world. She was alone and blind. She would say, "I am powerfully alone," and smile her secret little smile.

~4~

Ten years later, I was just starting to get used to my new name, Nina Williams Thomason, which I supposed would be what I called myself forever. But how wrong I was, how wrong we can be about our names. I had been married since March to James Thomason, and I was happy enough, but we had moved up to New Bern to start a contracting business. I missed the hubbub at my mother's house in Reelsboro, all the children, especially at Christmastime. So I begged James to go two weeks early, and he drove me down on December 12th, as a surprise, dropped me at the house on the way to bid a job. No one was at home. I recall I shivered when I took off my coat. In the front room, nobody had lit a fire, or even turned on the lights. The house seemed naked, not a hint of Christmas at the windows, no scent of baking from the kitchen. Here it was just two weeks to go, and there was no tree, no invitations for Christmas dinner. I did look forward to my first holiday as a married woman, but not to spending it with my husband's family. And if my mother didn't speak up soon, the Thomasons would ask us, and James and I would have to say yes. I still felt strange in their quiet, serious house, where there were no other children but my husband's brother, Nick, who was twenty-eight, and familiar with me in a way I didn't like. I had been hoping to find comfort and merrymaking in my mother's house, but the stillness and ghostly damp of the front rooms made me sad and lonely. I wondered sometimes at the constant presence of such feelings. I had never been like this before my marriage. It was as if taking the vows had peeled something away, instead of adding on, forcing me to see in a kind of true and piercing light. My mother had said in March, just before my wedding: "Don't look for him to be a companion. It isn't like that. And the men don't want it either. It's just an arrangement." And that night I dreamed we were in church and what James held out to me wasn't the gold wedding band, but a tiny circle of fire, a burning cogless wheel.

Why I was still standing in the entrance hall, in the cold, in the afternoon dim without calling out that I was home, I still can't say. To keep on listening to my old house maybe, but as I waited, my coat still over my shoulders, I became aware of a kind of low rumble coming from the small bedroom at the top of the stairs. It was the room all the new babies had slept in, and I had thought the house was so quiet because Emory was in there. Little Emory, fifteen years younger than I was. It would be strange, James had said, but nice, for Emory to grow up with our children, his own nieces and nephews.

I slowly recognized the voices as belonging to my mother and my father. Then I heard them cross the floor above me. Or one of them was crossing the floor. I started toward the staircase, but the tone of my father's voice froze my heart.

"We're moving down to Jacksonville, Laura," he said, "after the new year."

He opened the bedroom door a crack, and repeated the last part, then said, "There's no arguing with it." What I heard in his voice was astonishing, his usual willful calm, but drowning in sadness. I half expected him to cough or choke, the sensation of him submerged and cold was so strong.

In reply, my mother's tone was even, mocking: "If you move away from here," she said, "you will have to get another wife to go with you." There was a pause. Emory had started to whimper, and I heard the creak of the baby's bed. What my mother said next was only a little muffled. "And when you go, I will get another husband."

Some vague understanding drenched my bones, chilled them inside my skin. Jacksonville? I heard my father shake himself loose—that was the sound of it, keys or tools jangled and the door opened wider. He exhaled in a kind of low groan.

"I'm sick," he said. "I don't know what it is."

I moved into the shadows under the stairs.

"Did you hear me, Laura?" he went on. "I'm going out. Birdy needs a walk." And he called to his old dog.

I heard the bedroom door whine on its hinges and thought my father must have looked back in. He groaned again, and coughed. "Where are the boys?" he said.

"At Sister's," my mother said, in her suckling voice, the voice that is blind, that wants to talk only to itself.

"All right then," my father said, and closed the door. He picked up something from the corner of the hallway—his shotgun—and came slowly down the stairs, passed by without seeing me, walked through the kitchen and out the back door. He shut it quietly. He did not make much noise, ever, Michael Williams.

I sat in the hollow beneath the stairs for some minutes. Two or three years before, my father had outfitted this little corner with a wooden seat, nailed into the right angle. He had said to the family, "Someone is always standing in there, hiding from someone else or listening to talk he or she shouldn't be hearing. Right, Laura? So I'll just make it comfortable." And he did so the same evening, cut a triangular piece out of an old door, smaller beams to support it. From that corner then, a person could see part of the front door and into the front room as well, survey all the polite comings and goings, the society of the house. I had not hidden myself there since last January when I watched James Thomason wait alone for me, the day we decided to get married. I observed him for five or ten minutes, hoping to see something in his private behavior that would give him away, and wondering, too, if I would be forced to come out, reveal my little game. Finally, though, my father called James to the front porch, and I slipped out a minute later to join them.

I had hardly lived in the house since then, and what I had just witnessed between my mother and father made me feel even more of a stranger. I had not noticed before how unkempt the downstairs rooms looked, dusty, the furniture pushed about at odd angles. In the years after Grandmother Amos died, the front room slowly filled up with my mother's doll collection, as if it were important to keep some form of woman in there, staring out at the road without seeing. A few at a time, my mother had brought them downstairs, and now they all kept company, like an endless tea party, my father said, like deaf mute girls' night out. In the gloom of the winter afternoon, they were a terrifying, living stillness, half in shadow. I thought they might move. I wondered what they had overheard, what they knew, what was happening in this house. I felt three things in a particular order, the progression of which I would remember for years because I was ashamed. First, there was a kind of emptiness filling my heart, like the starless sky at night, as if my mother's dolls had sucked all the air out of the room. Then the world seemed to crumble beneath me, the whole universe held up by my parents' marriage. Finally, I realized they had always lived like this, each wanting to be free of the other, wanting something that could hardly be named.

What happened next was that my head felt heavy, seemed to nod of its own accord, and the room grew warm again, the yawning open space below my closed eyes. At the same instant, there were footsteps on the front porch, soft and cautious, as if the body they belonged to was approaching in the middle of the night, to do great harm. Overhead, the front bedroom door opened, and my mother stood still on the landing directly above. I understood, and the force of it caused me to nod furiously, the odd gesture of agreeing with myself. I remembered a moment after Thanksgiving dinner, three weeks before, when the Williamses and the Thomasons dined together, a look that passed between my mother and Nick Thomason, James's brother. I recalled, too, that their shoulders—my mother's and Nick's—brushed in passing through a doorway, the rustle of fabric. I had not dared to look any lower; I had not wanted to see their hands touch, or their hips through their clothes.

There was a light knock at the front door, and then my mother was flying down the stairs, lifting the latch, pulling Nick Thomason inside by his coat sleeve. I could not see all of their embrace, but I could hear it, the same crush of wool, a silence that seemed hungry, murmuring.

"He has gone out," my mother said.

"When was that?" Nick Thomason asked.

"Just now. He has gone. With his gun. Now is our time."

"Do you think so?"

"Yes." The word whispered, serpentine.

They would go upstairs, I believed, and it would be safe for me to come out from my hiding place and leave the house. I held my hand to my mouth, afraid I would be sick, or speak, or sob. James, Father, I tried to think who I might tell all this to.

But they did not go upstairs. There was silence, breathing, a rustling of clothes that sounded like dead leaves underfoot, and then Nick Thomason turned, passed by me and through the dining room, into the kitchen and out the back door. I tried to see his face, but it was turned so that I couldn't. From that angle, Nick's body looked like his brother's, and the resemblance at that moment made me feel faint. I put out a hand to steady myself, and my elbow knocked against the corner wall. My mother paused on the stairs, listening. I imagined her face at the moment: small, heart-shaped, dusky in complexion like an animal, the long regal nose twitching to get the scent of something, her great dark eyes locked in the middle distance, unblinking. When she was concentrating, I knew, my mother would often spread open her left hand and, starting at the scalp over her ear, run her fingers the length of her hair, separating the curly black mass into thin snakes. It was an alarming gesture—those small white fingers emerging from the sea of dark hair like vermin.

She knows I am here, I thought, *she can smell me.* The scent of onions, the peculiar soup-broth odor of the Thomasons' household. Someone was always boiling animal bones for stew, and it was always with us, inside our clothes. Like hell, my mother said once, if hell were a kitchen. *I have caught my mother in disobedience.* The thought was dizzying, and I argued with myself in the dark understair. What had I seen? Nothing. What had I heard? A kiss, maybe. Some instruction.

Charlie and Frank came into the house through the back door. I loved their boy conversation, the odd chorus of their quiet talk, voices swirling together, a rich language all their own. Before my marriage, I had been a second mother to them, more of a mother, I sometimes felt, than their own, the woman caught on the stairs. I knew now they were hungry, that they hadn't had their lunch or dinner. I heard one of them pull a chair across the floor, the sound of breathlessness, and then the sharp keen of the breadbox lid being raised. Frank, though he was the younger of the two, would be doing this, while Charlie watched. There was silence for a moment, until the boys' low murmuring began again. My mother crept the rest of the way upstairs, opened the bedroom door and went inside. She spoke to herself as she crossed the room, her footsteps ghostly above my head, like a stain spreading inside the wood and plaster of the ceiling.

I stepped from my hiding place, glancing left into the kitchen. The boys were out of sight, inside the pocket between the open door and the pantry. Then they went out as they had come in, silent as intruders, as strangers. I longed to go after them, hold their squirmy bodies to mine for a second or two, smooth their hair, but I knew the sound of my voice would bring my mother downstairs. Darling Nina, she would say, I didn't hear you come in. And I knew if I looked into my mother's face, I would see everything, betray everything. So I crossed the hall quickly to the front door, pulled it open, then shut it with the softest click. I did not turn to look back up at the house. Outside the late afternoon light melted, insubstantial, through low clouds that seemed like dusty wool, piled bedclothes. It was half a mile to the main road into Reelsboro. I could follow the road into town, find James, tell him that I felt like walking, that no one was at my mother's house. It was true. No one I knew was there.

The gravel lane between my parents' house and the road was hard and dry. There had been no rain for a few days, though the weather had been cold and wet the week before Thanksgiving, and then the freak snowfall, so tire marks still ran deep as canals. I thought suddenly that I should have my own car, and I pictured it, gleaming like a vision. Just below the house, the woods began, and there was Sampson Lee's place and then not another residence again until beyond the Baptist church and the tobacco barns. This time of year, anybody could see a good ways into the trees, pecan, pine, and oak reduced to gray scaly trunks and branches heaved up into the sky. I heard a gunshot, then another, and calculated how straight west from where I stood were the scrub and deadfall, the creek, and then the rise where my father liked to walk. There was a third shot. I thought if I looked hard enough, I might see him. It was odd how a person walking as I was could see for quite a ways into the trees, and then all of a sudden just couldn't. I'd said that once to James, and he had told me it was called perspective, the way sight was whittled down to a point, and then the eye could travel no further. "So it's a kind of blindness," I said to him, and he said, "No matter how well you can see, you can't see everything. You can't see all the way back."

~5~

"I'll get you out," was all I told her, but I didn't know I'd be able to until I saw Sampson Lee's face. Or rather, I didn't see. It was the middle of the night, but there was a hall light that he always kept on, and in its dull glow, I could see everything else, his uncombed hair, his nightshirt tucked into his trousers, his soft cloth house shoes and bare ankles. They were details in a dream, unconnected, waiting for the dreamer to wake up and make sense. He let me in and told me to follow him. Our eyes never met. "If I don't see you," he said, "then you wasn't here."

The back door was bolted and further secured by way of two locks. Sampson Lee slid back the bolt easily enough, but then it seemed a hundred years before he discovered the first key and the second on his ring. I wondered if this might be the moment in the dream when I cried out and woke myself. Then the heavy door came open, and cold air rushed at our faces. He stepped aside and motioned me out into the yard, which was pitch dark and bitterly cold, and for the first time I wondered whether we should go. The road was at that moment both very real and part of the geometry of my dreams: a narrow cylinder of darkness with a single streetlight at the far end, the stars glittering overhead. The near end of the yard was closed off by a shed of some kind, for storage, for drying or curing. I believed we would have to walk down toward that light, then turn in one direction or the other. I could, I thought, read the stars and follow them back to where I left my car. Sampson Lee stood there in the light of the doorway, his gaze trying to fix on something in the darkness. Then he motioned to us, a kind of slashing with his palm turned upward in supplication, which seemed to mean, *go, get away.* When I looked back, Sampson Lee's white, frightened face appeared in the column of darkness made by the open door. He still did not speak or seem to see us, but held up his hand in farewell. For a long time after, I saw that gesture, the five white fingers glowing around the palm. I thought of the way a child draws the sun shedding its rays over a house, a garden, a family of stick figures.

In the light, I looked at my mother and opened my mouth to say something, but she caught my hand, squeezed the fingers tightly, and whispered to me to hush. The door closed quickly, though Sampson Lee tried not to make any noise. I tugged on my mother's hand and we began to walk down the yard toward the streetlight. The stars moved with us in their vault overhead, a thousand tiny, bright eyes gauging our progress. At the streetlight, my mother seemed to understand the meaning of my presence, and the mystery of it. She was wearing the wool jacket I had seen my father wear every day during the winter, and underneath a flannel shirt I also remembered. In the blazing light on an empty road, she looked like the scarecrow of my father, his emissary from another world. I pointed to the left, the northbound road, away from Sampson Lee's house, and we began to walk in that direction.

In half an hour, we were out of town, and full darkness spread out on either side of us, fields of inky night. I thought not the darkness but the quiet was unbearable. The only sound was the scuff, scuff of my feet, and my mother did not make noise—she seemed to move without touching the ground. I knew where I was, and imagined I could hear the cotton in the fields, dormant, the sound of that like little rickety clicks, crickety mutterings. I knew this road was bordered with cotton, though I'd forgotten who owned it. I thought maybe my father had, fifteen years before, something about the way the land began to rise a little ways off, though we'd walked far way from his property. I remembered my father, my last vision of him, his eyes wide open, his gun on his left side with the muzzle over his shoulder. His hat had stayed on his head. There was not a particle of blood on the gun, but his left hand was a clenched red mass, like he was holding on to his heart.

"Where are we going, Nina?" my mother said when she believed we'd passed beyond anyone's hearing.

"To Rocky Mount."

"Walk to Rocky Mount? That's three hours' driving."

"I have a car."

"James's car?"

"No. My car. I bought it today."

"With James's money."

I didn't answer her.

"I see," she said.

She still held tightly to my hand, and I thought how she was really just a girl, like I was. We were keeping each other safe, out alone in the cold. So we walked on, and I felt as though we might fall asleep, but keep walking too, dream our way toward what lay ahead. We spoke, too, out of that dreaming.

"Mother, why did you do it?"

"He had some trouble finding your father, until he heard him shoot twice, and then he found him very easily. Your father had some cause to step aside, to wipe his face with his kerchief. He lay down his gun and Nick picked it up and got to sighting it around, and when your father got back close enough, Nick shot him, and your father threw his hand up to the wound, and said Nick don't do that again. Then he ran off a little ways and fell."

"I asked you why."

"Um hmmmm," my mother breathed out, with feeling, as though she were at a prayer meeting. Alongside the road, the sleeping cotton seemed to groan in its bed.

"Can you forgive me?" she said.

"I don't know."

All this time, my mother and I could not see each other. It was too dark and there was no moon, just our warm hands holding on.

"Nina, can you tell me how much farther? I might like to stop and rest if it's still a ways."

"We'll just keep on this road and we'll see the car."

"This road goes all the way to Raleigh."

"We just got to keep on it then."

"What would you do if I let go your hand and ran off in the dark?"

"I guess you'd find out."

"Tell me."

"I can't tell you unless you do it."

"I won't. I swear. Just tell me."

"I don't believe you."

She let go of my hand then, shook it loose because I had come to have a grip like iron. I slapped at her, fumbled crazy like a blind person hunting for a body, but she broke free and tore off into the field to my left, crashing down into a ditch and then out again, over the stubble and hard ground and kept going, away from what she thought was the road. Stalks broke and crunched with the heartbreaking sound of pottery, brittle and loud in my ears. I waited until I heard her stop to catch her breath.

"You're going to die then," I called to her, not yelling, but plainly, calmly, just so she could hear. "If you don't come with me, you're going to die, and prison may be worse than that." I heard my own voice as if from far away, a kind of weeping oddly removed from myself, for everybody but myself. I could imagine what my mother looked like at that moment, her thin arms in my father's jacket and shirt, the weight of a dead man's clothing hanging off of her as she stood in the middle of a field she couldn't even see the depths of, like our whole lives stretching ahead of us, unknown, dangerous, swallowing up our words. So she came back. She came back for the sound of her grown-up girl-child's voice, because it was what she most longed to hear. That's what I believe. I am convinced that no other sound in the world would have drawn her back to that dark road, not the report of a gun or the cry of a police siren, not Nick Thomason's sweet talk, not even the voice of my father.

"All right, Nina," she said and waded carefully, slowly back to the road, put her hand in mine again, and we walked on into the night.

I try to think how long we were on that road, my mother and I. It seemed like days. Whether we spoke much, of this too, I am not sure. What I dreamed walking along, and what my mother said—does it really matter now if the words actually passed out of her mouth and into the air?

At last we came to the car, where I'd left it, driven half into a pine grove. I thought this white car looked enormous, radiant and safe, and then I wanted to laugh at myself. I told my mother to get in back where I had piled coats and blankets from her house, and crawl under them, and stay there. She did this, and did not make a sound, except once, all the way to Rocky Mount: I turned on the radio, to an all-news program, and a minute later, she asked me to please turn it off. At the train station, I went inside and bought a ticket to the end of the line, Bangor, Maine, then came back out and sat with her for a while. It was just before six o'clock in the morning. Somewhere behind us, the town was coming to life, as if this were a day like any other.

"You can change at New Haven and go on to Montreal."

"Is that what I should do?"

"I packed you a bag. There's some money in it."

"He said he had to figure it out, so he wanted to go live near the base in Jacksonville. All those guys killed and not a scratch on him."

"Why did he do it?" I said this to my mother without looking at her. "Sampson Lee? Why did he hide you?"

"I don't know." She stopped talking then until it was time to go into the train. The sun was coming up, a blinding red line between the horizon and a skein of low clouds. "I think he can't forget what happened to my mother, how he found her."

"It follows you."

"You're a good girl," she said, touching my cheek. "I'm gone." She moved ahead of me then, out the door of the waiting room. The train was a dark point at the far end of the tracks, and I watched it grow larger, stop to take her in, and slip away to the north.

I believe she'll be back. I'm waiting for her. It may take a while, but I'm vigilant. I can still see her, walking away, down the platform to board the train. She's got my father's military pack, gripped tight to her chest, left arm under and the right held out, so it looks as if she's carrying a child. She's thinking of it that way, imagining it, I know. The child may be me, but it may be one of the others; I can't ever be sure: she's a blue dream in the early morning light. But it's a dream with a rattle, a little clank, a sound so peculiar and particular, it's like I'm seeing it too: my father's dogtag hanging off the strap, bouncing off her hip.

Quickening

I didn't call it a pact. That's not a word I'd use, not in a million years. I thought nobody here in Gloucester would have said that, here where we say *whippa* for party, *pissa* for awesome, *wicked* for good, *jimmies* on ice cream, *frappe* if there's milk in it. Drive to the *packie* to buy rum for your *frappe*. No. Pact is too normal, too obvious. I'd have said it was more like a dream. That dream you have of becoming famous, and suddenly a movie star comes crashing into your life, and she takes it all on: your chewed up fingernails, your bad dye job, your lonely Friday nights, your pissed-off mother, your dad, if he was around. You don't even know you're having this dream until later, when, can you believe it, there's Jane freakin' Fonda on CNN, with her perfect hair, her crazy huge blue eyes, her awesome biceps flexed while she clenches her fists and talks about your life, trying to get the emptiness of it. Jane Fonda said nobody offered us anything better. That was about the only part she got wrong.

For starters, Sabrina's brother Noah offered to buy us beer, and naturally we took him up on it, and then he drove us out to the waterfront in Rockport. We leaned up against that red barn the painters call Motif Number One, which looks like a horse at certain times of the year, the way the shadow falls on the ground. So it's like we were along its back, ready to ride away. Noah had just come back from two tours in Iraq, and he was totally messed up. He wanted to sleep with one of us, he didn't care which really, me or Meredith or Jordan or Rose or Toni or Chantrelle. I was pretty sure somebody would cave, but for a while there, we were all just trying to get him through the next thunderstorm. And the beer was fine.

It was January, old snow on the ground and colder than a witch's tit, as Noah liked to say. We were huddled up in the lee of The Motif, keeping still because some fool was actually trying night photography. In the winter. The camera flash was driving Noah to a whole new level of excruciation. Sabrina held him, pretty much in her lap. He's a little skinny guy, smaller now than two years ago when he was first deployed. You wince to look at him and imagine the mean fun the other marines had at his expense. Sabrina started cooing and calling Noah her baby, and that seemed to turn down the volume. We all took a drink. Noah had his liter of Old Grand-Dad, which he usually kept from us because he thought we were too young. But that night he was sharing. I don't much like the taste. It makes you warm though.

"Jill," Noah said to me, "you'll learn to like it." I wondered how he could see my face in the dark. "Don't be such a baby." He laughed and coughed, lit a cigarette. Then he started talking about the guys he knew who had babies, babies they hadn't even held, seen only in pictures. "It did something for them," Noah said. "More than wives or girlfriends. Like they could see the kids' faces clearer than anything else. They could tell you the shape of the little ear, where the teeth were missing or coming in.

They'd always talk about how white their kids' teeth were. This one dude, Bertram, big black mother, said his kid's teeth were a fucking beacon." He took a long swig from the bottle. "It took those guys longer to die."

We thought about that. The camera jockey finally packed up and left us to the shadows. In the dark, The Motif was just a barn, all creaking wood and empty on the inside.

"So." Noah stood up, unsteady. "Somebody give me a baby. Give us all a baby."

"What would Mom say?" Sabrina asked him.

"Tell her it's the patriotic thing to do. It's the new patriotism. Like those yellow ribbons," Noah said and fell back beside her.

We all got up then, walked away from The Motif. It seemed like the end of the evening. I felt a little queasy. I was thinking that very word *queasy,* and about words in general, how much I loved them, loved the strangest ones best, when Rose pointed to the sky and told us it was snowing.

"Check it out," Meredith said. She walked away from the barn's dark side, rolling a handful of snow along the ground, zigging and zagging past us until she had a ball the size of a fish bucket. Then she started over. Rose was the first to understand, and she started on the snowman's head. When she finished helping Meredith, she made her own snowman. We all went to work in the yard and the parking lot, helping out if we finished before someone else did. In twenty minutes, we had seven snowmen riding along the barn's shadow. I thought they should all have easels in front of them, and stick hands holding brushes. In the morning, the winter painters would see them and claim to have some kind of revelation.

"Wait," Noah said. "They're not happy campers." He handed

me his bottle of Old Grand-Dad and told me to drink up. "Get some practice, Jilly."

It took him only a few minutes to make seven little snowbabies and set them gently beside each snowman. "There," he croaked, out of breath. "I bet they last longer now." The snow fell down around us. We could hardly see each other for all the snow melting in our hair and sticking to our eyelashes. I was warm and tired, but I didn't want to go home. I wanted to lie down and pull that snow over me like a blanket.

Jordan was the first to do it, and she got the most ink, because she claimed that the father was this twenty-five-year-old homeless man. But nobody could ever track down such a person. Noah knew all those guys, and he'd look at Jordan whenever she told her story, and just shake his head. I still don't know who it was. Jordan's cute, and she gets along with everybody at school, the geeks, the preps, the emos, the skaters, so it could have been anyone. That's what we all discovered, actually. It could be anyone. Everyone was, as Toni said, up for it. When he heard that, Noah laughed until he cried, really cried, so hard I had to hug him until he fell asleep right there in my arms.

This was Valentine's Day. Jordan wanted to do her pregnancy test on Valentine's Day, and she did, and it turned pink, and we all thought that was so perfect. This makes us, I realize, sound silly and shallow and as stupid as a lot of people think we are. But I'll tell you something, you people: we were already smart enough to hate Valentine's Day, hate it so much we wanted to turn it inside out, take it back from Hallmark and Whitman's Sampler and Florists' Transworld Delivery.

"St. Valentine was a martyr," I said.

"Yeah, and he was also the first conscientious objector," Noah said. "He had a four-part punishment for it, too, imprisoned, beaten, stoned, decapitated."

"But look where it got him," Rose said.

"It got him like freaking everywhere," Meredith said. "Really. He's so *popular*." She made her voice do that mean girl's whine.

"It's not that hard to be popular," Jordan said. "Trust me."

I thought about that, about how popular we had become in the last six weeks, since the whole dream started. I thought about how the air in the hallways changed when I walked into school, how it parted to let me through, how heads turned away from the dark emptiness of lockers, how people really saw me for the first time in my life. I thought about the boys, how they had become human to me, knowable. They talked about their fathers, about college sometimes, what a dream *that* was, about our teachers, about the weather, about snow. There was so much talk in my life, all of a sudden, and it was all interesting. It was all different. They were like snow, I thought one night, suddenly, the boys. They were like snowflakes, no two were the same. My mother always said the opposite, that they were all exactly the same, men and boys. I wondered if I could ever explain it to her, how wrong she was.

Then there was the famous high-five in the school infirmary. That was Toni and Chantrelle, on the Ides of March; I happened to know because our English teacher had told us first thing. He was somebody you paid attention to, this teacher. He was different. He wanted us to call him by his first name, which was Jonas. He kept a bottle of white sand on his desk, a souvenir from a trip out west, when he walked from Carlsbad to Silver City, New Mexico.

On the Ides of March, he was wondering why Shakespeare might have written the date of Julius Caesar's death as the date Romeo married Juliet. Then he started talking about everything that couldn't be known about Shakespeare, that couldn't be known, period. Suddenly he got quiet and stared into the middle of the room. He asked if something was wrong. Toni raised her hand and told him she didn't feel well, then Chantrelle said the same thing. There was a moment when the earth seemed to spin off its axis. I thought, *this is really happening,* but I wasn't sure what I mean by *this*. Jonas asked if they wanted to go see the school nurse. His voice sounded like it was rising up from the bottom of the Gloucester reservoir. He was sitting on his desk, and as he spoke, he reached for the bottle of sand and held on to it.

Toni and Chantrelle rose from their desks, lifted their backpacks. They filed to the front of the room and handed over their copies of *Macbeth*. It was a ceremony, graduation in reverse, and they were more serious than I'd ever seen them, Toni who had some years back perfected the wide-eyed, dumb blonde act, and Chantrelle, who because of her height and huge breasts, and because she was the only black girl in our grade, couldn't complete a sentence without making fun of herself. They looked Jonas in the eye and he looked back. We all waited for the thing he would say to let them go, words that would bring the rest of us back to earth. He said, "Try to finish the play."

I listened for them to whoop and yell in the hallway, but they didn't. The nurse's office was in another building, so we didn't hear about the high-five until later. No one actually witnessed the moment except the nurse and the visiting doctor, which is a shame, because it must have been a beautiful sight—or maybe not. Maybe it was frightening. Maybe our world isn't ready for what it looked like: Chantrelle's huge black hand pressed up against Toni's little pale freckly paw. One of the television news crews tried to get them to stage a reenactment, but they wouldn't.

Later, in Rockport, Toni and Chantrelle sat quietly together, their hips touching. They were sharing a beer. "Just half," Chantrelle told us. "It's a lite beer."

"It settles my stomach," Toni said.

Noah laughed. "People really believe that?"

"It works for me," Jordan said. "And I don't have to worry about getting fat. Now I *am* fat."

"My sister is going to kill me," Toni said, and Chantrelle nodded. "She already thinks she's the only person in the world who's ever gotten pregnant."

"And she graduated from high school and went to college," Chantrelle said, "and she got married, and she was a virgin, right?"

"A *fucking* virgin," Toni said, and we cracked up.

"You'll give her some perspective," Noah said to Toni. "Everybody needs a little perspective."

"You can raise your kids together," Rose said.

"You're going to raise your kid with mine," Chantrelle said. Her voice seemed to shrink, to wither. "I thought that was the deal. That was the whole point."

"I thought it was all about me," Noah said. "It's not about your sister or your kids or raising your kids, or—" here he stopped and looked at Toni and Chantrelle—"whatever else is going on. It was my idea."

"Hey, Noah." Sabrina put her arm around her brother and pulled him close. "Chill, man. It's always all about you. You know that. We know that. We're your harem, right? Right?"

"You'd do anything to keep me from a third tour."

"That's right," I said.

"Little Jilly speaks." Noah gazed at me, his eyes half closed, his head shaking ever so slightly, the beginning of some palsy he shouldn't have for another fifty years. "What does *anything* mean, little wordsmith girl? What's this *anything* you would do? And why would you do it? Why keep me from going back?" He changed his voice, faked a southern drawl. "I got to kill me some more towel-headed terrorists."

"Because we know you don't really believe that," Sabrina said.

"How do you know what I believe?"

"I know," Sabrina said.

"How?" His voice was mean.

"Okay, Noah," Sabrina said. "Maybe I don't know. Maybe I just don't want you to die. How about that for a reason? Is that so hard to understand?" She was crying, and this time Noah held her.

"Ssshhhh," he whispered. "You're right. You're always right."

"So then why do you want to go back?" I asked.

Noah leaned his head against The Motif. He closed his eyes. "Well. Funny you should ask." He turned his face toward me, like a blind person. "Funny *you* should ask, smart girl. What the hell else is there for me? What the fuck else can I do? Fish? Go off in a little boat? Man, I saw that movie. I saw that Markie Mark bobbing there in the dark night on those huge waves, with his boat sunk under him. Nothing in Fallujah was that kind of alone, man. Nothing I saw is that kind of dead."

"It was just a movie," Rose said.

"That's actually what gets me," Noah said, "that it was a movie. Nobody really knows how those guys died, how perfect that storm was. At least over there, it's documented. Sniper fire, chopper down, roadside bomb, suicide bomber. Even if the enemy is invisible, there are witnesses. Buddies. *Semper fi,* man. What have I got here? A bunch of mommies? Over there I've got the four fucking horsemen of the fucking apocalypse."

"Where do you think you're going?" my mother said, night after night, the same question.

"Out," I said. "Far, far away. Crazy. I'm going crazy." She told me I was going to get myself in trouble, and I wanted to say *aroint thee, witch,* but I knew she wouldn't get it, the reference. I don't think she ever read a book, just price stickers and bar codes and the tabloid headlines next to her register.

Rose was the only one of us who had a steady boyfriend, though steady isn't really the right word for him. *Perched,* maybe. He was a private pilot, so he was usually flying off somewhere with a client, but he always seemed to land right back beside Rose. So we thought she'd be the first and the happiest of us to *live my dream,* as Noah sometimes said. And as the months went on, though, Rose's unencumbered state seemed to depress Noah more. He once said she was bad luck, and after that, he took to hanging around Dogtown, the stone-filled wilderness between Gloucester and Rockport. He'd sit on top of the boulders with his Old Grand-Dad, and sometimes we'd find him asleep, though it seemed like he was always careful to put the cap back on the bottle.

One night we woke him up, but he didn't want to go on with us to Rockport. He wanted us to stay with him or at least leave Rose.

"It came to me," he said. "What Rosie needs." Here he paused dramatically and waved Old Grand-Dad in the air, slowly, like a lantern or a broken bell.

"And that would be?" Rose said.

"Witches!" Noah called down from the boulder, then threw back his head so that the word rang off into the Dogtown night. "Witches, I say!"

That was part of the Dogtown history we all knew, Tammy Younger and Peg Wesson casting spells on fishing boats and oxen carts, spells for more and spells for less. The other part was that in 1935 a crazy millionaire named Roger Babson had paid unemployed stonecutters to carve words of wisdom on twenty-four of the biggest boulders. Noah thought the proper spell would fall on Rose if she sat with him on the boulder that said HELP MOTHER. You could see how it made a certain kind of sense.

"So who's going to call down these witches?" Rose said. "You?"

"Who else?" Sabrina said, and we all laughed because of her name. She tweaked her nose back and forth like the TV witch, and of course nothing happened. "See," she said, "it's got to be him."

Noah seemed to lose interest then, or forget. We could tell he'd been there a long time, alone with Old Grand-Dad. "The thing was," he began, "sometimes the world seemed really, really bright, and the air was clear, and the sky was that freaking miraculous blue, like it gets here in June. And I'd think, hot damn, I got away. I got outside time. I got outside the whole world. I'm perfect." He rolled over and looked down at us.

Rose went to the rock and put her face close to Noah's. "He doesn't want to do it," she said quietly, almost to herself. "Gary doesn't want a baby. He said it would tie him down." She laughed then. "He didn't even get it, the joke, tie him down, you know, the pilot. So a spell isn't exactly what I need at the moment."

"What do you need, Rosie?" Noah said. His voice was so gentle. I wished he was talking to me.

"Well. A job, for starters. A mom who's not mad at me all the time. A million dollars."

"You could probably get the job," Sabrina said.

"I want somebody to care about only me," Rose said. "I want to be number one on someone's list. I'm sick of taking the backseat. Gary's mom, my mom's boyfriend, Dad's stepkids. You know what I mean?"

"Amen," Chantrelle said.

"Then," Rose continued, "he says, oh, but you'll lose your childhood. Hello? I'm already eighteen. My childhood's way gone."

And anyway, I thought, what is childhood except stupidity? Children drown because they don't know how to swim. Children get into cars with strangers and disappear because they don't know any better. Children choke on toys because they don't know what's food and what's not. Children are small, and it's easy to make them feel smaller. So why would we want to hang on to childhood? Please, somebody tell us.

"Why do you think Babson had these rocks carved?" Noah asked.

"He wanted something set in stone," Sabrina said.

"He wanted unconditional love," Rose said.

"He wanted to make something that wouldn't cry for him at three in the morning," Jordan said.

He wanted something to last.

On Monday afternoon, Rose found me in the school parking lot. "Anybody asks," she said, "I'm at your house."

"Where are you really?"

"Those guys." She stabbed her finger toward a car facing away from us. I knew whose it was and who would be in it.

"How many, Rose?"

"Three. Maybe four. I'm not sure."

"That's like a gang. That's a crime."

"If we were fifteen years old, it would be a crime. This is called . . . I don't know. Sure-fire. No fail."

"You don't want to do that, Rose. You won't even know who the father is."

"Yeah, well, so what? What's the big deal about knowing? That's how it happens in the animal world. Cows, horses, lions. They don't know who the father is. They don't care."

"This is not the animal world."

"Isn't it?" She placed her hand flat against my chest and pushed, just a little. "You think this isn't the animal world? Go ask Noah."

So I went to ask Noah. He would be at home this time of day, home at his mother's house, before the evening's adventures began to unfold. I could go in without knocking, and when I did, I saw them there in the kitchen, Sabrina and Noah, frozen: Noah at the table with his head in his hands, Sabrina standing with her back to him, in front of an open cabinet, searching for something she would never find. When she spoke, her voice came from another world, or a ripped-open seam between worlds.

"Tell him not to do a third tour," she said.

"Don't go, Noah," I said, automatic.

"He's been on the phone with those guys all day," Sabrina went on. "They keep sweetening the deal. Money. Promotion. I don't know what the fuck else."

The room tilted, maniacal, cubist. I closed my eyes, felt my mouth open, my teeth move apart, in order to speak.

"Noah," I said. "I'll give you something money can't buy." I heard Sabrina make a noise like laughter, but the way it would sound on another planet. Noah looked up from his hands. Then he stood. He came around the table and took my arm, gently, like you would an old woman or a woman in some condition, a woman with a certain condition.

"All right," he said quietly. "Let's go."

We drove to Lanesville, to a friend's house. "They never use it," Noah said. "All the kids are grown. They gave me a key, but I never wanted to come back. We were so happy here it makes me sad now." He unlocked the side door, led me into the kitchen. "But they also left me this." He opened the refrigerator and lifted out a bottle of champagne. "Good stuff. For *eventualities*."

We drank a glass. I'd never had champagne before. I can see why some people never want to drink anything else. The rest of it was quick, quicker, quickening. Quick as in brief, as in out, out, brief candle, as in *adroit*, that crazy word, as in sudden, as in quickening, which I now know is a word, as if the world were turning but I was standing still on top of it. We stayed all night at the house. I called my mom and told her I was sleeping over at Rose's, that we were working on a project.

That thing they say to you: this will change your life forever. Like a dire warning, as if nobody would ever want their life changed. That's why we were doing it, you numbskulls, to change our lives. The forever part is just gravy, icing on the cake.

It was an identity, the newspapers said. It was something we could do, something we might even be good at, we who had failed so totally at everything else: school, sports, getting the hell out of Gloucester. Our last great failing was as daughters. All our mothers told us this when we gave them the news. Your life is over, they said. I'm so ashamed. This is killing me. Your father's gonna kill you. I don't understand you, or, well, you're on your own now, missy, or my personal favorite, how did this happen?

"You hate the people who make you feel afraid," Noah was saying. "You want them to die for the sin of forcing you to kill them." We were lying in bed, at the Lanesville house.

"Why would you want to go back?"

"You keep asking me that."

I thought eventually he would tell me the real reason, and I would know when I heard it. I thought if he gave me this real reason, he'd be free of it, like when you give something away, you don't have it anymore. "We could get married," I said. "I could go to work. You could stay home."

"With the baby."

"I guess."

"What if it cries?"

"You pick it up."

"What if I'm already holding it?"

"You rock it or feed it or change it."

"What if I've already done all that, and it's still crying, and it won't stop?"

"Then you kiss it."

"Kiss it?"

"Yes. A lot. All over its little face." I thought these things with happiness. Read it a story. Give it a bath. Make a fort out of blankets and get inside. Play horsey-ride on your knee. Imagine that you're magic. Let it bang on the pots and pans. Write letters to God. Tell it your dreams.

It was very dark inside the Lanesville house, so dark I could hear and smell everything. I could hear the sound of Noah's lashes brushing together as he opened and shut his eyes. I could smell his skin, which was like peanut butter, except for his scalp, which was like spaghetti. I believed I could hear the *click, click, click* of his brain, rolling certain thoughts over on top of others.

"They sent women and children out in front of the tanks," he said into the darkness. "Women holding babies. The convoys do not stop. The babies are crying so loud you can hear it inside. Inside a Bradley M2. Inside your bones, where the blood should be. And you get right up to them, so you see the babies' wailing little faces, and the women, but it's just their eyes. And they don't move, and the convoy does not stop."

Meredith said it, the word *pact*, after the story got out to the press, and she said it actually, unbelievably, to my mother in the checkout line at Star Market. My mother always liked Meredith, and so she said something to her, maybe, *I thought you had more sense,* and Meredith told her we'd made a pact, and my mother ran out from behind her register and flew home and came screaming into the house like a banshee. I screamed back. Doors banged shut and opened up again to pour out more screaming. What I hated about that hour was not the feeling of it but the words, how pathetic they were, like they came from television or a bad movie, out of the mouths of the world's worst actors. My mother really said, "This isn't how I raised you," and I really said, "You didn't raise me at all." She really said, "You're an ungrateful wretch," and I really said, "I hate you."

After the silence got to be too much for her, my mother turned on the television and spiked up the volume. So we both heard it, Frederika Whitfield's pretend-shocked questions and Jane Fonda's replies. My mother said, "Oh my God," and sank down into the couch. I stood in the doorway to my room and listened to Jane Fonda talk about us, saying we were lonely and bored, our lives *bereft*. The only other sound in the room came from my mother. When Jane said the fishing business in Gloucester had tanked, my mother retorted, in the voice of a tired child, *has not*. It occurred to me that Jane Fonda seemed not to know her lines, that her speech was slow, as if this part was new to her.

"So why are you doing this?" my mother asked when the interview was over.

"Why should you care?"

"Because I'm your mother."

Just like the idiot actor in the bad movie, I went into my bedroom and slammed the door.

Sabrina believed she was doing it for Noah. She was convinced he would never leave a pregnant sister. That it was more of a responsibility than if he had his own child. I thought she was right. She was the one who said "Sweet!" when her test came back positive, less dramatic than the high-five, only half overheard by the nurse, retooled later as gossip. It had become good manners not to ask about the father, so we didn't. And she didn't tell. I thought how Rose was right, this was the animal world, and the fathers lumbered forgotten, off into the distance, the tundra, the savannah, the prairie. I thought how Jordan's invention of the twenty-five-year-old homeless guy was perfect, how that father had disappeared before he even existed. And Toni and Chantrelle, whose feelings for each other had become real, a fact. They told us they wanted to go to California to get married. When Noah pointed out they could get married in Massachusetts, they just looked at us, struck dumb by our lack of imagination. California is the point, they said. To get away. To go to the end of the known world. They told Jonas, the English teacher, and he gave them his bottle of white sand. Dump it out and fill it up again, he said. Try to bring it back.

Which brings us to graduation, the end of the known world, but happening, ironically, on the Gloucester High School football field. We walked across a creaking stage at the fifty-yard line, all in order, at least alphabetically, and took possession of our diplomas. Only Jordan was showing, and really not that much, but she played it large and broad, as Noah said, waddling a little, leaning backward, her left hand open over her kidney. She was two in front of me, so I could see this. And I also saw all the people who would not look us in the eye, the principal in particular, who stared out over our heads as if searching for somebody else, the girls we might have become before we changed our lives forever.

Our families must have applauded and cheered, but we couldn't really see them, way up in the stands. The noise of relieved celebration was endless, seamless: cheers, some boos for exes and enemies, fireworks, popping balloons, all the chatter of people hoping and remembering. Can you believe it? we all said. For months, years even, we couldn't wait for the last day, and here it was, the grinding halt, the messy explosion made by a fast-moving object hitting a brick wall.

Afterward, after the diploma and the toss of mortarboards, the quick change out of those cheap heat-collecting robes, after the family dinner, after the twenty minutes of listening to Grandpa's advice, we were really, finally free. My mother asked where I was going, and I told her, Dogtown, knowing she'd be both enraged and powerless to stop me. Most of the senior class planned to meet there, literally to drink it in, the end of the road. There was going to be a sort of treasure hunt—this was the rumor—to find all the Babson boulders. People had formed unofficial teams, armed with maps and GPSs and coolers. Find a boulder, take a drink. *It's gonna be a whippa,* people said. *A pissa whippa.* The Gloucester police had agreed to look the other way.

As everyone knows, the first boulder on the trail says GET A JOB. So there it was, looming at the trail head, an extension of the principal's handshake. We toasted ourselves, a hundred and fifty strong, maybe half the graduates. A few feet away, at HELP MOTHER, somebody yelled, "God help the mothers." He didn't mean us. He meant our former teachers, our future bosses, army recruiters, local law enforcement, politicians, United States presidents past, present, and future. We all drank. Next was SAVE, then TRUTH, WORK, COURAGE, LOYALTY. We skipped BE ON TIME and STUDY. Jordan wanted to stop and rest. She'd already quit drinking, because she said she felt strange. She sat down and leaned back against a smaller, unmarked rock. "Hey guys," she said, and then something happened in her face. It was like she went off to the beyond. She stretched out full-length, with the beer can resting on her just rounded belly. "Watch," she said, and so we saw it, all of us, Sabrina and Noah, Meredith, Rose, Toni and Chantrelle. I saw it. The beer can rose, ever so slightly, then slid a little to the left.

"That's you breathing," Sabrina said. "Isn't it?"

"No," Jordan said. "I'm holding my breath." She inhaled and puffed out her cheeks. The beer can moved again. "It's in there," she said, her voice full of tears and sweetness, a voice I'd never heard, from anyone, not in my entire life.

"Let me feel," Toni said and dropped down beside Jordan. We

all held our breath, I think. The night was very still, as if we were alone in the woods or somebody had turned off the sound. Then Toni whispered, a long *wow*. Then she said again, over and over, *wow, wow, wow,* like a ghost barking. We all knelt and took a turn. Chantrelle cried. She said she couldn't wait for hers to move too.

Noah was last, and he asked Jordan for permission to touch, like an old man. Jordan was still holding on to the beer can, and it moved again, next to Noah's hand. "My goodness," he said, not in his own voice for a minute, but then he was back. "We'll call you Bud," Noah said. "Little Bud Lite." Then he looked at Jordan's face. "For now, I mean. But think about it. It's a good sign. They've got those Clydesdales, big strong beasts, pull like three times their own weight. You want a kid who can pull his own weight." He patted Jordan's belly. "Hey little Bud." We all drank, except Jordan. She just looked up at us in wonder. I don't think I'd ever seen her so happy.

So we were late arriving at INTEGRITY. And note was taken.

"Here come the Gloucester girls," a guy shouted. "Bringing up the rear."

"Dragging ass," somebody else said.

"Hey!" a girl yelled down from the top of the boulder. She pointed down to the word. "You Gloucester girls know what this is? Do you?"

The crowd got quiet, milling, humming like a hive.

"You girls are giving us a bad name, you know. People say 'Gloucester girls' now, and we're a joke. Gloucester girls will do it with anybody. Gloucester girls got no *sense*."

The humming grew louder. A few voices called for this girl to shut her trap, but there was a turn, a mood rising. You could feel it, a fading of spirits that seemed to go with the weakening light.

Soon we would be in full dark. There was only one boulder left. A guy carried a spotlight, the kind people use to jack deer, and he turned it on us, the Gloucester girls, all present and accounted for. Jordan leaned heavily into me, and I almost fell, thinking how that would satisfy them, the six of us going down like dominoes. I should have let it happen.

"Stupid bitches," someone yelled from out of the darkness beyond the lamp. Voices echoed his, and other voices told them to shut up. We all felt the rush of waiting to see how the fight would start. And so when I heard the great smash of glass against rock, I thought I would be hurt. The lamp swung back toward INTEGRITY, and there was Noah, gripping Old Grand-Dad by the neck, the jagged edges held out toward the crowd of us.

"Get on with you," he said. He swayed a little, and laughed. "The next stop, you assholes, is KINDNESS."

"Crazy vet," a guy shouted up at him.

"That's me," Noah said. "That sure as hell is me." His voice rose, wavered. "You don't know the half of it."

"Oh yeah?" someone said.

"Oh yeah, you . . . you . . . child," Noah yelled back. "You don't know fucking anything." He stopped and looked out over the crowd of us. "So let me tell you. Listen up, troops. No talking. Here I go. The enemy is completely unpredictable. The enemy is invisible. The enemy is everywhere. There are bombs in kids' clothes, bombs in girls' backpacks, bombs in the delivery guy's van, bombs sewn into the carcasses of dead animals. But then sometimes you find out they don't have a bomb. They don't even have a weapon. Sometimes it's an accident, and you find out you just killed the favorite son, you just killed the daughter who's going to college, and the mother falls to the ground and grabs on to your boots and begs you to kill her too. And all day long you're yelling 'die motherfuckers die.'" He looked down at the broken bottle. "What is this?" he said.

This was when I heard her right behind me, as if she'd dropped down from the sky, telling kids to go home, calling them by their names, her voice spellbinding, something about it reminding them how they'd given her money and she'd given them change all these years at the Star Market. She came up beside me and just stood there. The crowd moved backward, into the darkness, to the last boulder maybe, then out of Dogtown Common and on to the rest of the night's madness, the *pissa whippa*. Noah slid all the way down the front of the boulder and lay on the ground. My mother walked over to him, bent down, and said something we couldn't hear.

"No," Noah told her, "that's why I have to go back. I don't know how things work here. Kill or be killed, that's what I know. That's what I'm good at." He sat up and held his arms out to my mother. "I could have killed them," he said. "Every last one. Even the women. I would have done it."

I was good at it. It was something I could do. It was an identity I could have. I knew then he would sign up for a third tour. I felt it the way Jordan felt her baby move, the way I would feel mine a few months later, in August. I knew it, and I went to where my mother stood, and I held on to Noah, and he held on to me, but I could feel he was already gone.

My mother's favorite movie used to be *The Electric Horseman*. We saw it together, when I was a little girl. I remember Jane Fonda's long, skinny legs in those high-heeled boots, stumbling over the rocky terrain of someplace out west, trying to help free that horse. The day Noah left on his third tour, my mother said we should watch it again. "I bet it holds up," she said, "even after all these years. My favorite part is still when Sonny rides that horse out of Las Vegas, how all the little white lights strung all over his costume and the horse—they just go out. And I remember when I first saw it, in a theater, everybody in the audience kind of went, *ahhhhhh,* this big sigh of relief . . ." My mother let her voice trail off and glanced at me, then away. She got up and came to stand behind my chair, put her hands on my shoulders.

Maybe she was right about *bereft,* but this was the part of our lives Jane Fonda never saw, the small, unpredictable tendernesses. She only saw the lights going out, but not what happens after. She never saw the way an animal looks in darkness, when you're dreaming, the way the most familiar shapes in America can come to look like animals cowering in the dark.

For Tanya and Mary Kate

The River

Nearly every morning that summer, in North Carolina, their child told them what she'd dreamed the night before. Terrible, always: monsters and villains threatened, friends betrayed, parents died, disappeared, disowned.

No drowning, though. The mother took careful note of this, relieved. They lived now beside the Neuse River, just at the widest part, where it seemed to spill over the horizon.

"She's not afraid of water," the father said. He didn't add, like you are, or make his old joke, about the river's name.

One morning, very early, the child called from her room to theirs, saying, "Papa, are you alive?" The father told her he was, and the child went back to sleep. His voice woke the mother, and she said to him, "Let's get up." The father looked at her, this woman, his wife. Her eyes were wide open and dark as the night there on the river, away from the glow of town and the buzz of its roads. He wondered if he had ever seen her asleep. Her mother had said that to him before they married, "I don't know if she ever sleeps. From the beginning, when I went into her room, she'd be gazing up at me with those big eyes. Not crying. Just looking."

Though he would have liked to sleep longer, the father got out of bed, and the mother did, and they walked out to the river. They sat close together on the dock and peered into the water, catching flashes of silver, and wondering privately about the prowling life there, the pinch of crab, the odd submission of flounder, lying quietly in the mud, on its one blind side. They wondered about each other, still, after twelve years of marriage.

The child rose from her bed, went to the big window and watched her parents. She waited for them do something, reveal something about their life together, but they sat very still. Occasionally one looked out at the horizon while the other stared into the water. The child wanted to go to them. Every muscle in her body tensed, ready to run to the door, fling it wide, call to them, propel herself into their arms. But she could not move. They were outside in a kind of drama, a play in which she had no part. Her loneliness inside the house was frightening, but she knew she would have to get used to it.

Resolution Trust

The Muzak in the bank kept on going, that's the detail she remembers, and when it finally ran down, the sound was just this gurgle and crack, like water was rising inside the speakers. She doesn't really like to talk about it. Fifteen years ago, when my sister worked for the Resolution Trust Corporation, part of her job was this: she and three or four of her associates would enter a failing savings and loan, late on a Friday afternoon, and shut it down. In this manner, she closed S&Ls all over the state of Florida. It was not pleasant work: often the employees wept or cursed as they were asked for their keys and escorted out. Once, a manager slapped my sister across the face. When she told me this, I lunged forward, my arms out to catch her, but she did not faint or fall, or even cry. She only said that it haunted her, the way that Muzak went on, the broken notes echoing for a long time.

A year later, her marriage broke up on the rocks, as she put it. People who knew her had to take note of the parallels, the slow failure that all the rest of us could see quite clearly, my sister's denial that there was any real trouble, her husband's sudden announcement, late on a Friday afternoon. Curses were exchanged,

I feel sure, though I don't think anyone laid a hand on anyone else. Their infant daughter wailed in the background. He hadn't meant to do this, but when he left, her husband locked my sister out of the house. She was standing in the driveway, staring at the disappearing car, listening to the baby cry. She said later there was a strange moment when she believed the sound was coming from deep inside her hollowed-out self, a long interior wail from the empty corridors of her body. Only she could hear it. Then she realized who was howling, and she rushed back up the steps and flung her body hard against a door that wouldn't open.

She and the baby lived with me for a while, as she and I had before her marriage, but the arrangement didn't work this time. I liked my life and my home a certain way, and the habits and needs of a baby didn't fit. I'm not proud of this—my lack of flexibility, my hard heart. I think now we were two sad, lonely people, my sister and I, and the doubling of our griefs threatened to blow the windows out. I told her I thought maybe I wanted to live on a boat, and she could take the house. But I knew she couldn't make the payments by herself. She and the baby drifted north, state by state, Georgia, the Carolinas, finally Virginia, to be closer to the baby's father, who was dying and then died of cancer. We kept in touch by phone, on birthdays and Christmas. The baby grew into a girl, Elle, like the pronoun in French, and she became more real to me at a distance—in her elementary school pictures, and through the gifts I picked out for her a few times a year. In the thank you notes she wrote to me, Elle always included a story about the gift, about school, some funny thing her mother did or said. Three little stories in every letter, followed by the hope she would see me soon.

I went to work in real estate, selling houses on Marco Island, a boaters' paradise in south Florida. I did well. I lived on my boat, and for some reason this caused potential home buyers to seek me out. It was easy work. You could buy property for a song then, and everyone was singing, at the top of their lungs. It was a dazzling time, but I had a trick to keep myself sane: I'd go into these huge island mansions with my clients, and while they admired the swimming pool, the maid's quarters, the guest bungalow, the deep water dock, I'd think about how much work it would be to clean such a place. So I never wanted any of it for myself. My head was never turned. My forty-two-foot sailboat was paid for; the slip it rested in was paid for. I had secure investments, most of which my sister took care of.

I didn't need much. I took a three-week vacation once a year, usually out of the country, and meticulously planned. As part of this preparation, I thought in detail about what I would send Elle from Buenos Aires or Paris or Copenhagen. This was my little game: I would imagine some trinket, an Eiffel Tower lava lamp, a Little Mermaid radio, a Día de los Muertos comb and brush set, and then find, of course, that such a thing did not exist. And my failure would become part of a letter to Elle: "I tried to find [insert ridiculous object], but nobody had one." I'd send the settled-for gift, often a music box or a clock, from abroad so Elle could have the stamps for her collection, and I would imagine her and my sister laughing over my bumbling yet clever attempt. As soon as I was back home, I'd call to find out how my gift had been received, which was always happily. "You should come see how it works," Elle laughed into the phone. They invited me several times a year, but I never could go.

For my last trip, I decided on Patagonia, Tierra del Fuego. I promised Elle a picture from the bottom of the world, and that was in fact what I sent to her, a poster of Bahm Yendegaia, on the Chilean Pacific coast. I changed somehow in that place—I was still trying to describe it to myself at the end of the three weeks—I felt a terrific emptiness, that sound of rushing wind. Partly it was the elevation and all the hiking, but I was hollowed out; only my bones and skin were truly alive; I had no spiritual content. These were the phrases I worked out in my head. None of them, though, went to the heart of the sensation, which I resolved someday to understand. All I could say was that my body had become part of the place, the wind off the Pacific mingled with the breaths I drew: the trout in the *arroyo pescado* swam in my veins. Walking near Cape Horn, I was a ruin, broken columns and arches. The world swirled and whistled through me, and in my addled, breathless state, I imagined this was the nature of heaven.

I mailed the poster near the start of my trip, out of Ushuaia, the last city before Antarctica. I called Elle from the airport in Santiago, three weeks later, just before I boarded the first of my flights back to the U.S. I wanted to talk to her, and to my sister, before I lost this sense of expanse and abandon. As I hoped, my gift had arrived.

"It *is* the bottom of the world!" Elle shouted.

"The camera angle is really good," I said.

"It's scary. It's like you could fall off."

"I know. It felt that way too."

"I tried to hang it in my room," Elle said, "but it didn't work, so we—"

"Why didn't it work?"

"There wasn't any place . . . there wasn't any angle that . . . I mean if I looked at it from my bed, I'd never be able to sleep."

"Isn't it dark when you sleep?"

"Well, yes, but I knew it was there, even in the dark. I could sort of feel it. And over my desk, I just kept staring up at it. And on the other wall it's reflected in the mirror."

The telephone connection was scratchy and broken by delays. "So where is it?" I asked this question with some trepidation.

"Mom wanted it. For the door leading down into the basement. On the inside. You don't see it when you're going down the stairs, but it's right there when you're coming back up."

"That's pretty smart of your mom."

"I have my moments," my sister said, her voice whispering, crackling. "You'd be surprised."

"You should come see it," Elle said.

"I should," I said. "You wouldn't even know I was there. I'd spend all my time walking up and down the basement stairs." I thought my sister might laugh at that, but she was silent.

Two months later, when Elle turned sixteen, I bought her a car, actually a Jeep—perfect for her, I thought, quirky but safe—and drove it up to New Bern, North Carolina, where she and her mother now lived. Their house was in a small development south of town, a stunningly terrible place, the same one-story ranch repeated endlessly, like a funhouse mirror or the set in a science fiction movie, after the aliens have landed. The one redeeming feature was a sad little pond, surrounded by the only trees the developer had not cut down. I stopped there, a block away from my sister's house, to take stock, draw a breath. I'd driven straight through from Marco Island, twelve hours to Atlanta, where I slept briefly in a parking lot, then nine hours farther. I drank drive-thru coffee but didn't eat. I thought if I stopped for very long, I would not be able to complete this journey, this return to my sister and her child. I knew that's what it was, a return, which would undoubtedly culminate in a prodigal moment. Even though I had not yet sold my boat or its slip, I knew I would never go back.

Now I was giving myself one last chance to turn around. Though my sister and Elle expected me—I had called them as I left Florida to say I was coming, but not why—I thought they would not be surprised if I changed my mind. A woman in a white minivan pulled in behind me, but not too close, in order to enjoy the same little view. It was warm for November, so she rolled down the windows, then turned off the motor. She moved the driver's seat back, and then a large child, a girl, appeared and lay crossways on the woman's lap. The woman held this child—who was clearly too old and too big to be held any way in which gravity might be at work—in the crook of her arm, as one would cradle an infant. The woman kissed the child's forehead and nuzzled her face against the child's cheek. I found the sight dizzying. The emptiness of my own body took on the weight of a boulder. I could barely move to turn the key in Elle's new Jeep, shift the gears, twist the steering wheel to the left and pull away.

At my sister's house, they were waiting, in two rocking chairs. They rushed off the porch and clung to me, and I bore it for as long as I could. At first glance, my sister seemed mostly unchanged, her dark hair longer, below her shoulders, and shot with gray, her face unmade-up and winter pale. She appeared to be frightened, then surprised, by the Jeep. Elle swam into view, rangy and sweet-faced, and I had a moment of utter confusion before I realized she looked almost exactly like her mother.

"You're really, really here!" Elle cried.

She was, in fact, crying a little, I could see. My sister wept too, though she did not say anything for a while, until she managed to reach out, pat the Jeep and say, "Not what I would have pictured."

"It's for Elle," I said, turning to my niece. "Happy birthday."

"No," my sister said immediately. "You can't do that."

"Why not?" I asked.

"But," Elle sputtered. "Yeah. Why not, Mom?" She stepped away as she spoke, as if to touch me might cause the moment to disappear, to collapse.

"Well," my sister said, "the money?"

"It's all right, Jen," I said. "Really. I want to."

"I can't let you," my sister said.

We stood in a kind of suspended animation. I felt that years flashed by, both backward and forward, like strobe lights all around us, as in a time-travel machine. I had to say something to stop it.

"But I drove it all this way. Twenty-one hours straight. I didn't even stop to eat."

"Really?" My sister and Elle said this in unison, and their voices seemed to make a kind of shattering, and we were all back in place, back to our present selves. Elle flung her arms around my neck. "Thank you," she said, over and over, but not my name. I suppose she didn't know what to call me after all this time.

"And will you stay for a while?" my sister asked.

"I don't have any means of escape now, do I?"

We unloaded my two bags from the back of the Jeep, and they led me inside. The house was small but not crowded, though the main room was dominated by a grand piano. I had not heard that anyone played piano, and I said so, after which comment Elle cleared her throat in a somewhat dramatic fashion. I was shown to a guest room containing a double bed, a chair, and a chest of drawers. "Not fancy," my sister said, "but we hardly ever have guests." She pointed to a door. "You have your own bathroom. Maybe you want to sleep a little?"

"Not yet! Please!" Elle said and grabbed at my arm. "You just got here. There's so much . . ." I was interested to hear how she might finish that sentence, but she didn't continue, and the words hung there, swaying a little back and forth, like the hypnotizing pocket watch. I was indeed becoming very sleepy.

"You must be starved," my sister said.

"I'm all right for now," I told her, and turned to Elle, "but I bet you want to go for a test-drive. " I looked back at my sister: "You probably have to go along." Each of them gave me the same glum nod, and I laughed. "Good." I handed over the keys. "So I'll wash up and find myself a snack." Both Elle and my sister embraced me again. They went out of the bedroom and closed the door. I stood very still and listened. I heard them in their rooms, gathering purses, sweaters. Their readying seemed to take a long time. Then I heard laughter, and after that a silence I knew was raised eyebrows, fingers to pursed lips, an initial appraisal of me. The front door clicked shut, the Jeep growled to life, and they were gone.

I opened the bedroom door and stepped out into the hallway, feeling a bit like a thief. My heart beat wildly, ecstatically. I moved slowly into the kitchen—though my sister and Elle were gone, there was nevertheless an electric, mesmerizing presence in the house, a scent like women's perfume but softer: lavender, lilac. My sister once wore lilac oil, the memory came rushing back at me: I was picking out a vial of this oil at Christmas, in the mall, the store was The Body Shop. This was a thousand years ago, before my sister was married.

The kitchen was orderly, very clean. Coffeemaker, the kind that grinds the beans, microwave, toaster oven, gas stove, dishwasher. The front of the refrigerator was covered with magnets holding up notices from Elle's school, from various doctors, a dentist, but even these had been arranged with some care. The rectangular words of magnetic poetry seemed regimented, too, and though there were no actual poems, I intuited the ruin of some, words in proximity which might have made something lovely or clever or bawdy had they been closer together.

Inside the refrigerator was less order. I saw right away that my sister and Elle had an inclination toward, a taste for, hors d'oeuvres: sliced salami, olives, cheeses wrapped up on plates, two bottles of cornichons, packaged sushi rolls, a container of hummus. Yogurt, wine, milk, pomegranate juice, eggs, three varieties of cream cheese. All these items I could see clearly, but as I gazed on them, they seemed to lose meaning. I wasn't sure what I'd wanted—or wanted these things to tell me. So I did not open the freezer or the cabinets. For a minute or so, I stood looking at a framed poster depicting a French café, mostly noting the way my face was reflected in the glass. This only increased my sense of an observing presence, behind me, out of view.

In the living room, there were the inevitable collections, CDs and photographs. I saw that my sister's musical taste had not changed much since our somewhat misspent youth. The names took me back: Electric Light Orchestra, The Who, Billy Joel before he could fill a stadium, Blue Oyster Cult, Jethro Tull. I wondered if Elle liked this music too. Above these shelves, someone had made three poster-sized collages of photographs. I was surprised to appear in many of these pictures, holding the baby Elle or walking with her, on my boat, helping her with the tiller. I had not recalled so much photography during those years. We seemed, Elle and I, to make a contented duo, and again, I had not remembered this at all, only the noise and confusion of a baby in my house, and her silent, disappointed mother. There was no trace of this in the pictures. Even I looked happy.

But soon enough, my image was replaced by those of people I did not know, adults, other infants and small children, held by Elle or by my sister. Other seasons and settings: Washington, DC, of course one can recognize, and New York City. They had been to St. Louis, or Elle had—for here she was in the lean shadow of the famous Arch. Various oceans, or maybe the same ocean, and Elle in all manner of swimsuits—plump, thin, thinner, and her present self. The effect of all these photographs was very like what I had felt traveling in countries where English was not spoken: the speech I was hearing would be largely unrecognizable, except for a few words sprung up like floating spars, like lifeboats. In this sea of unknown persons, my sister and Elle were like *por favor* and *bitte* and *arrivederci* and *de rien*. And so, looking at these pictures was like listening to conversation in a foreign city; and the effort, the attention required, was exhausting.

I decided I would explore the rest of the house later—and really, poking into my sister's and Elle's bedrooms was not something I wanted to do—so I went back into the guest room and lay down. I was immediately overtaken by a leaden sleep, from which I awoke some hours later in total darkness, with the memory of a strange dream: Elle and I were walking, hand in hand, down a long, empty corridor. She was younger than her present self, perhaps nine or ten. After a while, I noticed we were passing unmarked doors, and when we paused, we could hear, quite clearly my sister explaining something; though we could not make out the exact words, her tone was patient, sympathetic, but also somewhat stern. When my sister's voice stopped, there was a sound of hands clapping once. After this, Elle and I moved to the next door, and these same sounds were repeated.

When I came out of this sleep, I felt I had to rise, as out of a black lake or perhaps some thicker, more sinister ooze. My room was, as I have said, dark, but I could see a thin band of light at the bottom of the door. I heard voices murmuring. My glowing wristwatch read 8:32. I felt my body return, limb by limb, and I realized I was very hungry. I went into the bathroom to wash my face, and for a hairsbreadth of a second, I did not recognize the person looking back at me from the mirror.

They were in the kitchen, seated at the table, my sister, Elle, and a man I did not know. In the middle of the table was a large—and, I felt, extraordinarily beautiful—lasagna, as well as a glass bowl of lettuces and tomatoes. My sister and this man were sharing a bottle of red wine and talking animatedly. Elle was taking in forkfuls of lasagna as if this might be her last meal. There was a place set beside her with a wine glass, for me, I assumed.

"Here you are," my sister said, and she introduced me to the stranger, called Kyle, who stood and shook my hand. He had a firm, assured grip, I noticed, and held on a second or two longer than was perhaps necessary. Elle looked up at us intently, her lips pressed together as if she were in pain. It was evident to me she did not like this Kyle. She brightened a bit when I inquired about the Jeep. Then, after she asked her mother if she could drive it to school, and Kyle said no, I got the lay of the land. And I decided to walk across.

"That's why I bought it for her, though," I said, "so she could have her own . . ." Here, I couldn't think of a word. "How far is it to school?"

"Four miles," Elle said. "Mom takes me."

"Well," I said, "she certainly can't get into any trouble on the way."

Kyle frowned but said nothing. My sister seemed oddly relieved.

"Great!" Elle said and rose quickly from the table. "Lots of homework." She stepped behind my chair, leaned down, and circled her long arms over my shoulders. She gently placed her face against mine, so that our ears touched. She stayed that way for a moment, as if to let me listen to something inside her head. I held my breath. Then she straightened up and walked out of the kitchen. I heard the door to her room close.

Kyle, it turned out, was a newly retired investment banker. He had come to New Bern for the sailing, he said, and because his son was up in Chapel Hill, but he and my sister exchanged a look that suggested otherwise, that in fact he had retired to New Bern for her. I didn't press them on this point, however; I believed that someone would fill me in later. I suspected and indeed hoped it would be Elle.

So we talked about boats while I ate a great slab of lasagna and we finished the wine and my sister brought forth a delicious apple cake. She stood at the stove to make a caramel sauce for it, and when this was done, she called Elle, who returned to the table for dessert. Kyle asked who was looking out for my boat, reminding me that hurricane season wasn't over for another two weeks.

"The broker," I said.

"Is it for sale?" Kyle wanted to know. I admitted it was.

"So you're going to move back on land." My sister said this with complete conviction.

"Maybe," I said. "Probably."

Elle looked up from her plate of apple cake. She gazed at me thoughtfully, dreamily, then across the table at her mother and Kyle, and finally over their heads, into the air. A kind of radiance came into her face, I thought, as she said, "So how long can you stay with us?"

I shrugged. "As long as you'll have me, I guess." I patted her arm, which lay next to mine. "I guess I could stay forever."

After Kyle left and Elle went to bed, my sister and I cleaned the kitchen, then she opened another bottle of wine, and we went out to sit on her front porch. "One more glass," she said, because she had to get up early. But then she corrected herself: not so early, since she didn't have to drive Elle to school. She thanked me again for the Jeep, saying it was beyond Elle's wildest dreams. We both remarked a moment later how that wasn't true, the Jeep wasn't beyond, and anyway, wasn't it inaccurate, that whole idea of something beyond one's wildest dreams; didn't it diminish the very idea of *dream*?

"So this Kyle," I said. "Elle doesn't care for him, it appears."

"No," my sister said, "she doesn't, but she's just afraid." I waited for her to finish, but she didn't.

"Of what?"

"Well," my sister began slowly, "he shouldn't have told her. I asked him not to, but he did." She paused and sighed heavily. I thought she might cry. "Remember when I worked for the RTC? And we closed those savings and loans? And that one bank manager in Naples slapped me? That was Kyle."

I couldn't speak. I wished suddenly I'd known this, so I could have hit him at dinner. A quick backhand with the spatula we used to serve the lasagna. Or the salad tongs. The violence of my thinking surprised me.

"He said he'd felt terrible about it all these years, so bad it ruined his marriage. He finally just had to find me and apologize. And he did." She smiled, I thought, though it was really too dark to see her face. "It was a very nice apology. You wouldn't believe all the flowers."

"I didn't see any."

"It was a while ago. Flowers can't last forever. He'd go broke."

"Couldn't he just apologize and go back to wherever?"

"I didn't want him to."

"Ah." I breathed, but I took note of the past tense.

She poured more wine. "After a while you get tired of being alone. You know what I mean?"

"I do."

"Which is maybe why you're here, preparing to stay forever?"

"I'm afraid, Jen."

"Of what?"

"Drowning."

She tried to laugh. She wanted me to be joking. "You live on a boat."

"That doesn't help."

"So it's a metaphor?"

"I think so," I said. "I know it's a lot to ask.

"I think you'll find us easier to live with than the last time we tried it."

"Jen," I said, "I'm so sorry about that. I just—"

"No," she said. "I know how it was. I know." She laughed a

little. "I wonder what it is about me that causes people to come to my house something like sixteen years after the fact and say they're sorry." She reached out and touched my hand. "So I should expect to see Elle back after she's turned thirty."

"What's she got to apologize for?"

"Not much, really. Maybe a little of the usual teenage stuff. She's a pretty good kid. Nice friends. The theater geeks, more geek than theater. They're here all the time, so you'll meet them." With that, she stood and stretched, and I did too. She hugged me and said she was glad I was back. I thought about that, as I was falling asleep in her house, my sister's use of the word *back* to designate a place I'd never been before.

The next day was Friday, and after school, Elle gave me a tour of New Bern. There wasn't much to see, not really: the two downtown streets prettified for tourists, the eighteenth-century manor house, called a *palace,* and grounds these tourists came to see, the waterfront and its sunny promenade, where we walked for half an hour or so. Several of her friends were making a video nearby at Union Point, inside the bandstand, and we stopped to watch. It was some sort of drama, but I couldn't get a handle on the plot, all glowering visages and complicated betrayals. Elle laughed a lot, which was nice to see. We sat on a bench just outside the bandstand, and she inched closer to me and linked her arm in mine. When the shooting ended, she introduced me to the players and suggested they come back with us to her house. They seemed to like the idea until one of the boys, the tallest, with a strikingly intelligent face, asked if Kyle would be there. Elle said she doubted it, that it was too early, that he usually showed up just in time for food.

"So about Kyle," I said when we were back in the Jeep heading toward my sister's house. "You don't like him, that's pretty clear. Your friends don't like him. How come your mom likes him?"

"I wish I knew," Elle said. She took in a breath, intending, I think, to say more, but then she changed her mind.

"*Why* don't you like him?"

Her eyes stayed fiercely on the road. "Well, you heard the thing last night about driving to school. He's always like that. Like he's my father, like Mom can't handle me or something."

"She seems to do okay with you."

"She does fine." Elle turned to look at me. "Do you know, in Florida, when she worked for the RTC, he was—"

"I know. She told me last night."

"Don't you think that's strange?"

It was all strange. "Which part?"

"That he would come looking for a woman he hit fifteen years ago? He just showed up with a billion flowers. She didn't let him in. They talked on the porch for a long time. I was ready to call 911."

"Is he at your house a lot?"

We made a left into the driveway. Elle stopped the Jeep and turned in her seat to face me.

"You're asking me if he sleeps over," she said calmly. "He did. But I told Mom I didn't want him there in the morning, when I'm walking around in my pajamas. And she said okay. But I'll tell you something. The reason I'm not freaking out about this is that I think he's going to be history pretty soon."

I can hardly express how deeply settled and happy this made me feel.

Her friends drove up behind us, in a silver minivan and a small red car. There were more of them now than had been at Union Point, eight altogether. Inside my sister's house, I was introduced again, and then I wondered what I should do with myself, go for a walk, take a nap. The group of them filed through the kitchen and out to the small back porch, where they milled about, not saying much, undecided about something. They looked at Elle, who linked her arm through mine and told them, "It's cool."

I still find the scent of marijuana delicious, transporting. If I close my eyes, Jen and I are teenagers again, in the woods behind our house, in a car parked behind a movie theater. We're watching a movie we can't quite understand, *Tommy* or *Close Encounters of the Third Kind*. We're talking and looking up through a canopy of pine trees, or sharing french fries. We're standing at the edge of the lake near our house, and my sister is afraid if she goes deeper, she'll drown, but I'm talking her in. We're at a concert. After a while I was saying all this to Elle's friends, and they were listening. They laughed when I told them about the time we were at a Yes concert, and I thought if Rick Wakeman played a particular chord on the organ, the world would blast to pieces.

The tall boy I noticed at Union Point suddenly seemed to wake up. He snapped his fingers and pointed at me. "So you're the one," he said. "You're the one who sends the wacky presents." I allowed that I was. "That's some great stuff."

"What did you like best?" I said to Elle, noting that my voice sounded gentle and far away. I thought I should try to talk like this all the time.

"You haven't had a viewing yet," Elle said and pulled me to my feet. We all trooped back into the house, down the hall to Elle's room. She pushed open the door, and at first all I could see was the late afternoon light outside, glittering along the tops of the trees. My eyes adjusted as she led me to the wall opposite her bed, where shelves were crowded with knick-knacks. When my mind caught up, I saw that this wasn't at all a jumble, but an orderly display, complete with hand-lettered cards bearing the names of the places I had traveled to, and the dates of each trip, and the stamps used for mailing. Behind each card was the gift I had sent. I was struck by how many of these were miniature architectural works that had some function, many of them clocks: the Parthenon, the Taj Mahal, the Little Mermaid, the Arc de Triomphe, Big Ben, which of course really is a clock. There were also the usual souvenirs, wishing dolls from Guatemala, a Day of the Dead skeleton from Mexico, still wrapped in cellophane.

"Remember this?" Elle said. "It's made of sugar."

"You wouldn't want to eat that," I said.

"No," she agreed, moving me down to the next display. "For a while, you sent rocks. The rocks years, we called them. A piece of the Berlin Wall, the Acropolis, which you must have stolen, the Coliseum in Rome. This is a piece of the abbey in Salzburg where *The Sound of Music* was filmed."

I noticed that most of Elle's friends had drifted away, into the den. Only the tall boy was still with us.

"Some of this is pretty cool," he said. "But a lot of it is really bizarre."

"I know," I said to Elle. "I always tried to imagine what you might like. But mostly I had no idea."

"How could you know if you never met her?" the tall boy asked, and Elle shushed him. "No, I'm good, I'm good," he said, turning to leave the room. "And then you show up with a Jeep. That's *interesting*."

The doorbell rang. Elle and I looked at each other as I knew Jen and I had all those years ago. Caught. Busted, as the kids would say. Then it occurred to me my sister wouldn't ring the doorbell at her own house. The moment deflated. "Kyle," Elle groaned, and went to let him in.

I turned back to the array of gifts I'd sent my niece, but I was thinking, too, of Kyle, and how this would be my chance to settle the score with him. The scene played out in my head: I would walk out into the hallway, right up to Kyle and say, this is for my sister. I could almost hear the sound of my hand on his cheek, like a box closing. Then I'd walk into the den and sit down with Elle's friends. I knew Jen wouldn't want me to do it, but still she would be glad, even if not right away.

Elle was at the door, talking to someone who wasn't Kyle, a young man, but older than Elle's friends, I thought. "He gave me this address," the young man said. Elle was silent. I moved closer. "Actually, I don't know where he lives." He was dressed in black jeans and a leather jacket. This and his dark hair brought out the pallor of his skin and made his blue eyes seem electric, unreal. I noticed he was holding a motorcycle helmet.

"I don't have his number," Elle said. "I could call my mom. They usually go out to dinner on Fridays. Come on in." Elle turned and saw me. She smiled. "This is Richard."

Richard held out his free hand, but his eyes moved to something over my shoulder and grew wide. Our hands were just clasped as he said, "Hey, that's my piano. What's it doing here?" The sound he made after the words was very nearly terrifying, a long, enraged wail.

"Your dad gave it to my mom," Elle said quietly, but Richard was already across the room, reaching to pull out the bench, sitting down. He began to play, a series of chords, arpeggios, glissandos, sounding oddly tuneless to my ear. Then he called out, to no one because he knew no one in my sister's house, "He ruined it. It's way out of tune. It sounds like junk." Still the notes came at us, big open rolling chords, pounded out on the wrecked instrument. Richard stood up suddenly and walked to the right side of the piano and raised the lid. As he turned back toward the bench, he saw the group we made, me, Elle, her eight friends. He stopped and gazed at us and seemed to compose himself. A certain pain left his face, or perhaps deepened, I thought a moment later, into something more familiar. "Requests?" he said, laughing a little, sadly, but he sat down before anyone had spoken. "Dedications?" he called over his shoulder.

"'Stairway to Heaven,'" the tall boy suggested, and his friends groaned, but seconds later, the famous opening notes seemed to roll out of Richard's fingers. I thought for a few moments that he was playing a minuet, or some other carefully choreographed dance. "It's everyone's first slow dance, right?" Elle was saying as if she'd read my mind, and then she and another boy stood up and began an authentically tortured parody, the hesitant hug, arms around each other's necks, staring off across the room, confused and out of breath. "I'm having an out-of-body experience," the boy whispered. Still, they held on for the full seven and a half minutes, until Richard said, "Here's the guitar solo," and the notes sounded like some live glittering thing, the sun off a glacier or a cold body of water. People think of "Stairway to Heaven" like a long joke, an endless, unfunny story, but it was impossible to stop listening, so accurate was Richard's rendition. On the piano, this song was like all those gifts I'd wanted to send to Elle, a transformation that completely reinvents the original, gives back its history. I thought then, of course Copenhagen's Little Mermaid should be a radio, blasting forth music that was both lovely and not.

And so, standing there, I thought of my last gift, the picture from the bottom of the world. As Richard continued to play—"Time for Cole Porter," he announced—I made my way into the kitchen and found the basement door, which I pulled open. There it was, held up by four red thumbtacks, the poster of Bahm Yendegaia. And I felt it all over again, with "Begin the Beguine" played angrily in the next room, I was emptied out, lost inside my body, but also a kind of ascension—that was finally the right word—I was risen above, released, come back from some kind of tomb. I remembered then what Elle had said about walking up the basement stairs toward the poster, and so I flipped on the light, took a step down and closed the door behind me. I descended slowly to the bottom step—I could see the washer and dryer, the chest freezer, the life jacket, the kayaks. I thought about the folly of basements in coastal North Carolina, a flood plain, then I turned and looked up toward the poster. I felt at first—how else to say this?—drowned. So real was this sensation that I raised my hands in order, I suppose, to fend off some vast, cold wave of sea water. I moved slowly forward, up the stairs, toward land, as it were. I felt acutely the force of gravity dragging me backward, down, under, but I kept going, to the lights of Ushuaia, the warmth and the noise of civilization. When I reached the top step and stood face to face with the Beagle Channel, the perils of Cape Horn behind me and out of sight, I turned and descended again to the bottom step, so I could do it again, fill myself up.

As I was making a third ascension, I heard voices, raised, angry. I guessed from what I could understand that my sister and

Kyle had arrived, that neither father nor son was glad to see the other. Soon there were many voices, loud but indecipherable. Finally, my sister's rose above them all, calling, "Stop it!" and then my name, twice, a question. I took the last four steps all at once, crashing into the poster and discovering to my horror and amazement that the basement door had locked itself behind me. For a moment I was so shocked as to be frozen, my cheek pressed hard against the spine of the Andes, but then I came back to myself and rapped loudly on the door, shouting for my sister and for Elle.

My niece came to the door and opened it, her face ashen, her eyes wide. The shouting between Kyle and his son had resumed, Richard nearly howling that his father had no right to give away his piano. In the front hallway, Kyle stood like the smug banker he had once been, legs apart, arms crossed over his chest, trying to drown out his son's voice with "I can" and "I did." Elle's friends clung together, farther away, near the front door, afraid, reduced to the children they really were, had been all along. My sister, however, who is not very tall or large, appeared to have grown, to have raised herself somehow, to have become radiant. She moved closer to Kyle, slowly angling her body between his and his son's.

"He's right," she said quietly, then again.

"What?" Kyle glanced at her, as if she were something he did not care to consume.

"I said, he's right. You can't give away his piano like that. You didn't tell me it was his."

"It's not his," Kyle said.

"It's Mother's," Richard said. "She gave it to me, and you know it. It was hers to give."

"It was hers to give," my sister repeated.

"You don't know anything about it, Jennifer," Kyle said.

"I know what I see. I heard him playing when we came in. *You don't play.* Just look at his face. Of course it's his piano."

"Stay out of it," Kyle said.

"Look," my sister said. "This is my house. You gave me the piano. So I give it to him." She turned. "Richard. It's your piano."

Kyle did something unwise then. He leaned in very close to my sister, and said, slowly, through gritted teeth, *"Stay out of it."*

I knew then I wouldn't have to do it. I knew as it was happening that my sister would cast her arm back and then bring her right hand forward to slap Kyle so hard he staggered. Spittle flew out of his open mouth. In the next moment, my sister looked at me, and I looked at Elle's tall friend who opened the front door, as if we had rehearsed all this. My sister caught Kyle as he stumbled and pushed him the three feet over the threshold and out onto the front porch. "Lock it," she said, and Elle's tall friend did as she asked. And there Kyle stayed, locked, for at least the second time in his life, out of a place he thought he might have managed.

I did not know what would happen next, but I was safe inside with all those children, my sister was smiling at me, and Elle was gripping my hand. If I closed my eyes, I could see us, my sister and me, all those years ago, chest-deep in the lake near our house, water swirling around us, seeping into our clothes. She is holding her breath. Her arms are around my neck, and I'm holding her up.

Body and Engine

Well, now I probably won't get into Harvard because you're going to put this in your notes, aren't you? *Applicant wrecked her car in my driveway.* I'm really sorry about the mailbox. And also about the tow truck tracks in your yard. I don't know what happened. The car just stopped. First the radio fell silent in the middle of "Heard It through the Grapevine," and the door locks clicked up and down, maybe twenty times, as if the vehicle were possessed. This was just as I found your house. Then the tow truck driver—his card says Lucius Wright—he just happened to be going by, or so he said. I wonder if those guys go out scouting for business, trolling the neighborhoods, looking for trouble. So anyway, Lucius Wright will tow the car to Diversified Body and Engine, and I'll find my way there after we're done.

I was. Yes. I was talking to him in sign language. After a minute or two I realized there was a problem with Lucius Wright. I was asking him where exactly Diversified is, and he said, "After lunch," and then he said, "Let me get you one." So I knew. It's in my application, about the signing. You must not have read my application yet. I've heard of interviewers who do that, read the applications later, after the candidate's gone, so they won't know what's coming, so they can wing it. Makes sense to me. Story of my life, winging it. Anyway, it's in the essay. Second paragraph. My interest in sign language, what I do exactly. The occasional public meetings, political rallies; mostly, though, literary stuff, usually poetry. I'm that person at readings, downstage right, below the poet, no jewelry, no fancy fingernails, a woman you hardly notice unless you need her.

That's actually the question everyone asks: why would a deaf person go to a poetry reading anyway? There's only one possible reason. To see. To see the poet. But I think there's more. Otherwise you could just look at the book jacket photo, right? But you want—how can I put this?—you want to make sure the guy's alive. Just checking, you tell yourself. Because next time, well, there may not be a next time. You wait and wait to go see somebody. You're too busy, or it's never the right place at the right time. And then the next thing you know, it's too late.

That's true: sometimes you do just want to see what such a person looks like. But of course, nobody's ever what anyone expects. For instance, am I what you expected? You're hesitating, so maybe don't answer that. You're certainly not what I expected. I expected you to be younger. I expected a suit and a tie— Harvard alum, lawyer garb. So—a poet? Who really looks like a poet? What's a poet supposed to look like? At a poetry reading, *I'm* the only one who looks like what you'd expect: a woman doing something with her hands. Doing it very fast. And quietly. I could be knitting. Darning your socks. Churning the butter, plucking the chicken. Any one of a million endless occupations. A woman seen and not heard.

Yeah, usually a woman, but not always. Probably not in ancient Rome. In ancient Rome—here's a little history for you—in ancient Rome, poets often hired orators to read their poems. If the poet wasn't a particularly arousing speaker, he could pay the B.C. version of James Earl Jones to get the job done. But the interesting part, at least for me, is that the poet stood right next to the orator and did the gestures and facial expressions. So think of it. One day, John Ashbery says to himself, I can't get rid of this droning midwestern injured animal voice of mine, but I can get Kevin Kline or maybe Patrick Stewart. Of course that was ancient Rome, true, and my work is a little different. I'm the gesture. In a way, I'm the poet, standing beside the orator. I'm ancient. I'm the poem before it was written down.

That's all in my application, the why of it, the personal story, the Oprah angle. Actually the sign for *Y* is just that, the little finger, a hook, the thing that gets to you, gets you in the heart. And so here it is. My hook: my mother is deaf. She came by it honestly, and slowly, working in the music industry, as a technician. Specifically, light crew. She's one of those little monkeys above the stage moving the big spotlights around. You see them at the beginning and the end of the show, scurrying up and down that ladder, the chain link contraption nobody ever owns but everybody wants when their house is on fire. My mom's one of the only women in the business. Most crew wear earplugs because they're positioned right in front of the speakers, but she never could because earplugs messed with her equilibrium. So thank you Nirvana and Pearl Jam and Steve Perry and Van Halen. Thank you from the bottom of my heart. She's touring with Springsteen now. He likes her work. He likes it that she can improvise. Bruce can drive the techies nuts because he's all over the place, but it's like my mom can read his mind.

Anyhow. By the time I was fourteen, she was about stone deaf, and gone all the time. No, I mean like gone, off the premises, Mom has left the building, gone. Literally. This is the sign for gone. See? Now you get it. The other kind of gone is this. See? Yeah, the bullet to the brain gesture. So I learned sign language, and I discovered an important truth: my mother paid more attention to me when I was completely silent. It takes time to sign or to fingerspell, a lot more time than talking. Sometimes I could get her to put down her backpack and pull up a chair and wait for me to get through a sentence. And my dad would stop what he was doing, look up from his lecture notes. And there we all were, silent, waiting for what would happen next.

My father was a professor—you might have heard of him—at the University of Georgia. That's how my parents met. She was his student and she got him tickets to an R.E.M. show. Yeah, no, don't feel bad. No one really gets R.E.M. Well, except my mom. "That's me in the spotlight." She loves that one. My dad taught literature, British Romantic poets. Blake. Now there's a weird dude. So that used to be their world: William Blake and Michael Stipe. Extreme craziness. And then Dad would take us to all these poetry readings, and Mom would whisper, "What? What?" Only she wasn't really whispering, since she couldn't hear herself. So I started signing the poems for her. And I got pretty good at it, and my fame spread, like a house on fire, as my dad put it. I was like a sideshow, this fourteen-year-old girl standing there, looking way too young for some of what some people weren't hearing. I learned a lot about the world, believe me, having all that poetry run into my ears and come out through my hands. I would say I learned pretty much all I need to know. Kids in my dad's classes used to ask him what poetry's good for, and he was always so patient with them. He'd explain at length, and they'd be textmessaging their friends and nodding uh hunh, uh hunh. He'd come home and tell me this, and I wanted to storm into the classroom and yell at them to listen, listen, goddamn it, listen.

Sorry. I'll be all right. Yes, he did. Six weeks ago. Yep, yep. Thanks. No it's okay. You didn't know. It's not in the application. Not that it would have mattered in your case. But I don't want people to think I'm playing the sympathy card. People like you. I have to say one thing, though. I hate that phrase *passed away*. This is the sign for it. See how stupid that looks? It's hard to do, too. You have to get your elbow way over here and then bring it back. But *died*. It's like this. See? To the point. Over. He died. No bringing back about it.

He thought I had a calling, my dad did. He'd watch me sign at a reading, and then he'd tell this story about when I was a baby, before I could really talk. We were all flying to London, and my mom was seated next to a Gypsy—the real thing, Romanian passport, wearing seven layers of clothes, gold teeth, spoke no language anyone could understand. Except me, apparently. The Gypsy and I did this thing with our hands—through the whole flight—and I would hand her a cup, a roll from my mom's tray, the in-flight magazine opened to the map of Heathrow, whatever she needed. See, my dad would say, it was already in her nature. And then he'd riff on from there—he'd talk about the great usefulness of signing poetry. He thought it made the poem even better, to reduce it to these signs. Made it elemental, he said, like the world before language. Like what went on between me and the Gypsy: all gesture and feeling.

One day, though, he's standing there in the kitchen reading "Tyger, tyger burning bright." He's letting loose with that poem, in his best crazy Blake voice, all color and thudding iron, and I'm signing right along, the sign for tiger, clawing the face with both hands, then for fire, fingers doing dancing flames. Then *bright,* fingertips of both hands together, then opening up like a sunrise. My mom's staring at us, and then she says, really loud, "So why is it good to go back to that, that elemental? What's so great about the scruffy dumb caveman sitting around his fire belching and pointing?" My father takes a deep breath then and says, "You're having an affair, aren't you?" This is the sign for affair, the first two fingers of the right hand open in a V and the left hand inserted in between them. Get it? For some time after that, I signed all their conversations, just stood there in the room, making the signs for *where, who,* for *when,* where the left index finger orbits the right, the sign for *disgust,* in which you claw your empty belly. They mostly ignored me, and everything else, mail unread, food burning on the stove. Sometimes I'd sign a line from Blake, *And what shoulders and what art could twist the sinews of thy heart?* Or R.E.M. *This one goes out to the one I love.* Or I'd do the obvious, *marriage,* which is a gentle clasping of the hands, or *husband,* which starts with a salute, or *wife,* which is the gesture of a woman pulling off an earring at the end of the evening. Then I started doing the names of times and places they'd been happy: Boston, Chicago, Christmas, Houston, New York, birthdays, Friday nights, London. I did it to remind them, even though they weren't watching. I did it to make their old selves alive again.

And it came to me then: what power I had. Power, yeah, that's right. See, even you know the sign for power, that Mr. Universe flex. What I mean here, though, is the power of revision. I realized I could help these poets make their work better. Say, for example, a poet is famous for setting all his work in Arizona, the sign for which by the way is that gesture elementary school teachers make for zip your lip. But these Arizona poems just aren't fresh anymore. How about suddenly I set his poem in Holland? Or instead of tired old lilacs and roses, I make them sunflowers, anemones, asters, delphiniums. No one would know except the deaf. And *they* wouldn't even know what they knew. And maybe, just maybe, the poet would be grateful. He's always had trouble with that line, he's sick of roses, his wife just left him, he never wants to see the godforsaken state of Arizona again.

    Are you going to put this in your notes, too, that I sometimes . . . what would you call it? Embellish? Beautify? Embroider? You're not? What kind of deal? You want me to read your poems? You write poems? I had no idea. Have you published anything? Oh. Oh, yeah, I agree. Dime a dozen. Much better to languish in obscurity. Emily Dickinson, for example. Sure. I'd love to see them. I'd be honored. Upstairs? I could wait here. No? All right, then. You lead. Is this your family? Isn't it interesting that people hang family pictures on the walls of stairways. The question is, youngest at the top or the bottom, growing up, winding down? She looks like you, this one. She's got your same eyes, wide open, like somebody just kicked her in the gut.

    What a great office. Yes, of course, right. *Study.* A person could write some fine poems in here, I'll wager. My dad would have loved this, the vaulted ceiling, all the light zooming in, all these books. Got your British Romantic poets, I see. Looks like it's all poetry. All poetry, all the time. Do you ever think maybe you missed your calling? Sorry. Right. You're the interviewer here. But aren't we done? No? Sure, I have time for one more. I'll bet it's something about my most memorable experience. See, I can read your mind.

It's funny though. In a way, it's always memorable, every time, living poet, dead poet, they all stay with you. Once I had a couple of beers before a reading. Don't look at me like that. *I* know I was underage. The poet was Sharon Olds. And she started in on that poem about her parents when they're young, about how they have no idea what horrible things they'll do to each other. My mind drifted, and I realized I was signing a Philip Larkin poem. Right. *That* one. It was like daydreaming, it was like passing outside time, like the poems were talking to each other, like they'd escaped their makers. Even so, I don't drink before readings anymore. Maybe after. But back to your question. The *strangest* was—well, I won't name the poet, but he has this perfectly lovely poem about a woman undressing. He's reading this poem, and it begins to occur to me that more people are looking at me than at him. I glance over, and I see *he's* looking at me. The words of the poem are wafting toward my face. I can see them, and it's as if I've become something else, some vision. The woman in the poem is mute and trapped and sad, and she's being watched intently by the poem's speaker. I feel this kind of overflow and collapsing, time and space certainly, but also like the edge of a cliff, that ragged lip of sand on the beach, the berm, the end of the known world. That's where I was, and I was bringing the sad woman with me. I was helping her get out of the poem. I thought when the poem ended, I might look down and find I was naked, that *I'd* become undressed. It was totally frightening and totally, well, *fabulous*. Like when you finally know what you're born for. Powerful. I keep waiting for it to happen again, that visionary blaze.

So that's it, right? That's all. But what about your poems? You didn't really forget. I know how you poets are. You wanted to be asked.

No, I don't mind. Hey, it's the cocktail hour somewhere, right? Me? Oh, no, thank you, but you go right ahead.

Wait. Was that a trick question?

Well, this one's interesting. Is this Latin? And this too? I guess you have to learn all that Latin in law school, and you might as well put it to good use, right? *Corpus delecti, caveat lector, quid pro quo.*

And there's French in here too, and I know *sueño* is Spanish for *dream*. Why are so many of your poems about dreams? Why do you think you use so many foreign words in your poems? Sorry, sorry! But I think about stuff like that all the time. Like bread in French is *pain,* right, but you spell it p-a-i-n. You sign it, *bread,* like this, like your left hand is a loaf of bread and you're slicing it. Which would cause pain, slicing your hand, pain, which is this. Your index fingers point toward each other and twist. So what would you do in a poem? And *milk* is this, like the act of grabbing a jug handle. In French, it's *lait,* two fingers in a V on your left hand lying down on your right. What do you do? Translate into English or use the sound of the word? Well, it depends. Sometimes the poet clues me in, and I can tell from his handshake. Or the voice sends a kind of message, like do the poems have more to do with sound or with meaning, body or engine, as old Lucius Wright might say. Sometimes, I wing it. *Sueño* you'd sign this way, the index finger to the forehead like thinking, then it twists away to show the thought is mysterious and elusive. And then, I'd do the sign for Spanish, like a hook into your heart.

Well, I have to tell you no one's ever wanted to do that before, get that close to their own poems. I don't think that's a good idea, right now, kind of a conflict of interest, wouldn't you say, though I know it worked miracles for Annie Sullivan and Helen Keller.

Still, it's nice of you to ask. How about this: I don't tell anyone that during my college interview you asked to hold my hands, and we forget all about it, and you write me a magnificent recommendation? That's my deal. That's my final offer. Where's your wife, anyway, the mother of those beautiful children? Oh, no. Oh dear, no. Oh. I'm so sorry. No, I don't mind that you say *passed away*. My mom? My mom would be kind of young for you I think, but of course she's her own person. And it was true, by the way, about the affair. Just so you know what you'd be getting yourself into. Oh, but, I thought you meant—anyway, right now, she's hanging over Bruce's head doing a light check in Greensboro, North Carolina. After that, it's Charlottesville, then on to London. Her favorite city on the planet. I'm supposed to meet her there and see the sights, all those big old echoing spaces. We'll go on tour she says, tramps like us. I'm not sure, though. I might have other plans.

This is probably the end of the interview—except, as you know, I don't have a car. No, that's not it. *This* is the sign for *shoe-in*. Sign language isn't about pointing, by the way. I should probably just call Diversified. Mr. Wright would come get me. Mr. Wright. That's a good one, isn't it? I could wait outside. It's a gorgeous day, and you have a nice front porch out there, great landscaping, good idea, by the way, about the Leland cypress and Bradford pear trees at the bottom of the yard so your view from up here is all sky. You wouldn't have seen me if I hadn't plowed into your mailbox. I could have had my mysterious automotive mishap completely unobserved. Yeah, maybe it wasn't my fault, but the question is, what causes a perfectly good car to just stop? There were a couple of warning signs, like the radio got stuck at a really high volume—it was—sorry, I have to say it—deafening.

Then a week later, when I'd start the engine, the back windows would open by themselves. Really. As if something needed to be let out, the soul of the car expiring. And you know I did the craziest thing the first time that happened. I called my dad. Even though he's dead. I forgot and called him, speed dial, and then on the third ring, the machine picked up, and there was his voice, and that made me remember. His old greeting: I can't come to the phone right now. Or ever, I said to the goddamned machine, as if it could hear me.

So can you tell me what you're going to write about this interview? Do they give you some kind of form? Was the candidate prompt, polite, behaved appropriately—well now you can answer that one honestly, right? Did the candidate arrive unaccompanied? I think that would be an interesting question, a telling question. Personally, I wouldn't want a freshman class stocked with clinging parents, parents hanging from the rafters, as it were, but that's just me. There's probably a question like, would you want to spend four years with this candidate? There's probably a question containing the word *unique*. Ha. I knew it.

And you know, that gives me an idea. *Unique* does. Because that's what it's all about, right? Distinguishing myself from the other ten thousand seekers of admission. It's brilliant. It's crazy. But here goes: we should take our show on the road. You and me. I mean I. You and I. We'll go pick up my car, and then I'll say good-bye to Mr. Wright, and we'll burn up the highway to Cambridge, to the Admissions Office, and present your findings. You could read your recommendation, and I could sign it. It would be mesmerizing. I mean with your dreams and my visions. You could sort of write the poem of me. I promise not to lie or embellish. You might, but I wouldn't. Actually, if you lie and embellish, then I won't have to. It would be like Wordsworth, his definition of poetry, the way my dad explained it to me years ago: spontaneous overflow of powerful feeling recollected in tranquillity. I never liked that word much, I have to tell you, those two *l*'s or the idea, that business of recollected in tranquillity. I keep wondering what happens to the powerful feeling. Where does it go? Like the spirit, the essence of the dead. Where? I guess it trips the automatic windows of the poem and just flies away.

So when we stand up in front of the Admissions Committee, you'll be the tranquillity. I'll be the overflow. How does that sound? Doesn't *that* sound fabulous?

Slip, Out, Back, Here

The darkness in this bedroom seems to ask a question: what if you'd never been born? The voice it uses is my mother's, even though she's not in the room with me, not in the house, but in her own house with my father, a hundred yards east. I am trying to think how to get back to her. I promised to spend the night here, but I don't think I can make it until the morning. I am ten, and I believe that if I don't see my mother's face right this minute, I will disappear forever.

My friend Alexis sleeps on the floor, snoring, just a little whistle, and twitching in her sleep. Awake, she's never still, and so I'm thinking, how would Alexis do it? How would she rise out of this bed so fast, as if she'd never been in it, as if she'd always been in the air, between the ground and the clouds? How would she turn the knob on the door? Fast for speed or slow for silence? I ask this question, and my mother's voice answers, slow for silence, and then I hear her say it again: what if you'd never been born? Outside is the river, and I hear it along with my mother's voice, its little rushes, moving where the wind sends it, slow for speed, coming into the shore but never staying. The river is like my mother, like my dream of her, her dream of herself, never staying, this river called Neuse. The other meaning, the rope around the neck, I have just learned this spring: you can slip out, but it's not easy. Still.

How to do it? How to get back to my mother? If I think about my mother, if I put her inside my head like a starlight mint in your mouth, I can get back. I can concentrate, and the feel of it, the waft of her moves in my head. My mother in Paris, in New York, in Southern California, and all her stories of escape, which I know now are all about me, about my not being born. So I know I have to think like my mother in order to slip out, in order to be born.

The strangest story is that my mother followed a rock-and-roll band for a year, maybe longer, she won't say, all around the West: Denver, Colorado Springs, Albuquerque, Las Cruces, which is a terrible name, worse than Neuse, and Phoenix, which is much better, a West-word. She drove by herself for a while, from city to city in a red pickup truck, and then she didn't do the driving anymore. She bought tickets for a while, the most expensive seats. She was making a lot of money in those days, but didn't have anyone to spend it on. She paid for the tickets, but then she figured out how not to have to. When she says this, she and my father exchange a long look, and in his face there is something hilarious but frightened. I'm sure I'm wearing this same expression, in the dark, in Alexis's inky bedroom, trying to imagine myself free of her house and moving back toward my own. My mother in Las Cruces, moving toward the door of the big traveling bus, its generator drowning out the sound of her footsteps in the parking lot, the fairgrounds empty, finally, except for these seven buses, circled like wagons, she thought, here in the wild, wild West.

The door opened and she stepped up, inside. A man offered her a beer, and when she took it, their fingers touched, just barely. It was very quiet after the blare of the concert from her third-row seat. She never paid for another ticket. It was easy. She could slip out, and nobody saw.

She'll tell me how it felt, years later, to be standing in the hysterical light of Barnes & Noble, in Fresno, California, listening but not really to the classical Muzak, reading how this man in the traveling bus had married a model from Texas—they had so much in common, the magazine writer said. She'll say she wanted to slip out of the store into the night, to be alone. When she tells this story, I'll remind her that she has me and the Texas model doesn't, but it scares me to say this. I know I'll look like my father, that mixture of delight and fear, and she'll say so, you look like your father, but there will be daylight, and I'll be in her arms, and I'll exist.

I sit up in bed and swing my legs over Alexis, the way she swings hers over the balance beam to dismount, once, twice, like a lever going around. I can't vault like that, though, even now. I'm slow and steady, like my mother usually, like my father always.

Now I'm standing on the other side of Alexis, and she turns toward me in her sleep, turns so slowly, I think it can't be her, or she must be injured to move at that speed, or she's my mother, and I've dreamed this, this slumber party. I'm standing, and it's my mother here, sleeping like a child, and I'm watching over her to make sure she doesn't get lost, get away, as mothers are always trying to do in their waking lives.

The cat makes her strange whine and chatter on the other side of the closed door. The cat's name is Mischief, but she's no trouble at all, compared to what I'm about to be.

My mother, again, in Los Angeles, in the Hollywood Hills, frozen in this same moment, with her hand on a doorknob, leaving a house, so that I will exist. She'll tell me this story when I find her, when I slip out and walk one hundred yards in the dark, by the Neuse, past Jadyn's house, between the swings on the swing set, the river sounding like the wind in my ears when I swing. I'll slip out, and my mother will be there in the doorway of her house, waiting for me.

And she'll tell me all about it, how the year before she met my father, she went on a blind date in the Hollywood Hills, blind, in the dark. A friend of friends. They talked a few times on the telephone, this man and my mother, and he told her he was a writer for the entertainment industry. He asked her to the premier of *Death and the Maiden,* but she couldn't go. Then he was interviewing the young woman who made Prozac famous. Cute but crazy, he said about this woman, and my mother felt an infant jealousy, like she did when her sister got a bigger slice of pie. Would she come down to L.A., he finally asked, to a party with some writers. She'd like them, he was sure. Stay at my house. All right, she said. It's not far. I can get away.

So my mother spent a whole afternoon at Macy's, with her sister, enthralled by the possibilities, all she'd missed in her years of mail order. A pair of linen trousers and a little black dress, lacy, sleeveless, over her head in a whoosh—and then seeing it in that huge mirror. OK, her sister said. That should work. My mother picked out a silk vest, the color of rust. What's that for? her sister asked, and my mother just shrugged. I like the color. I want it.

The drive to L.A., late Saturday afternoon, every song on the radio an omen, foreshadowing. Full dark by the time she gets close, hard to read the directions, missed turns in the canyons, before cell phones, this was—she'll have to explain that to me. Finally, though, the house stuck on the side of a hill, glowing from the street side. Hard to park, parallel, set the brake, pray it holds, pray some more. When he opens the door, she knows the voice, but it doesn't match the boy who stands there, not a boy, a man, of course, but small, slight, his fashionable hair and glasses like a costume. My mother will say she is ashamed of herself for judging this way until she sees, unmistakably, the same judgment on her blind date's face. Distaste. Not at all what I thought. Oh well. She wants to turn and run away into the night.

But the house! She would have liked to date the house, fall in love with it, marry it, have little houses all over the world, which was certainly possible, she saw. My father just sent these from New York, the blind date says, flinging his little hand at the cherry dining table and eight chairs. Not a bad view, he says, and my mother turns to see the whole city, laid out below her, like diamonds, she will tell me. In here, the blind date says, I'm watching something, which was Elton John on the largest television my mother has ever seen. She knows the song he's singing, but now she can't remember, so she'll think of the ones we've heard in the movies. "The Road to Eldorado," "The Circle of Life." Elton John sings all his hits, his head on the screen as big as a car tire. They watch for an hour without speaking. My mother believes the blind date is thinking about something else, entertainment, media, Prozac. Who knows?

They leave for the party. The blind date drives, an old Buick Skylark, which makes my mother like him until he curses the car, explaining that his Triumph is in the shop. My mother thinks, though she might not tell me this, how long it's been since a man has driven her anywhere, let alone on a date, how the feeling of it is pleasant, a relief, how she'd like it to go on. He'd opened the door for her, this man-boy, and now he reaches over to pat her hand as it lies on the seat between them. He talks and talks. He says he's read her books. This is nice, she thinks. I could do this. I could settle for this.

I'm carrying quite a load now in my backpack, my clothes, my books, a comforter, my shredded baby blanket, of which not much is left besides its gender. It is a he, which amuses my mother. Every night before bed, I say, where is he? and my mother tries not to smile. I am standing with this cargo outside Alexis's bedroom. Across the hall, I see her father, at the computer. Her mother is nowhere, probably fallen asleep with Nicole, Alexis's sister, the way my mother falls asleep with me. This thought makes tears swim in my eyes. I have to get to my mother before this night is over, so I can slip back into the story.

At the party, her blind date introduces my mother and then leaves her alone. My mother finds a drink, gathers her courage, talks to a few people. She meets a man who writes for the movies. He has lived in Utah, as my mother has. They talk about Salt Lake City. He says the word *fiancée,* drops his fiancée gently into the conversation, and my mother feels a different relief, cards on the table. They sit next to each other at dinner. The blind date is farther away. A woman, a publicist, arrives late, drunk and unhappy. Everyone but my mother knows why. The publicist slides into the chair across from my mother and admires her rust-colored vest. That's nice silk, she says. What would you call that color?

As dinner proceeds, my mother and the writer agree that Salt Lake is a hilarious and frightening city: the bilious lake, the many wives hidden away in the canyons. The fiancée is not at the party, but everyone there knows her, asks how she's doing. The publicist is particularly interested. My mother slowly realizes the publicist is staring at her, imagining my mother a flirt, gold digger, home wrecker, worse, words I don't even know yet. My mother gets up, goes into the bathroom, stares at her face in the mirror. Her eyes are hazel, a color nothing else really is, except other eyes. She comes back to the table and begins a conversation with the woman on her right. But she turns back because Salt Lake is too compelling, oddly excessive, like Hollywood and screenwriting. The publicist is very drunk and listening intensely. My mother sees what will happen just before it does.

There is wine everywhere, red wine, from the bottle, from the publicist's glass and my mother's, swept forward over the table, across my mother's chest and into her lap. Your vest, the publicist says, smiling. I'm so sorry. The table is in an uproar, ten people moving out of the way, sopping up wine. Dinner is over now anyway. Dessert is later, in another room. Send me a bill, the publicist says. For the dry cleaning.

In this moment, time collapses. My mother and I collapse across time in our longing to be gone. I'm inside her body again, our old conjunction, but she is in mine too, as if each of us has swallowed a billion little mirrors, and we see each other repeated endlessly down the long hallway of her past and my future. She would say, if you swallow a mirror, it would have to be in pieces, all jagged edges, all sharp corners waiting to be turned.

And so I do. I turn the corner, and the back door of Alexis's house swims up before me, the river beyond it, hushing into the shore. I think how to navigate, out the screen door, through the garden, around the trampoline, past the flagpole. The new neighbors' dog will bark. He will give me away, I think, and he does.

In the car, on the way back to his house, the blind date does not mention the crazed publicist, the spilled wine, my mother's ruined clothing. My mother wonders if she imagined the whole incident, but then she looks down, inside her coat, sees the wine stains blooming on her vest, deepening over her legs, darkening the black of her trousers. She has a thought then: what if her blind date is really blind! This is the only possible explanation for his silence on the matter. She stifles a giggle, a guffaw, a sob. What? he asks her, what's so funny? Nothing, she says, just—and she points to her throat. A blind date! And oh God, she thinks, he's driving a car. Tomorrow I'll give you a tour, he says. Tomorrow we'll go to a bookstore and look for your books. That's okay, my mother says, thinking to spare the blind date the mortification of reading all those words.

    At his house, they admire the view. It really is just like Salt Lake, she says, up in the hills, the Wasatch Front. I used to ski in those canyons, she says, cross country, down into the woods so far you think you might never find your way out. The blind date says he's been to Aspen, Vail, Steamboat, Sundance, but downhill. He interviewed Redford once, he says, but my mother can tell he's lying. She thinks she could never marry a man who skis downhill, but my father will prove her wrong about that.

    After a while, the blind date says, you must be tired. He offers to pull out the sofa bed, but my mother tells him she can do it. Okay, he says, with one last look. Then he disappears down the stairs to his room. My mother hears the door close. She thinks this is the last she will ever see of him. She arranges the sheets and blanket on the couch so that she will be able to look out at the lights of L.A. She will never see this view again, but she believes she will see others like it, maybe better. She walks into the bathroom.

Because I am ten, this is my favorite part of the story. I think it is my mother's favorite too, but for another reason: because it is a metaphor. Because in this astonishing house in the Hollywood Hills, she meets up with the self she would be with this man. The blind date left her no towels, no soap, no toilet paper. Her overnight bag is open by the bathroom door. She reaches in and finds a pair of clean white socks. She can hardly believe what she has to use them for.

I stand outside under the moonlight. I see the front door to my house, a hundred yards east, the magenta-colored calla lilies on the steps, the impatiens glowing like neon, the petunia covered in small purple trumpets. You must make my mother leave L.A., I say to the moon. She can sleep for another minute, but then she must wake up. She must slip out of that house in the Hollywood Hills so that she will be waiting for me when I get to the door. You must wake her up, whoever you are, and wherever. Otherwise, I will be stuck here, or I will make a mistake and walk south and the Neuse will swallow me.

My mother wakes suddenly. Where the lights of L.A. glittered, there is now only a gray soup, like a blanket, a cloth with pinpricks and a dull glow behind it. She sits up and listens. She hears nothing, or maybe a small, slow whisper of air, like the feet of a child moving over the grass at night. She reaches into her bag, finds some paper, writes a note for the blind date. Sick. Sorry. Going home.

Her heart beats wildly, the pressure of two hearts, another one under her own. She's moving like a dancer, every gesture connected to the one before, every gesture with a purpose. Shoes, bag, keys, to the door, open it. The early morning air rushes in at her, cool and soft, like the breeze off a body of water. There is weak, happy sunshine. The street is still, cars parked neatly. She sees her truck wedged between two others, on the downhill. This will be difficult. She can't remember ever having to extricate herself from such a situation, the clutch, the brake, reverse, all against the force of gravity. Quickly. Before the blind date sees.

The river is on my right, a path of moonlight you could walk into. What if Alexis's mother hears me, makes me come back? Already I am past the trampoline, almost to the flagpole, where I could walk along its shadow, reduce myself to a line of darkness, to nothing. I hear Alexis's mother, I think, calling to her husband at his computer. I hear their door open. I must make myself invisible.

Then my mother is free, blasting down the hill, toward Westwood, the freeway north. She's gone so that she can meet me in the yard by the Neuse River under the moonlight, so that she can bring me back. Alexis's mother is calling my name now, but the door to my house opens and there she is, my mother, her hair blasted wild from the wind on I-5 because she drives with the windows open because she sings along with the radio, and she wants me to hear her coming.

Then I'm in her arms. Alexis's mother is talking, talking, but my mother waves her away. In a moment, there will be only darkness broken by the perfectly round beam from the moon, the pulse of the river, the smell of my mother, which is always wine, lemon, another scent like clothes just out of the wash.

We have conjured each other. We have slipped out to bring each other into being. This is the first night again, alone together in the hospital room, my father gone home to sleep, a single light shining on us, the rest of the room, the maternity floor, the hospital, the whole city, gone to darkness beyond this one light. My mother holds me. A nurse comes in, but my mother waves her away. She will tell me this, and later I come to know the story of it so well, I can tell it back to her. How it all happened. How I just slipped out, and she was there.

Daniel V. Stanford

Liza Wieland has published three novels, two previous collections of short fiction, and a book of poems. The recipient of grants from the National Endowment for the Arts, the Christopher Isherwood Foundation, and the North Carolina Arts Council, she has also won two Pushcart Prizes. She teaches at Eastern Carolina University and lives with her husband and daughter in Arapahoe, North Carolina.